The Purple Bike

Tamsin Stanford

For information: www.tamstanford.com

ISBN 978 0 6486572 1 7
eISBN 978 0 6486572 0 0

Cover photography:
Purple bike by Simo M./Alamy Stock Photo
Background by Ivan Gromov on Unsplash

First edition: October 2019

10 9 8 7 6 5 4 3 2 1

For Joe

1

Tom scraped back the thin curtains, one at a time. The metal on metal set my teeth on edge and even heavy condensation on the inside of the window couldn't disguise the grey day outside.

I was always nervous for the hairs on his tanned legs as he turned on the gas fire, holding my breath at the long hiss before the flame licked across the front of the grille. Six seconds today.

Warmth would follow, but an involuntary shiver made me inch the quilt up further, trying not to expose my toes.

We'd been talking about his ex-girlfriend and the embossed cream wedding invitation that had arrived the day before, care of the Law Faculty. My indignation that Sandrine felt entitled to invite him merged with anxiety in case he accepted.

I knew their history and her reputation from the stories Tom and others had shared. Her ability to lie without hesitation, including empty threats of self-harm if he ever left her. Her tendency to feign illness for sympathy after being unfaithful.

She had spoken often, Tom had told me when we were first seeing each other, about engagement rings and a midsummer wedding, with no attempt at subtlety. I couldn't relate to this fixation and less than a year after their split, she had got what she wanted from someone else.

Tom leant against my desk while he pulled on his jeans and socks, then paused, head tilted: "Would you marry me?"

The look of expectation on his face brought my heart to a stop.

A dozen panicked thoughts rushed through my head before I realised he'd said "would", not "will". No bended knee, no ring in a box; this was not a proposal.

"Of course I would."

I forced the words out with a smile as my heart thudded back into life. The response was a reflex, the answer Tom expected.

He smiled, satisfied, as he tied his shoes.

I loved Tom – at least I felt what I assumed was love – and we'd been in a relationship for nine months, but marriage had never crossed my mind.

What if his question had been serious? Would he accept my polite refusal if I explained that vows are pointless if people split up the moment things get tough? Would he understand that the thought of being a bride conjured up the image of a corpse on the autopsy table, people poring over every inch of me?

Probably not. He knew I disliked being the centre of attention, without knowing why. It wasn't his fault; I'd always been so careful about what I said, he couldn't know that time in the spotlight as a child had left me with no desire to be there again.

All I'd shared with Tom is that I grew up in a small town in Cornwall. Before my parents separated in 1983, we'd been happy, like any other middle-class family in the 1970s: Dad worked in a bank, Mum took care of the house, and we spent summer holidays with my grandparents. That was enough for him to know.

I'd never told him about Jenni.

Jenni was my big sister, almost three years older than me, and I adored her. She protected me from ghosts and kept me safe during thunderstorms and let me hang around when her friends came over.

On midsummer nights, when it was past bedtime but too light for us to feel sleepy, we would lie in our beds and play word games or make up quizzes. As the sky faded from blue to fuchsia to burnt orange we whispered questions and giggled the answers, hoping our parents couldn't hear us over the television downstairs.

True or false was our favourite. One night she asked whether the number one song in the charts was *C'mon Eileen*. Definitely false, I said, until she sang it to me. Eileen was our mother. She still is, but not the one she used to be. In the years since Jenni and I last played that game, whenever I hear an unlikely song title I still whisper, "true or false?" and hope for a response.

Tom was saying my name and I faked a yawn. "I'm sleepy, I'm staying here for a while."

He ducked to kiss the tip of my nose and brush a stray hair away from my face.

"I'll see you later?"

"See you later."

Then the sound of someone closing a door quietly.

The centre of the bed was still dark and warm. I lay there for a while, curled into a ball and thinking of Jenni, while tears slid sideways down my face.

2

The first time I saw Tom was shortly after the start of my second year at the University of West Wales. I was living with a couple of friends – Zoë and Katrina – and Stephanie, a fellow Art History student who often made me laugh at inappropriate times.

Tom was in his third year of a four-year Law degree and lived in the house next door to mine in a street filled with students. The unweeded front gardens and discarded beer bottles were a giveaway.

He was cute, I thought, with his brown hair flopping casually over one eyebrow. But not very friendly, as he merely tilted his chin while we walked up our adjacent front paths and extracted keys from our pockets. Later on I found out he was having girlfriend trouble but had thought he was just rude.

Despite being neighbours, after our initial encounter I only saw Tom from a distance as our circles were entirely different. Plus, there was the girlfriend, Sandrine. She was French and worked as a language assistant at the university, on exchange as part of her teaching degree.

Katrina and her friends in the Languages Faculty had

plenty of salacious stories about the language assistants: it was tradition, or at least not uncommon, for them to find a partner among the student body. Officially the behaviour was prohibited; unofficially the faculty turned a blind eye, as long as they stayed away from the students they were teaching.

Sandrine, one of the newly arrived group, was a bit older and quite a few years more experienced than her predecessors. She had decided in the very first week when she saw Tom at a student bar, he told me later, that he was 'the one' for her year abroad.

He found her accent attractive and her persistence flattering and she was naturally beautiful in a way I could never hope to be. My friends and I dressed in black because it was an unspoken uniform that suggested nonchalance. Sandrine dressed in black because her clothes – better made and better fitting – accentuated her figure and gave her an appeal we could never match. Shiny chestnut hair hung thick and straight past her shoulders. Her petite size gave her a misplaced air of vulnerability, which she used to full advantage, along with her large, dark eyes and long lashes.

At the time I was unaware how volatile their relationship was. Screaming fights were followed by tears, leading to soothing words and promises. Tom always backed down, usually as he shielded himself from her angry slaps and scratches.

The day Tom and I met properly was a mild Saturday in May 1991, towards the end of my second year. Sandrine had flown to Bordeaux for the weekend to attend a cousin's wedding. I was in one of the local pubs packed with people, mostly students watching Nottingham Forest and

Tottenham Hotspur in the FA Cup Final.

Tottenham had been my team for years, in the absence of any first division football within 60 miles of home. Jenni and I used to play a game, our ritual before dinner on a Saturday, when Len Martin read out the day's football scores on Grandstand. We'd cover our eyes, listen to the first team's score – "Southampton 2 …" – and scream out our guesses for the other team, based on his intonation. We were only right about half of the time, but it was one of my favourite moments of the week. Tottenham Hotspur would be my team, I decided, for no other reason than the name sounded funny. Jenni chose Crystal Palace, a place she said sounded magical, fit for a princess, and they would be her team forever.

During the match, Tom's housemate Paul recognised me, and raised his pint in greeting. Tom was wearing the Spurs strip so, as post-match celebrations were kicking off, and fuelled by a few cheap pints on a near-empty stomach, I left my group and went over. I was glad I'd made the effort to smooth my hair and dab on a little make-up that morning. At first I thought Paul was interested in me, but he soon disappeared to the bar and didn't return, leaving me with Tom. He had intriguing eyes: cool grey with a hint of blue, which made his expression slightly stern until they lit up with his smile.

He was over the moon at the win. I didn't explain why Tottenham were my team but as we talked about how the players had performed he seemed impressed I was a genuine supporter.

I have no idea what else we talked about in the pub – anything but not quite everything. We got back to his room around nine o'clock, picking up newspaper-wrapped chips on the way after a day of nothing but alcohol. We lay on the bed, talking, while Sinead O'Connor played on repeat. After the third or fourth time around, we were bellowing all the lyrics to *Nothing Compares to You* until someone banged on the ceiling.

Tom was open about being in a relationship with someone so I had no expectations, not even when he assured me the next morning – when we both woke up coy and fur-mouthed – that their break-up was imminent. He would be clear with her when she came back from France. His nervousness was appealing and I assumed it was because of me, not the prospect of delivering bad news when he knew what the reaction would be.

He went to the kitchen and before long the smell of toast made my mouth water. I heard a muffled conversation – one of his housemates must have been up already – before he backed into the bedroom balancing plates and two steaming cups of tea.

I tried to act more casual than I felt when I got dressed. He kissed me and said we should meet up later, adding that Sandrine was still away, as if that was the only reason he wanted to. I made an exaggerated show of climbing over the low wall between our two houses before disappearing inside to face the interrogation from my housemates.

"You do know his girlfriend is a psycho, don't you?" Stephanie asked, peering into my eyes as if I had gone mad myself.

"They are about to break up. He said it's been coming for a while and he's waiting for the right time." My cheeks were aching from the stupid grin stuck to my face.

"From what I know about her, the right time would be

when she is far, far away. Like on a rocket ship to Mars. Anyway, it's his funeral!"

She threw her arm around me and asked for all the details of our night together, none of which I was willing to share.

That afternoon, Tom and I met up for a walk along the promenade and out along the pier. To push through my hangover I'd had more tea and a hot bath. I hoped to look as good as possible after too many pints and a night squashed into a single bed, trying not to move, snore, or do anything to make Tom regret asking me to stay.

As we strolled along in the sunshine, not quite holding hands but occasionally bumping shoulders or brushing fingers, he assured me again his relationship with Sandrine was over. He'd told her a few times that things weren't good between them and she refused to hear it so it was dragging on. Now was time for it to stop. He didn't want me to think he was the sort to be unfaithful, he said, which sounded chivalrous and mature.

The way he was talking, it sounded as if we were seeing each other, which scared me and gave me butterflies. I liked him, but he didn't seem quite my type, even if I wasn't exactly sure what my type was. He was more self-assured than the boys I knew from school and he must be clever if he was studying law. It was clear he'd been brought up in a nice family and I could join the dots and work out they had money. So why was he interested in me?

He didn't know I'd never slept with anyone before. It wasn't important. The opportunity hadn't ever come up until last night when he'd asked and I'd thought "why not?". Before leaving home I'd never been on a date. The options were limited in a small town and I was wary of what someone's motive would be. Once I reached university, relationships and casual sex were both readily available, but I preferred to hang out with my housemates, yelling at them over the music in pubs or going nuts on the dancefloor after a few drinks.

Tom told me more than I wanted to know about Sandrine, as if satisfying himself he was doing the right thing. He pointed to where she had scratched him after he told her, two months earlier, that he couldn't accompany her to the wedding in France in case Spurs reached the FA Cup Final on the same weekend. Her nails had left two fine, parallel scars on the side of his jaw.

I agreed, that sounded pretty unstable.

"She's back tomorrow so I'll talk to her then. I won't mention you. She wouldn't take that well at all," he said, then carried on as if I wasn't there.

"I should have ended it as soon as she cheated on me. That would have been way easier. Except she said she was so sorry, she'd acted crazy. She promised I could trust her, and I was naïve enough to believe her. No-one would have blamed me for breaking up with her after the second time."

If it had been one of my friends I would have said "hell yes, you should have ditched her the first time she slept with another man. And, by the way, everyone knows she's a bunny boiler".

"I wouldn't have found out, except she told me, like she was testing my reaction. Well, this time it's over, I can't be with someone I can't trust," he said, still convincing himself. "It's definitely best I don't mention us."

Us. A shiver gave me goosebumps as I walked beside

this cute, sophisticated, intelligent man who thought we were an 'us'. To keep my smile under control, in case he thought I was crazy too, I stared down at our feet stepping in unison along the pavement.

True to his word, he sat down with Sandrine the following day and made sure she understood the relationship was over. She did; she left him with several slaps to the face and more scratches – this time down his left arm, which would leave thin white lines that stood out against his tanned skin.

After that we fell into a relationship without really thinking about it. I still went out to clubs with the girls, but once Tom arrived I'd spend the rest of the night dancing with him, hoping the alcohol gave me more rhythm than I felt and praying nobody else caught his eye. Instead of joining the girls for late-night pizza or curry, I adopted Tom's habit of late-night chips, smothered in vinegar. Several nights a week I slept at his place and sometimes he stayed at mine. The first few times, I heard him leave via the back door, through the kitchen. I asked Zoë if that seemed odd and she told me she'd seen Sandrine one morning, leaning against the garden wall opposite Tom's house, "looking like she could murder someone". Thank God he hadn't mentioned me.

As the end of term approached, we spent as much time together as possible, knowing we faced a long summer apart. At his father's instruction, Tom spent at least part of every holiday gaining work experience. A six-week legal internship in London, followed by his family's regular summer trip to the French Riviera, meant we wouldn't see each other until the end of September.

They didn't disapprove of me, he promised, these plans had been in place for ages.

I thought back to what Zoë had told me and hoped Sandrine didn't have the address in Nice.

Over the summer I missed him in an odd way. Each week when we spoke on the phone he relayed stories of the cases he was working on and how much he admired the lawyers he was working with. He was learning so much, making connections that would be important once he graduated. One evening he called me unexpectedly, triumphant about spotting a detail overlooked by the other lawyers that had turned a probable loss into a victory. It was a side of him I couldn't easily relate to, but it was always good to hear his voice and I was proud he was clearly doing well. We wrote letters, too, and in those he was more personal, less full of stories about how much he was impressing other people and more about us.

My fruit picking job was trivial in comparison but gave me time to daydream about what I would buy with my meagre earnings. My only desire was to become an artist, so any money I earned I spent on materials and bus tickets to places around Cornwall that wouldn't be over-run by tourists and I hadn't painted a dozen times before.

The only friend I kept in touch with from school was Ally, but she wasn't interested in hearing what university life was like. She had attended the local college briefly before deciding it wasn't for her and now worked in a shoe shop on the high street. It never occurred to me she might be jealous, not even when she hurt my feelings by calling me "la-di-da" for having a boyfriend who would one day be a lawyer.

Red, my cousin, lived nearby and had her driver's license, so a few times we went out in her rusty Mini when she wasn't working. She loved driving too fast down narrow, winding lanes to beaches the tourists hadn't yet discovered. In the 18 months since she dropped out of university, only weeks before her final exams, she had struggled. Business Management had not inspired her and she'd complained of becoming "a Jack of all trades, master of none".

Her decision to quit, made without any discussion, caused friction with her mother for "wasting a bloody good education". Aunt Vera expected her daughter to be on the corporate ladder, not renting a bedsit less than 10 miles from the town she grew up in. Red had taken a job in a supermarket while she worked out what to do with her life. Her goals were modest: as long as she had time to enjoy a chat with customers, avoid too much pressure and come away with money in her pocket, that was enough for her.

By the end of the summer I was freckled and healthy and ready to go back to Wales.

"It's good to see you happy," Dad told me as he turned a sausage on the barbeque, jerking as it spat hot oil on his arm. His girlfriend, Fern – not that I would use the term he hated in front of him – and Aunt Vera were hooting with laughter over something in the kitchen where they were preparing salads.

"Joy's in luuurve!" Red sang out and clapped with delight at my flushing cheeks.

"I am not!" My face undermined my protests. "We've only been going out a few weeks so it's too soon for all that."

"So? When you know, you know, there's no time limit."

"We haven't said 'it' yet and I'm not in any rush."

Red knew how to wind me up. I'd told her a bit about Tom and showed her the photo I'd taken the week before the end of term, up on the headland with the wind blowing his hair in a way that he knew suited him.

"Mmm, very cute," had been her response.

Aunt Vera emerged, balancing two large salad bowls and a bread basket, followed by Fern with a tray of drinks.

"What are we missing?"

"Joy was telling us how dreamy Tom is."

"Aunt Vera, make her stop!"

How could I tell whether I was in love when I had nothing to compare to? That fluttering I felt the first night we were together had never gone away, but neither had the feeling of surprise he had chosen me. Our conversations over the summer reminded me how different our lives were away from university, so I was keen to be back on common ground. Everything else would sort itself out.

3

For his final year, Tom moved into a house 15 minutes away instead of being next door. It was larger, better furnished, and had only two other students, also at the Faculty of Law.

"Dad gave me a big lecture after what happened in my last year at school, when I got a bit lazy and distracted," Tom explained. "He still hasn't got over the fact that I didn't get into a London university and he's probably calculated how many extra minutes I can study by being closer to the library."

It made little difference to our relationship. We still drank too much and danced until midnight or shouted ourselves hoarse over too-loud music at parties. We still took long walks to clear our hangovers, where Tom would tell me about trips he and his family had taken, all of which sounded incredible.

Occasionally I shared stories from my childhood – pre-planned tales that omitted key details – but even this had me on tenterhooks in case I accidentally blurted out Jenni's name. Many times I questioned my reluctance to tell Tom about her. I'd imagined how the conversation would go and each time it ended with my happiness bursting like a bubble.

Jenni belonged to another life and another place. I had escaped the grief that hovered over Cornwall like a fog; I didn't want it to find me in Wales.

On an unseasonably warm day in late autumn, Tom and I took a picnic blanket up to the headland. The sea was sparkling in the low sun and I told him it reminded me of home, so enticing until you dipped your toe in the water and realised you might catch pneumonia.

"You should go to the Maldives," Tom said, as if that was as easy as popping down to the shops. "The water is like a warm bath and you can swim with turtles, which is amazing. Not as incredible as the reefs off Australia, though. You can't imagine how many different fish are right there below the surface. One day I'm going to dive the Great Blue Hole. Have you heard of it?" I hadn't. "Jacques Cousteau discovered it off Belize and it's so deep only dive masters can get to it."

He wanted to explore places I would struggle to find on a map.

"Next summer I'll take you sailing, around the Isle of Wight," he continued. "It's a magic feeling, skimming across the waves at 40 knots with salt spray hitting your face. I love it. You'll love it," and his lips brushed mine gently. "In fact, I love you, Joy Carter," and he kissed me again, deeply, before I had a chance to speak.

My heart should have been singing at the words every girl wants to hear; instead, I wondered what I would have done if he'd waited for me to say it back.

I liked being with him, a lot. A man like him could have had his pick of girlfriends, so I felt lucky it was my hand in his. He was good-looking and smart and now he loved me, too. It should have been easy to say it back, but I wanted to focus on what we had here and now. Declarations of love might result in conversations about the future, and that could lead to conversations about the past.

~ ~ ~

I met Tom's family in December, staying for a few days at the start of the Christmas break. Like me, he was from a family where the father worked and the mother kept the house. That's where the similarity ended. Our three-bedroom end-of-terrace house was neat and modest but also slightly dark and stuffy, although the garden was large and ran from front to back down the side. Their sizeable house in Surrey was airy and immaculate. Mrs Fitzgerald – Valerie – played tennis on their own court when she wasn't lunching with other wives or looking after Tom's younger brother, Ben. She took French classes to enable her to flirt more eloquently with the waiters when the family stayed in their villa on the Riviera each August.

Growing up in the country, I suppose I was proud my father was a bank manager. It gave him a certain status, which is what drew my mother to him. How naïve that seemed now. Tom's father Edward was a senior partner in a commercial law firm in London, head of a wealthy family and respected by everyone who knew him – even those across the boardroom table.

His parents were friendly, though, and greeted me with warm embraces. Mr Fitzgerald ("Call me Edward!" he boomed) sounded formal and reserved but he kissed his wife in front of his sons, hugged them, and would play-wrestle as if they were still five years old. Valerie made it clear they were her whole life and she would do anything for her family's happiness.

In their presence I felt awkward and unsophisticated and was on edge trying not to do or say the wrong thing. Observing them as an outsider, I experienced jabs of envy at seeing how a loving family behaved and knowing I would never feel part of it.

After my visit, Tom asked whether I intended to take him home at any point. I skirted the question, instead playing up the bitterness of the divorce, how little time I spent at home, and how boring it was with nothing to do. I was buying time. Eventually he would have to visit and, when he did, I would have to tell him about Jenni. The scene had played out in my mind so many times I had memorised it:

"Welcome," Dad would say, stiff and full of nerves at meeting the first boyfriend I had brought home. We'd go inside and start with a cup of tea and a nice plate of biscuits laid out by Fern.

Tom would glance around the lounge searching for something to compliment, until his eyes landed on the photo, recognising a younger Dad next to me and Mum, but with someone else who clearly belonged. He would pause, assuming the other girl was Red, who he'd heard so much about, before noticing more pictures of the same girl: an annual school photo; another of her and I perched on the garden wall with our legs stuck out straight, giggling, with matching white shoes and frilly socks.

Then he would turn and ask me who the other girl was, at which point my Dad would look at me, then at Tom, and reply with a puzzled tone, "Well that's Jenni, of course" and my story would be known.

Years ago, I realised that once people know certain things about you they can never un-know them. Their mind starts weighing up what to say, considering the context: Is this choice of words insensitive? Will this comment upset her? So I made sure they knew very little.

I knew I had to tell Tom, but when it made me sad even to think about her, I just didn't know how.

~ ~ ~

In the New Year, with only months to go before graduating, we threw ourselves back into study. Tom's workload was immense in comparison to mine and his father's lecture had the intended effect. While my housemates dressed up to go clubbing, I'd go to Tom's for a quiet night on the couch watching TV. I would lie with my head on his lap while he wound my hair around his fingers, which always sent me to sleep. On the days I made him leave his books for a couple of hours, we wrapped up warm and walked up along the cliff to the monument on the headland.

It didn't matter where we were; next to Tom, with my hand in his, or his arm around my shoulder, I felt content enough.

Until the cold February day when I thought he was proposing.

At a time I should have been focused, studying hard and preparing for my final exhibition, my head became a cloudy mess. Marriage had never crossed my mind and even though Tom's proposal was hypothetical, it worried me that it had crossed his.

I hadn't planned any of this. I hadn't left the house the day of the Cup Final hoping to be with somebody by the evening. I hadn't started dating Tom thinking it was the start of a lifetime together.

Tom loved me. After that day on the picnic rug he told me regularly. The fifth or sixth time, I blurted the same in response – afraid if I didn't that he might soon ask me outright – and hoping I would sense whether it was true as I said it out loud. From the smile on his face, I was believable. I wasn't sure whether the knot in my stomach was because I loved him or because I didn't.

I needed advice. One evening I hovered until all my housemates except Stephanie had gone to bed, and casually started a conversation about men. Compared to me she was experienced – she had dated her first love, Gavin, for more than two years before she'd moved to Wales. Since then she'd had a mixture of intense flings and longer-term relationships.

"Apart from Gavin, have you been in love?" I asked her.

"Only once, in our first year, before I got to know you. Rory. He was a gorgeous blond Scot with the sexiest voice you've ever heard. We had that instant spark, we couldn't take our eyes off each other from the moment we met. We were inseparable – it was quite nauseating, probably, but I was head over heels and he acted the same. The sex was mind-blowing! He told me he loved me right after we started seeing each other and I was absolutely sure I was in love with him, too."

"So, what happened?"

"He came back after the Christmas holidays and told me he'd met a girl on New Year's Eve and they were going to try a long-distance relationship. He broke my heart. In hindsight I think he loved me in his way, but he loved the thrill of a new relationship more and was constantly on the lookout for someone else to fall in love with."

"That's my point: how do you know when it's really love?"

"You mean, with you and Tom? How does he make you feel?"

"Lucky. Important. He's easy to be with."

"No trumpets or fireworks or wanting to rip his clothes off all the time?"

I'd never talked about sex with anyone apart from Tom – in fact, not even with Tom.

"Well, yeah, sort of," I mumbled. "At first, maybe. He makes me feel like I fit into his life so I'm happy with where we're at, as long as I don't think too hard about it."

"And what if he turned around tomorrow and said it was over?"

What a huge question. "I think I'd be gutted."

"Don't overthink it then. It sounds like you're in love."

~ ~ ~

I dream of Jenni that night, finding myself up on the windy headland. The town below is familiar, a combination of multiple places I know well.

Out to sea is a colour that doesn't quite fit, a white shape, larger and whiter than the tips of the waves as the breeze catches them. Squinting, I see it's Jenni waving at me and I strain to hear her voice on the wind. The current is moving her away from shore and I must reach the telescope before she disappears so she can tell me where she's going.

A group of older boys, teenagers, laugh and jostle each other as they pan the telescope across the town. They want to spy on people sunbathing on the sand; I want to save my sister.

Meekly, I ask if they are finished and one of them turns. It's a boy from our school, one of the mean ones who steals crisps from smaller kids at lunchtime and doesn't give your ball back until the bell rings. He sneers at me, "Carter", and turns away to let me know I'm not important enough to mention to his friends. Jenni is growing smaller so I have to be brave. I step forward and tap a boy on the arm who's sniggering at what he can see through the lens.

He wheels the telescope around so sharply I have to step back and suddenly it's pointing at me. He hoots louder, tells his friends to look, he's found Joy Carter's giant, ugly face. I try and tell them why I need them to move but their laughter is too loud and anyway they don't care. Jenni becomes a dot floating towards the horizon and I've missed my chance.

4

Jenni and I were out on our bikes in the middle of August 1982, early in the morning.

For close to two years, Jenni had done a newspaper round before school. By the age of 14, she was working almost every morning during the holidays, as well as sometimes after school in the newsagent, to earn money she spent on magazines and lip gloss.

Despite the difference in our ages, we were closer in height than we had ever been. I had started to shoot up like a beanstalk, outgrowing Jenni's hand-me-downs and causing our mother grief that she had to buy two sets of clothes. My sister was average size, her poker-straight light brown hair cut in a perfect bob, framing a pretty face. I was becoming gawky and my hair was a bit darker and a bit curly but our bright blue eyes made it obvious we were sisters.

During the school holidays I sometimes jumped up before 6.30am to help her deliver the newspapers. She gave me my own satchel for the first dozen or so customers, so my bag would be light early in the five-mile round. And I got half her earnings.

Our small town spread along the floor of a valley and

up one side, but Jenni's round had a few stops in nearby villages. She liked to start with the big climb out to the furthest point – five customers in the village of St Marow, all Mail readers in the days when it was respectable.

It was a Thursday, the latest in a long run of warm, hazy mornings that would turn into hot, muggy afternoons. The sort of day when kids, already bored after two weeks of summer holidays, would go down to the stream to cool off or see who could jump the furthest from bank to bank without getting wet.

The day's regional paper was fat with notices of cattle markets and farm sales, so my bag was heavier than usual and my legs were tired after a long ride the day before. But I had cycled this route many times and wasn't worried when Jenni pulled away as we climbed the hill out of town.

Standing on the pedals to give me more grunt, I huffed and puffed all the way to the top. My legs complained at the incline until the road levelled out towards St Marow. It was silent in both directions, apart from my loud panting as I paused at the verge.

How far ahead was she? I was becoming annoyed. All the papers for St Marow were in my bag, so she wasn't saving time by racing away. Slowly I took off again, wobbling with the lopsided weight of the satchel until I picked up speed.

I rounded a bend and there it was: Jenni's bike, lying carelessly in the middle of the road, one wheel on either side of a painted white line. The back wheel hung a few inches off the ground, spinning steadily.

I frowned and turned around, expecting her to jump out from a farmer's field. The tick, tick, tick of the wheel was loud against the coo of fat summer pigeons.

"Jenni?"

No reply.

"Jenni!" Louder this time, making a dog bark up the road.

"I'm not coming to find you," my voice petulant.

Still silence.

I began to sulk, bracing against the "boo!" I feared was imminent, and cross that Jenni would play around when we had papers to deliver and breakfast waiting. My angry kick scraped the chrome handlebar across the tarmac and ripped off a piece of the silver streamer. Now she would be furious, but it was her fault.

I can't say how long I stood there. After I shouted a few more times the stillness became overwhelming and I started to cry, hoping it might bring her out of her hiding place. It didn't.

At the chug of an approaching van, I wondered what would happen if I let it run over Jenni's bike. Would the tyres pop like balloons? Would it flatten the metal into the road like a cartoon or push it along, scraping more of the chrome?

I picked up her purple bike and leant it against mine. The driver was Eric, whose parents owned Tremayne Farm, just up the road. He always waved when he saw us, but I must have cast a forlorn figure because this time he slowed to a stop and leaned out of the open window.

"Morning Joy. Everything OK? You're not lost, are you?"

"Did you see Jenni? I don't know where she went. Her bike's here but she won't come out."

Eric surveyed the quiet road. He'd come from the direction of St Marow but hadn't passed her. Perhaps she was hiding over the hedge? Or had fallen while trying to hide?

He shut off the engine and jumped down and together we started calling. "Jen-ni, Jen-ni". My high voice overlapped with his deep shout. Eric clambered over the hedgerow, making sparrows twitter away in protest. The field was flat and empty; nowhere to hide, and no sign of the girl.

Scrambling back over the high hedge was harder, and Eric grabbed handfuls of bracken leaves to pull himself up as his boots slipped. The thorns of a bramble caught his bare arm, leaving a fine line of crimson dots that he smeared away with a curse.

"Nope, she's not there. You girls aren't playing a trick on me, are you?" He frowned.

I wiped my nose on my hand and shook my head. His face showed he believed me and was starting to worry. When he jogged away down the road I cried out, even though he was only checking the field opposite. After less than a minute he reappeared and shrugged. No Jenni.

I climbed into the van's dusty front seat as he loaded the two bikes into the back and manoeuvred an awkward U-turn. Curious to hear the van back so soon, Eric's mother appeared in the doorway in her dressing gown. She found me a hankie while his father called the police, who said they would come straight away, then my parents, who were in the middle of breakfast. Before long the front entrance was crowded with cars and people.

Dad greeted all the police by name and they treated him respectfully, given his stature in the town. Charlie was the only one I recognised, the young PC with ruddy cheeks who had visited our school only a few weeks earlier to remind us to say no to strangers.

What followed was a blur of tears and navy uniforms

with brass buttons. Of my mother's white knuckles as she clutched my father's arm while he sucked wordlessly on a cigarette. Of the click-whirr-click-whirr of photos being taken.

That was the day I lost my sister. The day I discovered that the flashing blue light on top of a police car feels even more ominous without a siren, like a silent scream.

Even when I closed my eyes I saw noiseless flashes of blue.

Dozens of questions were asked – or, more accurately, a small number of questions were asked again and again. I lost count of how many times I replied, "I don't know". Had I seen anyone, or had Jenni mentioned anything suspicious on other days? Was she in with the 'wrong crowd' or have an older boyfriend or did I ever hear her argue with our parents? I heard the police questioning Eric. Why was he out in his van so early? What was his relationship with Jenni and Joy? He said he saw a light blue car pass his house, moments before he left, so why had Joy not mentioned it?

We walked back to the spot where Jenni's bike had lain and the questions continued, although this time Eric was moved a distance away with his back to me as three policemen formed a barrier. He was considered the first suspect, which didn't make sense to me but still I wasn't allowed to talk to him. In my mind, those first minutes I had been alone on the road stretched out into hours. I tried to picture the light blue car. Did I remember it before Eric mentioned it? Had I seen it the week before, or not at all? I don't know.

Was Jenni having any problems at school? I don't know. Had she taken anything unusual with her, like a prized possession or an extra bag? I don't know. Did she have any money hidden in our bedroom? I don't know, I don't know, I DON'T KNOW.

The sun was high in the sky and burning the top of my head by the time we travelled in convoy back to the small, beige rooms of the police station.

In separate rooms my parents were asked the same questions about their eldest daughter, and about whether she would have got into a stranger's car or had any reason to run away.

My Aunt Vera lived in the next town and was the first person Mum called, as soon as the police allowed her to.

Most people found it hard to imagine Vera and Mum as sisters, and not only because of their physical appearance ("I prefer 'big boned' or 'larger than life'," Aunt Vera would say with a wink and a chuckle). Aunt Vera was lively, funny, and proudly independent. She had married badly, hoping a child might make things better, but when her husband ran off before their daughter turned one she wasn't terribly disappointed. My mother was smaller and quieter. She had a demure smile and a tendency to let other people make decisions for her.

While Mum was training as a teller in the local bank, batting her eyelashes at a man she suspected had management potential, Aunt Vera was building her reputation with a flourishing Tupperware business, successfully encouraging large numbers of housewives to save their leftovers in tubs of lime green and orange. Her flair for selling enabled her to send her daughter to a respectable boarding school an hour away, even though she missed her intensely through the week. She filled the empty house with casual and intimate dinners and noisy cocktail parties, always careful to have the latest Tupperware on show. She enjoyed her status as a divorced-yet-successful woman; it gave her a certain mystique.

Aunt Vera and my mother had gone through their pregnancies together, developing a new closeness after growing up with a six-year age difference. In the first few weeks of her pregnancy, before anyone else knew, Vera told her younger sister she wanted to name her child Freda, after their mother, or Frederick if she turned out to be a he. My mother would tell people Jenni was an early baby, but the truth is she was newly pregnant when she and Dad married, something she didn't want people to find out.

Both women had girls, a few days apart in June 1968. Freda arrived first, crimson and angry with a mop of dark hair. Jenni was a rosy pink and much calmer from the start. She was also bald for weeks, much to her mother's distress. Eileen wanted to name her daughter *Jennifer Juniper*, which she'd played over and over while she was pregnant. Len put his foot down at Juniper for a middle name – it was far too hippy to have a child named after a bush – so it was shortened to June. In those days Eileen rarely challenged her husband and chose not to point out his mother's name was Myrtle.

Red – which was what my headstrong cousin Freda renamed herself when she turned nine – often visited at weekends and stayed over during the holidays. She and my sister became even closer as teenagers. I often caught them giggling in the garden at the latest agony aunt column in *Jackie* magazine, trying on the free lipstick and squabbling over posters of Rod Stewart and Duran Duran. Those were the times I felt like the little sister, when Jenni needed me less. Pop stars and make-up didn't interest me: the posters on my side of our bedroom had puppies, and my teddy bear still slept with me because he got lonely by himself.

Even though Jenni and I had been delivering papers on our own, the police wanted Aunt Vera's permission to interview Red, in case she and Jenni had plotted anything. Red was sulky with the officer asking her questions, indignant at his suggestion she might be hiding something that would help find her cousin. She had nothing to give him and ended the interview in tears, as worried as the rest of us and racking her brains in case she had missed any signs. I wanted her and Aunt Vera to stay with us but my aunt said they needed to rest and would be back first thing in the morning.

By the time we returned to the house we were stunned and speechless. My distress over Jenni's whereabouts was mixed with confusion over why the police would say things that weren't right. She never gave our parents a second's worry. At school, teachers loved her cheerful willingness to take part in anything – sports day, the choir, the Christmas play. The suggestion that my sister had found herself in some kind of trouble and had taken off for a few days to sort it out wasn't possible: she wouldn't leave me on an empty road and go off with a stranger, not even someone she knew – not without telling me.

That night when I wearily climbed the stairs to bed, alone in our room for the first time ever, I cried tears of fear and bewilderment into my pillow and fell asleep with strands of damp hair stuck to my face.

Almost before I knew it, sunlight was hitting me through a gap in the curtains. Relief at waking from a nightmare was replaced by panic as the events of the previous day flooded back. The house was already awake and the smell of toast seemed out of place.

If a person dies, everyone knows what's expected. They bring lilies and chicken casserole and talk in hushed tones while the kettle boils. Planning a funeral gives a family purpose as they choose songs for the church and decide which style of satin will eternally line the coffin.

But when someone disappears, people don't have a script to follow. They aren't sure whether to bring food. They daren't take flowers, in case their gesture is misinterpreted. And when a family is entombed in its house, every nerve on edge waiting for the phone to ring, people can't even call.

Instead they gather in small groups, clumps of women clutching each other's arms on the high street, and old men drinking slowly while their elbows polish the solid oak bar.

In the days that followed, we spent hours at the police station and officers spent hours at our house. Aunt Vera buzzed around quietly, making cup after cup of tea for the police and for us, dishing out comforting food we hardly touched and taking every opportunity to hug me and kiss the top of my head. Her uncharacteristic quietness filled her with a vigorous, fearful energy that made it impossible for her to sit still. Every time I moved to another room there she was, dusting or tidying, cooking or re-arranging books on the shelf.

On the second day, all the grandparents arrived.

The grandmas clacked their needles as if they were in a race while Grandpa Opie and Grandfather Carter sat and smoked in unison with Dad. After the initial questions, each of them was lost in their own thoughts, needing few words and uttering even fewer.

'Kidnapped' was the word on everybody's lips but mine. My conviction that I would have heard her fight and scream made me cling to the belief she had simply vanished and was 'elsewhere', intact and unharmed.

Clouding my thoughts was the car Eric was adamant he had seen. It had passed his gate while he was clearing out his van for market, he'd said, but he had barely glanced at it, assuming only a neighbour would be around at such an early hour. It was feasible, the police admitted, that a car was lying in wait; in one small stretch the road widened into a grass verge, built so cars could pass the slow tractors that often went that way. It meant we were both telling the truth. What didn't make sense to me was why someone would choose such a quiet road if they wanted to kidnap someone. Unless they knew the bank manager's daughter rode past here on her paper round, ensuring people had the headlines to read and crosswords to complete while they ate breakfast.

It was an extraordinary occurrence in our small town. Police would not rule out the possibility Jenni was simply a runaway – after all, no-one had found a ransom note – but they called in officers from the next county to help with the search. A television appeal, they suggested on the second day, would show any kidnappers Jenni's parents were beside themselves, which might be enough to make them release her. Or, if she had run away, she might see the news and come home once she knew she wasn't in trouble.

Dad declined at first. He said he didn't want their faces plastered everywhere, people judging whether they looked innocent or guilty. It was Charlie, the young constable, who convinced him – the first 72 hours of the investigation were the most critical, he said gently. Every avenue had to be explored. Dad agreed, on condition I would not be part of it. If Jenni were watching, he didn't want her upset by the sight of her little sister, pale and hollow-eyed. As it was, Mum sobbed audibly throughout the filming. Dad held her hand like he was told to and stared into the cameras as he read out the carefully worded statement, saying how much we all care about Jenni, Jenni isn't in any trouble, we just want Jenni to come back to us.

Seeing ourselves on the evening news with the sound turned down was surreal. There we stood, huddled between two police cars as hundreds of townspeople – some we knew and many we didn't – trudged in slow but meaningful lines across the recognisable landscape. They wore heavy shoes and wellington boots and used walking sticks, poles, or wooden bats to poke and smack clumps of grass and gorse on the uneven ground. Mounted police from the next county guided them in an organised and systematic fan shape and used their vantage point to hunt for things that might otherwise be missed. We were grateful people were helping.

The police took me and Mum and Dad back to the meandering road four or maybe five times in those first few days; I lost count. Every click-whirr of the police photographer's camera made me flinch and wish I was as invisible as my sister. I did everything they asked. Again and again I showed them exactly where I was on the hill when I lost sight of Jenni. They even loaded a satchel with the right number of newspapers that I slung over my shoulder before I set off pedalling; they wanted to work out the number of seconds between me losing sight of her and turning the corner to see her bike, based on my wobbling speed.

I was terrified in case I remembered the details wrong

and was in a slightly different spot, or travelling at a fractionally slower speed, and because of me they might not find her.

Eric was there too, recreating his part in the horrible spectacle with his parents looking grimly on. I watched from a distance as he showed, yet again, where he'd gone over the hedge, and the photographer snapped away at the damaged ferns. Crime scene specialists took cuttings of the brambles, hoping to find blood belonging to someone other than Eric. They dusted the metal gates leading into the fields on either side; the weathered iron and rust gave them nothing. They examined every inch of the road, trying to prove or disprove Eric's insistence he'd seen a car pass his front gate moments before he set out.

The final time we were there, when I saw a policeman drop Jenni's bike casually on the ground, I began to cry. He spun the wheel hard and started a stopwatch to see how long it took to become stationary. Over and over I was made to walk towards the bicycle, even after tears began streaming down my face. Officers followed close behind, bending down to my height to see exactly the same as me.

"Enough," Dad said at that point. "She's had enough, we need to take her home."

I didn't want to be at home either, as the quiet house only emphasised Jenni's absence. My ears were constantly straining for the sound of the squeaky floorboard next to her bed. Mum had no-one to tell off for "galumphing down the stairs like an elephant".

Our parents sat separately in the living room – one on the couch, one in the brown armchair – while the clock on the mantelpiece softly ticked the hours away. The most enduring image I have of my father is him sitting silently in his chair, smoke from his cigarette rising straight up before catching an unseen air current and curling across the room.

5

The police organised posters to help with the search.

'MISSING!' shouted the heading, '£1,000 reward for information leading to the safe return of Jenni Carter'. In her school portrait her young smile was innocent. A second photo at the bottom showed someone riding away from the camera on the road to St Marow. It wasn't Jenni; the police found someone about her size and appearance and used Jenni's bike to recreate the scene no-one had witnessed.

Frogmen searched a reservoir a couple of miles away and turned up nothing but old bikes and a shopping trolley. From the local army base, a group of soldiers volunteered to abseil down the dozen or so disused mineshafts in the surrounding countryside that were big enough to accommodate a body. All of this I saw on the television, watching silently from halfway up the stairs so my parents wouldn't notice. They thought I should be sheltered, but I was desperate to know what was being done to try and find Jenni.

Still the countryside refused to give up any clues, leaving the locals to focus on Eric as the sole suspect. His van had been confiscated for forensic examination and someone had slashed the tyres on his father's car, stranding them on the farm.

Three weeks of school holidays loomed ahead but offered no trips to the beach with my grandparents, no dancing under the hose in the back garden, shrieking with delight at the icy water. Most days I did very little. My friends didn't call around because their parents didn't know what to say and thought we shouldn't be disturbed. I didn't want to go out because my sister's smiling face was staring at me from every shop window.

Instead, I sat in my room and drew. Inspired by films I loved – The *King and I* and *Gone with the Wind* – I sketched elaborate dresses with enormous hooped skirts for ladies with long wavy hair. Their faces were left indistinct but I perfected every flounce and ruched hem and set them in formal gardens with trees in blossom and a backdrop of green rolling hills, until every inch of the paper was covered.

The ladies in the pictures became my company now that the other half of the bedroom was empty. I made up stories about their happy families and introduced an imaginary love rival, causing two of them to argue in high-pitched voices.

At the start, I talked to my sister constantly. Over and over I asked her where she was and why she hadn't come back. From the time I woke up until I drifted to sleep each night my chest was full of a strange feeling. The aching pressure was hard to describe. I hadn't experienced the true grief reserved for permanent loss and this was only temporary, surely? But an impenetrable sadness weighed down our house like a woollen blanket, muffling all sounds and dulling the light while we stewed underneath, not knowing what to do.

Local police and special crime force detectives continued to come and go, sometimes with more questions, sometimes to search through her things once more. I told her how hard everyone was trying to find her. If she came back, she'd be able to see the adorable, droopy-eyed bloodhounds who were doing their best to find her and we'd laugh together at the clairvoyant with wild orange hair and an enormous bosom who was convinced she was receiving messages.

When the first day of the autumn school term finally arrived, I thought it would be a relief. Mum made me breakfast distractedly, packed a cheese and pickle sandwich for lunch – forgetting I hated pickle – and gave me a shiny green apple Grandma Opie had bought from the market.

At school, the children fell into one of two camps: the kids in my class and those who knew Jenni mumbled "My mum says we're very sorry" and kept their eyes down, not knowing what else to say. A handful of the older kids, feeling brave, asked for details about the police and Eric and the mysterious blue car to experience the excitement of being involved in a real-life crime.

My best friend, Ally, simply gave me her beloved rainbow slinky and took me outside to sit on the steps and watch the other kids play.

6

It's difficult to remember the order of things in those first few months. Like the possible sightings (always unproven), the ransom note (a cruel fake) and the girl's body found two counties away (someone else's grief). They all fell into the hazy limbo that follows a disappearance.

Unfortunately for my parents, the incident highlighted that they had few close friends, mostly acquaintances who kept what they believed was a respectful distance at such a difficult time. Our house was either a hive of activity when the police arrived to check something or as quiet as the grave.

We stopped having the newspaper delivered – in part because of Jenni, but mostly because of the unexpected headlines that dropped onto our front doormat, making my mother weep before she had even prepared breakfast.

"WAS JENNI PREGNANT?" screeched one front page.

"JENNI'S SECRET LOVE IDENTIFIED" promised another.

"ARE MINESHAFT REMAINS JENNI'S?" teased a third.

The pitying stares and whispered conversations we hated were nonetheless preferable to the accusations. My parents tried to protect me at home but children will be children and repeat what they hear their parents say. The idea of someone in our family harming Jenni or doing something so terrible it would drive her away was inconceivable to me, but that did not stop the rumours.

One day as I arrived home from school, I found what I thought was a playing card on our doorstep. As I turned it over, my mother opened the front door. She snatched the tarot card from my hand, tearing it into small pieces before marching straight to the dustbin.

"Superstitious nonsense," she said with tears in her eyes.

Despite being so junior, PC Charlie was heavily involved in the case and brought us every detail he could. How many volunteers were searching, how many people were calling the incident room. Like starving children my parents gobbled up every word that might take them a step closer to Jenni, only to have their hopes dashed as a possible suspect produced an ironclad alibi and definite clues turned out to be red herrings.

This yo-yo of emotions took a huge toll. If she was alive, was she safe or suffering? If she was dead, had she died painlessly? If she was alive, why had nobody found her? So she must be dead, but then why has nobody found her?

The stress of not knowing transformed my mother from the woman she used to be into the one Jenni's disappearance made her. The dutiful wife, the mother, the one who ran the household and entertained Dad's colleagues and local businessmen, shrank in front of me.

She stopped asking me about school, as if she didn't want to hear I'd had a good day while she was stuck in the house waiting for the phone to ring. She stopped having her hair done, to avoid the way conversations around her suddenly fell silent mid-sentence. Sometimes she would sit so quiet and still on the couch I would check she was breathing then creep by without making a noise.

My father disappeared too, in his own way. Whenever I walked into a room and found him there, he looked sheepish at daring to be at home when he could have been out searching. This was in spite of the countless hours he had spent walking and driving the same hills and farmland that had been combed over and over. He was often absent in the evenings, sitting in a more comfortable silence at the Royal Oak down the road – a place he had never been on his own before this happened – pretending he was part of the real life going on around him.

Their world shrank to fit their new reality and it seemed this world barely had room for me. All their exchanges were about the case. Had Len seen the message from Charlie or the Inspector, Mum wanted to know. Had Eileen heard about the increase in the reward money, thanks to an anonymous benefactor, asked Dad. They were tethered by fear and anxiety, instead of being separate Mum and Dad.

If I wasn't in my room I was hovering in the kitchen, hoping someone would talk to me, or kicking leaves in the garden and trying not to remember how much fun Jenni and I had each autumn, piling them up and diving onto them like a giant cushion.

I can picture the looks my parents gave each other, the way they stared through me, and the pitying, or even accusing, expressions on people's faces in the grocery store as Mum and I traipsed through the aisles. What I don't recall are the conversations or the songs on the radio. Life continued without its soundtrack.

I didn't know how to ask if they felt as helpless as I did

that Jenni appeared later and later in the main news bulletin, in reports that dropped from minutes to seconds. The day the weather forecast started before anyone had mentioned her sent a bolt of anguish through my body.

That first Christmas the four grandparents rallied around, doing their best to pretend it was like any other year. I received hand-knitted jumpers, one from each grandma, a wooden box one grandpa had carved and lined with pale green felt, and a stack of new books from the other. From my parents, an upgrade from roller skates to roller boots (they hadn't noticed my old skates, untouched under the coat rack since August) and a beautiful notebook, its orange fabric cover embroidered with colourful birds and each page waiting to be filled.

My favourite present, though, was the one Aunt Vera gave me. Without asking, she knew exactly what I wanted: a set of 12 pristine graphite pencils lined up from 'H' to '9B' in a smooth metal tin that gave the most satisfying clunk when I closed it. She and Red weren't there; Red needed a bit of 'normality', which meant a few days in a nice hotel in Bath. If she'd been there, she would have known straightaway how much I loved her gift.

What I remember most about that first Christmas is what was left unsaid. No-one spoke about the fact that Jenni had always taken charge of decorating the tree and had made, at the age of seven, the lopsided foil and tinsel star that took pride of place on top every year. Or that she and I would wake up on Christmas morning to open our stockings long before dawn, sniffing and feeling each item in the dark, then shoving everything back so we could be excited all over again when we woke up properly. Even deciding the order of opening presents was Jenni's job as the first child. Christmas had been hers and I had been content to sit and watch because she always gave me the first present to unwrap and knew exactly how long to leave me fidgety with anticipation before she handed me the next.

None of this was mentioned, and nothing was said when Mum disappeared upstairs after the presents were opened, leaving scraps of wrapping paper littering the carpet. She reappeared an hour later with puffy eyes and busied herself in the kitchen without making eye contact. Nothing was said, either, when Dad left the house. He returned shortly before lunch with a more relaxed demeanour and beer on his breath.

It was tradition to wrap up warm – us girls in our new clothes or shoes – and drive the three miles to the nearest beach. "A brisk stroll before lunch" is what my parents liked while the turkey was roasting and that is usually what they got. Only locals venture out on days when the sea and sky have merged into the same angry steely grey and the seagulls are screaming overhead on the wind.

One of my earliest memories is of Jenni and me on Christmas Day running after Wally, our dopey King Charles Spaniel. We chased him on legs barely longer than his as he scampered, yapping wildly, towards every seagull stupid enough to land.

I waited, but no-one suggested we go anywhere even though a faint sun was pushing through thin cloud. Instead, my grandparents spent the morning trying to distract me from the horrible atmosphere until it was time to eat and everyone pulled crackers and put on the paper hats in a show of forced merriment while the radio played festive songs we didn't want to sing.

Later that day, when everything had been cleared away and all four grandparents were snoozing, I noticed two presents left under the tree: a box in silver paper covered in dancing Father Christmases and a misshapen package with a frivolous red bow. I knew whose name would be on the gift tags but I felt compelled to check anyway.

On Boxing Day we took our first outing as a new, incomplete family. Not since mid-summer had we ventured out together for anything other than official police business. At the cinema in the next town, we pretended it was Elliott saying goodbye to E.T. that made us all cry. If Jenni were out in space somewhere, I hoped she had a kind extra-terrestrial to take care of her.

~ ~ ~

Broken sleep made me tired and irritable during the day as occasional bad dreams, which had been lurking for months, were replaced by increasingly vivid nightmares. Since Jenni's disappearance, the dreams I remembered were often unsettling: in one, I was on a beach, pointlessly washing the sand with a hose even as the waves foamed around my feet; in another, I was shouting to Jenni across a wide road, knowing she had no chance of hearing me over several thundering lanes of traffic.

More and more frequently I woke up with an anxious jolt, sometimes with tears on my cheeks. If I was lucky, the details would remain fuzzy, leaving me sad and exhausted all day. If not, the disturbing images stuck in my mind for weeks. Some nightmares I won't ever forget, like the one a few months after Jenni's disappearance: our family gathers together, distraught with the knowledge she isn't ever coming back. We swallow pills that will kill us peacefully and painlessly so we don't have to miss her anymore. Only then do we receive the news Jenni has been found, safe and well. It's too late, and we know we are about to die and leave her alone.

Worst of all, though, is the recurring nightmare about the purple bicycle. Over and over I see the pleasant and meandering country road, its smooth tarmac bordered by high hedgerows covered in grass and moss and brambles. The white lines down the centre disappear around a corner and I'm following them, moving forward but not of my own volition. I try to resist because I know what's coming and I don't want to see it.

The inevitable happens and I come to a stop in front of the bicycle. It's Jenni's. The purple frame is lying on the tarmac and I recognise the lilac seat with the white flowers I always wished was mine. Silver streamers on the ends of her handlebars are twitching in the light wind. The back wheel is not quite touching the ground so it's spinning, slowly, as if it has been spinning for a while. It doesn't stop no matter how long I stare at it. Now I want to move but I'm paralysed. I want to catch up with my sister, to ask her why she left her bike in the road. But Jenni is nowhere to be seen.

That nightmare was the hardest to bear. The scene was so clear, sometimes I was afraid I dreamt it first, and made it happen. More often than not, I woke myself up calling out. When I did, I was usually lying on my back, arms and legs rigid, fists clenched so tight my fingernails had dug angry half-moons into the palms of my hands.

7

January in England always arrives on a current of hopelessness after the colourful lights of Christmas have faded and spring is a long time away. The start of 1983 was particularly desolate and right after new year came one of the cruellest blows: a rare heavy snowfall I should have enjoyed with my sister.

Snow to Jenni was more magical than Christmas, and much less common. While she was supposed to be sleeping she would sit for hours in front of our bedroom window watching the silent flakes descend in the glow of the street light, willing them to settle and turn the world white. If she dressed up warmly enough to go outside, she would catch them one at a time on her mittens, turning each flake this way and that with a reverent expression.

The last time it snowed I was too little to enjoy it. The snowman Dad and Jenni created had scared me: its dark coal-for-eyes, lopsided grimace, and scrawny, pointy arms had stayed with me for years. In Dad's arms I had wriggled and screamed as he encouraged me to stick a carrot into its blank face.

By the time I was almost 12, we would have built a

snowman together. Jenni would have given it a lady's scarf and found a way to add pink lips and a floppy hat. Then we would have had a snowball fight, scraping up dry flakes that stuck to our woollen gloves and turned our fingers pink with cold. Instead, I watched from the front window as children threw snowballs up and down the street. A soft, white layer muffled everything, from the sound of the few cars brave enough to venture out to the shouts of "Mind the windows" and "Don't you dare!".

"Come back," I told Jenni, "I miss you and I want to play."

Was she cold, I wondered, or did she have a fire to dry out her gloves and a hot water bottle to warm her bed? I wanted to show her the sketches I had done, trying to recreate her face from the photo on the mantelpiece. They weren't very good. Perhaps if she came home I'd do better.

At school I isolated myself. It was easier sitting in the library than explaining why I didn't feel like running around the playground or listening to people whisper and point. Ally and I walked to and from school together sometimes but we never talked about Jenni, which was fine with me, although I'm sure Ally missed her too.

My marks were good enough for my teachers to leave me alone – I did my homework, read what I was supposed to read, and flew under the radar in class. Secretly they were probably relieved they didn't need to intervene or call my parents in over poor behaviour. They had no more idea of what to say to me and my parents than the other townspeople and were relieved to let me be.

The exception was Miss Robbins, my Art teacher. She knew I loved her class and when I proudly showed her the pencils I had been given for Christmas she said I was welcome to use the art room any time I wanted. Her father had passed away when she was my age, she told me. Although that wasn't the same as Jenni being missing, drawing had helped her when she was sad, and she hoped it might help me a little too.

She was right. Ignoring the winter outside, I spent hour after hour practising. Drawing allowed me to hide away at school when I wanted to be alone, or to be in my room without noticing Jenni's side looked the same as the day she disappeared. Her single bed was made, her green quilt cover pulled halfway up the pillow, which was plumped expectantly. On her white bedside table sat a small pot of strawberry lip gloss I was not supposed to touch (after she disappeared, I opened it at least twice a day to inhale my sister back to me) and the *1982 Jackie Summer Annual*. Her clothes hung on her side of the wardrobe and the tan sandals she had kicked off the night before she disappeared were lined up, ready for her to slip them on.

As mid-March approached, instead of looking forward to spring I became uneasy about what I should do for Mother's Day. Traditionally Jenni and I would bake a cake, buy a card if we hadn't made one at school, and pick daffodils from our garden.

I didn't want to bake on my own. Half the fun was watching Jenni in the kitchen, weighing out the ingredients and giggling while she impersonated the Swedish Chef from *The Muppets*. Jenni let me scrape the bowl and lick the spoon. Last year was the first time she let me use the electric mixer, with the warning not to splatter anything up the walls. The sticky, sweet chocolate mixture was so irresistible it didn't make it into the oven and we had to mix a second batch, hoping Mum didn't notice how many eggs were gone or how our appetites seemed so small at lunchtime.

Shuffling in my seat over breakfast, I asked Dad for money to buy a cake. He handed me a pound note without putting down the newspaper or seeming to register my question. I needed help with what to write in the card – should I sign it from me and Jenni, or me alone? – but I couldn't work out how to ask him. In the end, I threw the card away and gave Mum the cake and flowers. We ate the cake in silence and that night, before I went to bed, I put the flowers in a jug of water so they wouldn't die.

Losing Jenni had not brought my parents closer. My hearing was extra-sensitive from listening out for her, or so I thought, but she had been gone for months before I first heard them argue. Perhaps they had done it quietly, behind closed doors until now, or perhaps this was new.

The telephone had become a weapon they used against each other: if my father went out too frequently, my mother accused him of not wanting to take THE phone call, if and when it came; and if my mother spent too long talking to her parents or Aunt Vera, he would walk up and beep at her like the engaged signal, playing on one of her greatest fears.

They reached breaking point 10 months after Jenni disappeared.

As I dropped my bag inside the front door after school, Dad's voice, loud but muffled, reached me from upstairs. He should have been at work and I could hardly breathe when I thought Jenni must be back. Bolting up the stairs, I came to a sudden halt when I heard my mother yelling, her voice shrill with tears.

From the third-from-top step, through the bannisters, I

could see their bedroom door was closed. Someone was moving around the room, changing the line of light under the door. I picked at the edge of the stair carpet where it had come unglued.

They were yelling about the telephone again. Dad came home from work early, feeling unwell, to find Mum on the phone to her mother. This was just two days after the last bill, which had caused an argument because of the number of calls at peak daytime rates.

Why couldn't she wait until the evening, Dad had yelled after dinner, or better yet, why didn't she save money by visiting her mother and talking until they ran out of things to talk about? She was scared to use the phone in the evenings, my mother had told him, because she dreamed Jenni would call, needing her more after dark. Dad was scornful. It was June, approaching the longest day of the year, and any sane person would be asleep while it was dark.

"You don't know," she had sobbed. "You don't know what it's like to sit at home and wait for the phone to ring. The only time I know it won't ring is when I'm talking to someone on it."

That had stopped my father. He'd grabbed his hat and left the house, not coming home before I was in bed, fighting sleep, my ears alert as ever for the sound of the front door.

This same argument was continuing 48 hours later when I came home.

From my vantage point I knew it was my mother walking around as her voice wavered louder and then quieter. She was packing a suitcase, taking up Dad's suggestion that she should visit her mother.

I caught "unbearable" and "miserable" and "house" but

no more before she opened the door and came towards me, struggling with the weight of the case. She reached the top of the stairs before she saw me. She exclaimed "Oh!" as if she had forgotten I lived there, then kept moving, her case thumping down each carpeted step.

She rested her hand fleetingly on the top of my head as she passed but didn't say anything. Nothing about where she was going or when she would be back or what to do if anybody needed her in the meantime.

When the sound started, I didn't recognise it at first; I'd never heard my Dad cry. The weeping was too high-pitched and the sniffing too childlike. He cried and cried while I slipped downstairs and out the back door and down to Ally's house, where her mum opened her arms the moment she saw me. I lay on her lap like a baby while she shushed and rocked me and kissed my hair and didn't complain when my nose ran all over her t-shirt.

No-one even mentioned it was Jenni's birthday.

~ ~ ~

We're out in the garden playing one of our favourite games. In the centre of the lawn, we join hands and start to spin, slowly at first, then faster and faster, until one of us lets go and falls down and the other is the winner. Jenni's hand is gripping mine and I don't want to be the first one to fall, not this time. I'll be told off about the grass stains on my jeans, but I love holding my sister's hand tight as we spin.

I close my eyes so I can focus more intensely on moving my legs as fast as they will go and we're circling so fast, faster than we've ever managed before, and I'm hearing Jenni laugh and I'm out of breath, not wanting to give up before she does. Then I'm falling backwards, bracing for the lung-emptying whump I know is coming. I open my eyes and drop my gaze: Jenni's hand is still in mine but its bloodied wrist is detached from the rest of her, and Jenni has vanished.

I wake up with my head buried under the pillow and my body chilled with the sweat that has soaked my nightie.

8

My parents were separated. My sister was gone. I had no-one to tell me off for scuffing my shoes along the road as I walked or for wearing a shirt to school that wasn't quite clean. No-one to run to the corner shop with on a Saturday morning, coins jingling in our pockets, to agonise between lemon sherbets and cola cubes. My art project – the one I spent weeks working on to make sure it was absolutely right – was given an A, but I didn't feel like telling anybody.

Dad was rarely at home, it seemed, and when he was there his tired body was sunk so far into the armchair I thought I would need a rope to pull him out. All he did was sit watching TV, a cigarette burning in his left hand and smoke wafting towards the ceiling.

The wedding photo disappeared from the mantelpiece at some point that summer. It was there a few days after Mum left, I know, because I had stood in front of it wondering how she could walk out – and how could Dad let her – when they had promised to be together forever. Scenes from films I'd watched with Jenni came into my head. For better or for worse, 'til death do us part. That's what Mum must have said, and Dad. What was the point of making a promise only to break it when 'for worse' came true?

After the occasional attempt to cash in on Jenni's disappearance with a recap of what had already been printed, the newspapers rubbed their hands at the separation of my parents. The once-sympathetic local journalists knew they would shift a few more copies with innuendo and accusation.

Had Eileen left out of guilt? Did Len uncover an affair, or was he caught being unfaithful? Maybe Eileen thought Len, the upstanding bank manager, had been somehow involved in their daughter's disappearance?

No journalists had spoken to my parents in several months and they didn't bother checking the facts. People my parents thought trustworthy were happy to contribute their insights into a marriage apparently long in trouble, possible affairs, and raised voices. Even I wasn't spared. "Joy is sullen" and "withdrawn", apparently unacceptable despite what I'd been through.

The first anniversary of Jenni's disappearance was marked by page after page in the local newspapers of possible new witnesses and alleged perpetrators, regurgitating (or concocting) the outlandish theories of how a 14-year-old girl can vanish.

We hated the people who ran the media as much as we needed them, but the police said having Jenni's face on the front page and the six o'clock bulletin might lead to a break in the case. Thankfully they replayed the footage from the year before – Dad's appeal with Mum at his side, locals combing the countryside, and the ever-present purple bike lying in the road. Was Mum watching? Did it make her wish she hadn't left us?

The police were, quite simply, baffled at the lack of evidence and admitted as much in their press conference. Despite the lack of progress, they wanted us to know they had pursued every lead and would continue to do so. On that first anniversary, dozens of officers were stationed around the town and on the roads leading to St Marow, stopping every car to see if they could jog anyone's memory or find a returning holidaymaker who'd been unaware of what happened a year before. Again, posters appeared in the windows of shops and houses around town. The reward was now £2,000. Everyone who had previously provided a statement – there weren't many, given the odd circumstances – was re-interviewed in case they revealed the slightest detail not mentioned before.

We were all grateful for their efforts.

At Mum's insistence, a pair of officers travelled all the way to Kent where Eric was temporarily living, to put him through the wringer once again. A phone call was not enough, she told them, because she wanted the police to "see his eyes, so they know he's lying".

In our ever-decreasing household, Dad and I kept going because we didn't know how not to. I took over the hole left first by Jenni then by Mum. Breakfast was on the table when Dad came downstairs. He was always freshly shaven but his blue eyes were tired and sad. Each morning I made my own packed lunch because it never occurred to Dad he should.

He occupied much less room than Mum had. The flowers, the magazines, the books, and letters that formed part of the surface of our living space were absent. Even the bathroom echoed more and smelled different. No more bath oils or disposable razors along the edge of the bath and only two towels, not four. Only Dad's cigarettes on the kitchen bench, the open packet with a matching lighter lined up alongside, suggested I was not alone in the house.

Thankfully Aunt Vera was there to step in. Each weekend I made a grocery list as best I could and she took me to the new supermarket on the edge of town. She made quiches and plates of cheese and salad while the weather was warm. As autumn arrived, our freezer filled with casseroles and crumbles, and basics like ham, eggs and potatoes that even Dad could cook after he finished work.

At least once a week she had dinner with us to check we were looking after ourselves. Although she was never directly critical of her sister, Aunt Vera's pursed lips and the way she shook her head ever-so-slightly whenever I mentioned Mum spoke volumes. She was conscious never to stay overnight, refusing to add fuel to one inflammatory article that made Dad leap up and grab the phone, shouting at the switchboard operator that he wanted to speak to the editor RIGHT NOW.

Any stranger who walked in and saw us might have assumed we were a family – me, Dad, Aunt Vera and Red, when she was home from school. By the time Jenni had been gone for 18 months, I struggled to picture her face without running into the living room to check the photo of us on holiday in front of colourful beach huts, noses wrinkled as we squinted into the sun.

Mum didn't come home. First she moved in with Grandma and Grandpa because she needed a break from being in the house, Dad told me. She made sure the police knew where to find her when they had news. "When", she said, not "if". Then, after a few weeks, once the anniversary of the disappearance was past, she rented a flat on the other side of town that she would not let me see and picked up the rest of her clothes while I was at school and Dad at work.

I had no idea if she and Dad talked on the phone or saw each other. Dad never discussed it, and simply accepted his wife was no longer there, as he had accepted it when Jenni was no longer there.

On Wednesdays Mum met me from school and we walked to the local coffee shop for hot chocolate and a toasted, buttered teacake.

I struggle to remember our conversations. I would have talked about Ally and things I was learning that I thought she might want to hear about. She would have talked about my grandparents and any gossip about other people in the town.

Her mood was bright but detached, as if she was recounting news to an acquaintance. She never apologised for leaving or offered me an explanation. Had she had enough of a break, I wondered, and was she ready to come back and be a mother, even though she hadn't been much of a mother for the last year? Not brave enough to ask, I concluded from her behaviour that if she couldn't have Jenni, she wasn't interested in having only me and Dad.

Occasionally she remembered to ask about my end-of-term reports. She'd flick absent-mindedly through the B minuses and C pluses and pause to read about me being "a quiet girl who keeps to herself somewhat" and "answers questions willingly, when asked".

What was she thinking, I wondered? Was it "Hasn't she done well, in the circumstances," or "Jenni would have done better"? I always left my reports on the kitchen counter for Dad to read and he always signed the acknowledgement slip for me to take back to school. We never talked about what was in the reports, though, and for all I knew he never read them.

I loved the weekends I spent with Aunt Vera and Red, when we would bake crusty white bread and eat the whole loaf smothered in butter and homemade blackcurrant jam before it had time to cool. She braided our hair and painted our fingernails, ensuring mine were cleaned off before she dropped me home. It was Aunt Vera who took me to the school uniform shop after I was sent home one Friday with a note that my skirt was unacceptably short, due to a recent growth spurt. Aunt Vera, too, who took me to the chemist when I whispered to her one weekend, crimson with embarrassment, that I had my first period. Instead of treating it as something shameful, she took me out on my own to celebrate with a towering ice cream sundae, covered in whipped cream and nuts, and told me I should be proud because I was becoming a woman.

She did everything with me I thought a mother would do. More than that, though, instead of just listening to me talk about the same things I told Mum, she'd remember what I'd said and ask me questions the next time she saw me.

I was lucky, too, that I still had Red.

She and I had inherited the rangy build of our grandfathers and I was delighted when I grew tall enough to fit her cast-offs perfectly – the skinny stonewashed jeans she was tired of and flimsy summer dresses that were no longer the latest style.

She and Jenni were alike in many ways – outgoing, energetic and fun to be around. Jenni had been serious about becoming a clothing designer and she used to pore over the fashion magazines Mum left around the house. As kids, the three of us loved to play dress-up in our mothers' clothes. Nothing made us laugh quite as hard as tottering around in high heels many sizes too large, wearing dresses over bras stuffed with socks. My favourite was the leopard print cocktail dress Dad didn't like Mum wearing, with a string of pearls and an exaggerated smile of pink lipstick. Jenni had good taste even when she was only nine or 10: she would pick the black chiffon evening gown, add silver beads, sweep her hair up the way she'd seen it done on TV, and dab on enough eye shadow and lipstick to look fancy, not cheap.

When it was just Red and me, sitting in my garden on the tartan rug, she'd backcomb my unruly hair into the latest style and fix it into place with hairspray that made us both cough. She applied make-up more expertly than Jenni had done, and I loved the frown of concentration on her face, her nose inches from mine.

Over time I became used to my own new reality, comfortable in my bubble of school and Aunt Vera and Red and taking care of Dad. On summer days when Red and I took glasses of fizzy Tizer onto the lawn and lay on our backs as fat bees hummed above us, it was possible to believe Jenni had never existed. Some nights I dreamed I was Aunt Vera's daughter and Red's little sister, and one day we would live together, happily ever after.

That bubble burst when Red went to university seven hours away in Portsmouth. The jabbing pain in my stomach made me feel like I had lost my sister all over again. She wrote letters that were infrequent and filled with tales of parties with cheap wine and illicit cigarettes. It was all too foreign. I couldn't picture what her world was like, in the same way as I failed to picture where Jenni was or what she was doing, no matter how hard I tried.

In a way, losing Red was harder. Jenni didn't leave me willingly, I was sure of that, and although my mother moved out she remained nearby. But Red had chosen to leave. I was old enough to know I was being petulant and unrealistic and young enough to feel I had the right to be. My sister had vanished, and now Red was abandoning me too.

I hated waving goodbye at the start of each term knowing I would not quite recognise the person who stepped off the train a few months later. It was like watching a slide show in the dark, where Red was a child for slide after slide until, with a single abrupt click, she turned into an adult.

The first term she was gone I withdrew a bit more, not that Dad noticed. It was easy to keep out of his way, telling him I was busy with homework – which was partly true, although after I gave up trying to concentrate on Geography or Biology I would read or draw for hours. The quietness of my bedroom was preferable to the silence of being in a room with another person lost in their own thoughts. With Aunt Vera I found it possible to pretend I was OK for a few hours at a time, although I suspected she saw through my façade.

Ally tried her best to get me out of the house and invited me to hang out with the newer friends she had made in my absence. The damp autumn weather was my excuse for staying at home, and I was aware without caring that I was causing us to drift apart.

Less than three weeks after Red left, right before my half-term holidays, Grandfather Carter passed away and Dad drove up to Bristol to make the arrangements with his mother. I wondered how adults knew about organising a funeral if they had never done it before. Perhaps Mum and Dad had planned one for Jenni, to be ready.

I considered myself mature enough to stay at home on my own but Dad was less keen on the idea. I could have stayed with my aunt, or Mum could have slept in our spare room for a few days but I knew that would never happen. In the end, Dad said I'd be sleeping on Mum's couch for a few nights.

The day of the funeral, Aunt Vera drove Mum and me to Bristol, leaving early in the morning and coming back late the same day. Red was excused as it was too far so soon after she'd moved to Portsmouth.

In the front row – the family pew – the imposing oak coffin was within reach. Aromatic white lilies made the air thick despite the cool church. I couldn't shake the image of my grandfather lying in such a horribly confined space. As the first jarring notes of *The Day Thou Gavest* began, I remembered one of my first assemblies at secondary school, watching Jenni in the choir lead the rest of the pupils in song. Over dinner that night I'd asked her what 'behest' meant. She'd laughed and said she had no idea, it was probably a made-up word because they needed something to rhyme with 'rest'.

On the unforgiving wooden seat, sandwiched like a buffer between my parents, I started to cry, not exactly sure who I was crying for.

Afterwards, I wanted to stay and spend a few days with Grandma Carter, drinking tea and talking about my grandfather. Mum said we should leave her and Dad be. I'm sure Dad would have been glad to have me there, but I didn't ask.

~ ~ ~

We've run out of bread and Mum sends me to the supermarket with 50p. As I approach the entrance I notice Jenni's bike leaning against the wall outside and am filled with relief: I didn't lose her, she just went to the shops. The car park is full and every car is light blue. In fact the same car is in every space, the one Eric said he saw.

It's totally quiet, so Jenni's voice is clear when she starts to yell and bang but the sound isn't coming from one place, it's coming from all around. I'm seized with the panic of knowing I have to rescue her before her kidnapper comes back.

I dash from car to car, putting my ear against the cold steel and calling her name, but all the doors are locked and even if I knew which boot she was in, I have no way of opening it.

I've been up and down every lane when men with blurry faces begin to pour out of the supermarket. I've missed my chance.

I run home to tell Mum she needs to get help, but she won't listen and shouts that the bread was for Jenni and Grandfather Carter and now they will both starve.

9

My teenage years were defined by a feeling of restlessness, of not wanting to be where I was, without knowing where I did want to be. Sometimes it was hard to breathe, like being stifled by a thunderstorm that creeps up so slowly you don't notice how loaded the air is until the first startling clap of thunder.

At almost 16, still with a couple of years before I could leave for university, it took all my energy to stay patient. I studied hard enough to avoid any unwanted attention and even welcomed the homework and assignments at school that kept me busy. Art remained my favourite subject, whether I was learning about Renaissance architecture or the Impressionists or experimenting with everything from pottery to screen printing.

Only when I was painting, though, did I feel as if the thunderstorm had passed. For hours at a time I would lose myself at my easel, learning how to be delicate with oils and bold with watercolours, and vice versa. Each Christmas and birthday, my list was full of finer and finer brushes, books on techniques requiring special paint I could hardly pronounce, and a never-ending supply of paper.

After my parents divorced, communication between them was minimal and I was expected to "tell your father" and "ask your mother" anything relevant. It took me by surprise, then, that they came together to stress the importance of making the right A Level choices.

At the parents-and-pupils careers evening, Mum was impressed by the Legal Studies teacher and thought Law, English, and Psychology would set me up for a lucrative future. Dad was keen on Maths or Economics, even though I had shown no aptitude for either subject previously. Neither of them would accept my plans of becoming an artist – "That's not a career," Mum told me while Dad nodded – but I refused to compromise completely and settled on Art, Psychology, and English.

I began to count the days until I would be moving to a town where I knew no-one and, hopefully, no-one knew me. I daydreamed about how I might introduce myself and who I would be. At last my bedroom would contain one bed, not two, and there would no longer be one set of sheets that lay gathering dust until I washed them. Stripping Jenni's unused bed always made me feel guilty, as if I was admitting defeat, but afterwards – when the pillow slip was fresh and ready for a weary head – the ache of emptiness would stay with me for days.

~ ~ ~

Several women had sniffed around Dad after he and Mum split up without him showing any interest. Some of them seemed attracted in a way I found quite disturbing; others saw him as damaged and in need of saving, which he possibly was, but didn't want.

He'd always been a quiet man, tall and dark-haired, with a serious air that made it inevitable he would end up as a bank manager. His old-fashioned haircut made him appear older than his years, even when he had an obviously younger wife on his arm. When people first met him, they found themselves waiting for his straight mouth to break into a smile, but it rarely did. That's not to say he was miserable; his shyness made him seem standoffish and he appeared more comfortable in work attire, behind the shield of a suit, tie, and waistcoat, than in social settings.

My Aunt Vera told me no-one in the family – not on either side – could fathom how my parents got together, fell in what felt like love, and got married. And if Jenni hadn't disappeared? Who knew, Aunt Vera shrugged. Maybe they would still be together without having faced anything more testing than mumps and measles, the death of the family dog when I was four, and arguments over whose turn it was to have the skin off the custard. Or maybe, once Jenni and I left home, they might have discovered we were all they had in common and separated anyway.

I loved talking about things with my aunt I would never dream of discussing with Mum or Dad.

In the bank, a woman named Fern came in to apply for a car loan one day, as her ancient Cortina had at long last joined "the great car yard in the sky" as she put it. As Dad guided her through the paperwork they began talking. She knew who Dad was – everyone did – but they found conversation surprisingly easy.

Fern lost her only child in 1981. It was different from our loss, because Molly was 18 and was killed by a man who had gone out to commiserate losing his job and ended his evening drunk and driving through a red light. But Fern's husband had left less than a year later. His way of grieving turned out to be incompatible with hers, even though they thought they loved each other enough at the start. They sold their house, left behind the bad memories, and moved on.

She came closest to understanding what Dad had been through, so I was happy for him when he told me, with more than a hint of wonder in his voice, that he'd been asked out to dinner and had said yes.

I had questions, but wasn't used to talking about the important stuff, like whether he was content or lonely, fulfilled or over-worked. Selfishly, I was pleased at the thought he might not be alone when I went away to university, the last one left in the home that used to hold a family. I never understood why we didn't move to escape the reminders that drove Mum away. With his date looming, I caught him flicking through an old photo album when he thought he was alone in the house so I asked him the question.

"I couldn't bear to think of Jenni knocking at the door one day and finding strangers. Your Mum felt the same at the start, until it became too hard and she wanted us to move, but I vowed I wouldn't sell, even after she left."

The irony was not lost on me: Mum and Dad started to turn into strangers the day Jenni vanished. She would not even recognise them today. Dad's moustache was greying and his hair – once clipped immaculately – often grew past his collar if he forgot to get it cut; Mum had a bigger perm than she would ever have dared when she and Dad were together. More than that, though, the loss of their daughter never quite left their faces.

The night of his first date with Fern, Dad was home before 9 o'clock and all I was able to prise out of him was that he'd enjoyed his evening "immensely". A second date soon followed, from which he returned with his tie loosened and top shirt button undone.

I was curious.

"Is she nice Dad, do you like her?"

"Yes, she's a very nice woman. I do like her."

"Well then, ask her for dinner so I can meet her. It doesn't have to be a big deal. I promise I won't do anything to embarrass you, like ask if I can call her 'Mum'!"

It took a few weeks, and I had to practically dial her number for him, but he invited her round. When the evening came, he was as nervous as a teenager.

She knocked lightly and Dad rushed to the front door. They stood talking quietly for a few moments before he brought her through and formally introduced us.

"Fern, this is my daughter, Joy. Joy, Fern."

She and I simultaneously started to say "nice to meet you!", which made us all laugh and Dad visibly relaxed. The scent of freesias touched my cheek as she kissed me. During the meal, she and I made most of the conversation and Dad seemed happy to watch on and occasionally chime in.

Sitting opposite Fern while she and I chatted about school and my love of art, Dad looked smitten and it was clear why. She was one of those women who exudes a lightness of being, a sense of peace I had never seen in my mother, and which rubbed off on my father. She wasn't over-confident like Aunt Vera. She was Dad's age, not a decade younger as my mother was. They discovered they had both been evacuated to Cornwall during the Second World War –

living only a few miles apart – which is what led them to return as adults. Her expectations of Dad seemed simple and clearly they enjoyed each other's company, which made me happy for him.

The next time I saw Mum – gradually our weekly catch ups became fortnightly, and were now roughly monthly, which suited us both since we never seemed to have enough to talk about – she made a sly remark: "I hear your Dad is doing very well for himself."

I didn't rise to the bait.

"Have you met her?" she asked.

"Fern? Yes, she's been round once or twice." I felt no obligation to provide details. Mum and Dad had been divorced for four years so it wasn't any of her business.

"What's she like?"

"She's friendly, chatty. She and Dad have a lot in common." I was as non-committal as Dad had been.

"Does she stay over?"

"Mum!" I screwed up my face. "Don't ask me things like that. If you want to know, ask Dad. Or, better yet, don't even think about it."

She hmphed with annoyance and asked for the bill the instant a waitress came near.

10

As the fifth anniversary of Jenni disappearing approached, I developed a strong urge to go back to the spot she had last been. Like one of the many psychics who begged us to involve them in the investigation, I wanted to see if I could detect her presence – or her absence – from changes in the air pressure.

Often I took long walks on my own, especially in the summer, but this would be my first visit to St Marow since the police took me there, over and over. How far behind her were you, exactly? Which way was the wind blowing? When you called out, how loud were you?

If my parents had been back there, together or alone, they had not told me.

Compared to being on my bike, walking felt like moving in slow motion, while the incline of the hill and a growing apprehension combined to make my pulse race. Despite the desire to be there I had no idea what I was expecting.

Jenni's road – as I thought of it – was lined by the same hedges. The painted white lines were the same as the ones in my nightmares, except where patches had worn away. In the adjoining fields, small trees had become taller and wider and created a horizon that was recognisable even if it did not quite match my memory.

The long grasses at the tops of the hedgerows swayed as if someone was running a hand over them. Traffic noise from the by-pass reached me on the breeze and mixed with birdsong and the sound of the blood beating in my ears. The silver tassels twitching on the handlebars of the bike as it lay in the road were vivid enough to touch, along with the blue flash of the police car's light.

I didn't know I was screaming until a man came running out of the field nearby, his farm boots and his fear making him lope clumsily. He grabbed hold of me, one hand on each skinny upper arm, and pulled me towards him, wrapping his arms tightly around me until my face was pressed into his cotton shirt and I couldn't scream any more.

I had only seen Eric from a distance over the years and we hadn't spoken since that day. I knew he was the very first suspect, the obvious choice.

The police had questioned him for hour upon hour to try and catch him out. My parents forbade me from approaching him or talking about him, and my whiny insistence he had nothing to do with it fell on deaf ears. Mum was adamant: it could only have been him and either the police had missed something, or more likely he had used his cunning to convince them he was innocent. She would not be told otherwise.

The newspapers loved the idea of Eric the villain. He was young enough to have been interested in a 14-year-old girl, strong enough from farm work to have overpowered her, and naively open enough that he answered every question thrown at him, in case it helped. His blushing, rugged cheeks and shaggy blond hair made for a great front-page photo on more than one occasion.

As soon as the police told him he was no longer their main suspect – they weren't entirely convinced he was innocent but had no evidence of his involvement in a crime – he moved to Kent to work on his cousin's farm and study at agricultural college. Even if his face reminded the locals of someone, his short-cropped hair and beard meant people couldn't quite place him. Now he was back, managing his ageing father's 80 Friesian cattle and holding me in the middle of the road.

Against his chest, the smell of laundry powder mixed with the soft earthiness of the fields. Maybe it took me back to my childhood or maybe I had missed being held this close, but I felt instantly safe.

Five minutes later we were in the farmhouse kitchen, dark despite the sunny afternoon, and too warm from the Aga that ran year-round. Harry Tremayne had lost his wife to a stroke the previous year and it showed. He wouldn't let Eric tidy away her things, so her armchair was draped in a half-made summer cardigan, knitting needles sticking out of the pale-green wool. Jars, once clean in anticipation of stewed fruits, covered half the kitchen worktop but their lids were coated in dust. One corner of the adjacent sitting room was permanently inhabited by the Singer sewing table neither Harry nor Eric would ever use.

Eric made me tea – strong, with unchilled milk from the morning's milking, and more sugar than I normally liked – and we sat down at the kitchen table. He brushed away breakfast crumbs self-consciously and screwed the lid back on a jar of honey.

We cradled our tea. My middle finger barely fit through

the handle of the delicate china cups Harry insisted they still use.

"It wasn't me," Eric said in a low voice.

I looked up, but his eyes were fixed on the floor.

"I know that. I know! I told them it couldn't have been you, you weren't there. Nobody was there. Only me."

His shoulders sagged as he exhaled, not lifting his eyes.

"It wasn't your fault, either," he said, and his voice was so gentle I was afraid I might cry. At first, people seemed reluctant to say it wasn't my fault, in case they planted a thought that wasn't already there. The policewoman who sat with me while her colleagues interviewed my parents had told me I wasn't to blame. I was never quite sure if that was the same thing.

I'd always assumed Eric was older – to an 11-year-old he seemed like a grown up, but as I examined his face I realised he could only have been about 19 or 20 when it happened. Hardly more than a teenager, dealing with the suspicion of a whole town, and not being able to prove his innocence. Only Jenni's return, or proof of someone else's guilt, would have done that.

He managed a half smile and met my gaze for the first time with what could have been sympathy.

We drank our tea and talked about everyday things although it was mostly me doing the talking. I was sorry his mother had died and I hoped his father was managing and the farm was doing OK. He knew Red had gone away to university and asked what I had chosen for my A Levels.

As he drove me back into town we made a vague commitment to catch up again. Without needing to ask, he dropped me off several streets away from my house to avoid any wagging tongues.

Only back home did I remember what I had set out to do. Sitting on my bed, still keeping to my side of the bedroom, the plan I left the house with that morning felt foolish: the only way I would know she was alive was to see her. Slow tears of self-pity turned into heaving sobs that I couldn't stop and didn't want to. I bawled into my pillow until my body was aching and I had exhausted myself into calmness.

When Dad came home to me in the kitchen he glanced sideways as if to say something about my red, puffy eyes. I stayed mute. If he remembered today was five years since Jenni disappeared, he probably wouldn't want to talk; if he didn't remember, explaining myself would make both of us uncomfortable.

11

After the arguments over my A Level subjects, it shouldn't have surprised Mum and Dad that I wanted to apply for 'Art History with Fine Art' at university. Except my need to avoid causing drama meant I wasn't used to doing things they disapproved of.

"Not academic enough" they insisted, coming together in their second show of unity to ask me repeatedly "what can you do with fine art?". My teachers were predicting respectable grades, which only fuelled my parents' determination to see me take a more professional path such as teaching – progressing to headmistress status one day, naturally – or using psychology in a medical setting.

Miss Robbins continued to be my guiding light. She had a talent for nurturing the creativity of her pupils. She knew how to handle parents, too, and reassured mine that my choice had the potential to open doors into academia, travel, even television.

"Joy has great instincts," she told Mum and Dad. "She would benefit enormously from learning more techniques than I can teach her here and she should do that alongside the theory and history she'll need for a career in the Arts."

'The Arts' was the magic phrase that finally won them over.

Miss Robbins's advice also led me to choose the University of West Wales. Students sometimes found it lonely, moving away from home, she said. In her experience they fared better if they picked a university either because they knew other people, or because they knew the place.

I had no intention of going where other students might know my name, so that left places I knew. The nearest university was 100 miles away, in the small city where my grandparents lived. Mum would suggest I live with them, which was not what I had in mind. With a map and train timetable, I carefully ruled out the options that were too near, too far, or too urban for someone wanting to specialise in rural landscapes.

Wales seemed the best fit and, when I checked, no-one from my school had gone there in the past decade. The prospectus showed an area resembling the coastal towns of Cornwall and Devon, right down to the sandy beaches and untamed cliffs. Miss Robbins was complimentary about the course, and although I visited three universities to appease my parents, the instant I arrived for an overnight visit I knew Wales was where I wanted to be.

The small-town feel was reassuring, and the seafront reminded me of holidays with my grandparents, while the sense of distance made it easy to pretend home was a world away. The Art department was the opposite of our small pre-fab classroom at school. The century-old building was formidable outside and in, but as soon as the unmistakable smell of paints and chemicals hit me, I was at home.

My parents' focus on my choice of career intrigued me.

Dad had worked for the same bank since he left school and had reached his peak back in 1979. Mum abandoned her embryonic banking career when she married the boss and decided she preferred taking care of her husband, their house, and children instead.

It occurred to me then to consider what either of them might have become, had Jenni not disappeared. Dad was smart, I knew that. He might have ended up running the regional office or taking us further afield to a mid-sized city. We would have left behind the nightmares and lingering whispers to start afresh.

For her part, Mum had been planning a return to work in the early 1980s. By the time I was nine and Jenni was eleven we were old enough to get to and from school unaccompanied, and Mum was finding her days at home a little uninspiring. She had started an evening class in book-keeping the year before Jenni disappeared but dropped out afterwards, with neither the concentration required nor the wish to be away from the house.

It took her a couple of years to pick it up again and find work. I never knew what she did for money until then; she was disparaging of people on welfare, turning up her nose at the queue outside the Unemployment Office on sign-on day. Despite headlines about the struggling economy, she still considered unemployment to be caused by laziness, not a shortage of jobs, so I couldn't picture her waiting for her cheque. Dad gave her what she needed, I assumed, or let her take the Child Benefit payment she saw as an entitlement rather than a handout.

Fern was the exact opposite. She worked at the Job Centre, helping people explore opportunities, writing their applications with them, and preparing them for the occasional interview. In her opinion, a big part of where you ended up was luck. With her practical and non-judgmental approach, and plenty of firm nudging, she got the best out of people and made them feel they had achieved it all on their own.

~ ~ ~

Leaving home to go to university was a magic moment. By the end of the 1980s, other major crimes and high-profile murders were fresher in people's minds so it was unlikely my fellow students would remember a story from when they were 11. Moving to a new place, I could introduce myself however I wanted instead of being "Joy, you know, Jenni-that-disappeared's little sister". I wouldn't have to put up with furtive glances and whispered conversations or – worse – questions about where they recognised me from (I always lied) or a clumsy attempt to acknowledge who I was.

On a cool Saturday in late September, a small group waved me off at the train station. Mum was typically unemotional but Fern and I hugged and sniffled as if we had known each other for years. She knew I was worried about leaving Dad on his own and in her usual gentle way had made me feel better.

"It's OK, love. No-one expects their children to stay at home forever. He's happy you're spreading your wings – and don't forget I'm here to look out for him now."

I cried as I said goodbye to Dad, too, even as we embraced with our usual slight formality. He waited until the train was pulling away before dabbing at his eyes as Fern put her arm round his shoulder. He didn't know I saw, but it meant a lot to me.

Excitement outweighed my nerves of living with people I had never met. They were from around the country, but despite our different courses and backgrounds we were all enjoying our first taste of freedom.

Initially I'd been nervous about the course, too – was I worthy of being a Fine Art student? – until a class tour through the gallery of alumni work in our first week gave us a shared sense of inadequacy.

I had an instant social life, happy to follow the lead set by my housemates. We drank cheap wine while we got ready to hit the town, raiding each other's wardrobes for whatever would fit. In pubs, in giggling groups, we got drunk and flirted with boys. On dancefloors we formed a circle and threw ourselves around to Boney M and Abba. Anyone spotted in a dark corner or caught sliding the key quietly into the lock the next morning was teased mercilessly.

It was easy to hide in a crowd; no-one noticed how rarely I mentioned my family or childhood. Guilt flared up from time to time that I wasn't being honest with my new friends, but I justified it by believing the past was less and less relevant. In truth, it was a relief to block out thoughts of home for weeks at a time, writing letters instead of phoning to avoid the world that I was pretending didn't exist.

Miss Robbins had prepared me well for the types of essays and practical assignments I would be doing. I studied hard enough to find myself at the middle of the pack and relished being allowed to focus so much on what I loved doing, like a guilty pleasure.

Sometimes I tried to look at my surroundings through

Jenni's eyes to imagine what she might have studied, who she would be friends with, and which boys would have caught her eye. She'd been too young to have a proper boyfriend but she told me which boys she fancied at school, one of whom tucked a Valentine's card into her bag when she pretended she wasn't looking. And the day after a school disco that I was too young to attend she explained what proper kissing was like. She laughed at my screwed-up nose – the idea of a boy's tongue being anywhere near my face was revolting – and tried to stick her tongue in my ear until I tickled her and we rolled onto the floor, breathless and crying with laughter.

Often after a few drinks I had to hold myself back from telling the others about her, not wanting to mess with what was – at last – a nice, uncomplicated life.

<h1 style="text-align:center">12</h1>

On our first anniversary, Tom surprised me with a bunch of exquisite red roses and a night in a beautiful Edwardian country house. Since the Easter break we had seen very little of each other and, when we did, all he wanted me to do was test his recall skills and listen to him recite arguments. I told myself it would only be short term and it seemed our romantic night away was an effort to make up for it.

To my relief, the topic of marriage had not come up again.

During dinner, Tom shared his news: he had been accepted to start his Legal Practice course in September at the University of London. His plan was to study while working part-time in his father's firm and he wanted me to move to London with him.

"Dad wants to take a step back this year, so he'll spend more time at home and fewer nights in London. He has a place in South Kensington where we can live rent-free, as long as he can stay every now and again. You'll love it. It's a great area, close to heaps of shops and restaurants, and the Tube is just around the corner. I can show you all the sights and you can visit galleries and museums and we can have people round for drinks."

My mind hadn't drifted beyond graduation day and the long, lazy summer I was planning to enjoy, and he was talking about us living together in a city I'd never even visited.

He had it all worked out.

"So, what do you think?"

His face was so eager, his confidence in our relationship was unquestioning – yet images of noisy, dirty streets and gridlocked traffic filled my mind. What sort of landscape artist could I become in that environment? But moving home is no guarantee you'll become an artist, whined the voice of doubt in my mind. And do you really want to go back to Cornwall?

Two options, neither of which seemed particularly appealing. I had to make a choice but didn't want to. One decision might seriously damage my relationship; the other required a leap into the unknown. Stephanie's advice came to mind – "don't overthink it!" – so I took a deep breath, reminding myself of London's reputation as one of the greatest cities in the world for art.

"I think we're moving to London!" I exclaimed, hoping the panic in my voice sounded more like excitement as we toasted ourselves and our future.

Tom was largely absent in the weeks that followed, intent on studying hard enough to come away with the first-class degree his father expected. I didn't mind. I was dealing with my own final-year pressures and found it easier being around people like Stephanie, ready with encouragement whenever the urge struck me to throw my paintbrush out the window, followed by myself.

Fern called me unexpectedly one evening, under the

pretence of wishing me luck with my final assignment. Her tone became immediately apologetic as she revealed the real reason for her call: she and Dad had discussed who should tell me they had ended their relationship. She was so sorry about the timing, right before my exams, and she assured me they both wanted to remain friends. Romantically, though, it just hadn't worked out.

"What happened? Did he do something?" I couldn't hide my disappointment. Fern had been so good for Dad and they made each other happy.

"He didn't do anything, which is exactly the problem."

She sounded sad and a touch bitter.

"Everything has been going fine – so well, in fact, that a few weeks ago I suggested we look for a house together. I love the old bugger and, although he never says it, I thought he loved me.

"He shut me down straightaway, said he has no intention of selling the house. That's it, no compromise, no explanation. If we were living together, I told him I didn't feel it should be where he lived with your Mum. I didn't think he even liked the place!"

"He didn't tell you?" I was astounded that he would rather break up with Fern than share with her what he told me the night of their first date. "He won't leave because of Jenni. Mum couldn't stand being there with all the memories but Dad has never been able to move out, just in case."

Fern groaned with exasperation, but her voice was gentler when she spoke: "He should have told me. I don't know that it would have changed things completely, because I need more from him if we're going to be a couple, but at least we'd have had the chance to talk about it."

Tom and I survived our final few weeks of late nights fuelled by takeaways and caffeine pills, and nervous, fidgety days of assessments and exams. My hand ached from hour after hour of writing, interspersed with planning and perfecting pieces for my final degree show. I was quietly proud of my dissertation – a lengthy comparison of two female artists from the 19th century, Billie Waters and Mary Jewels – and an interpretation of their Cornish harbour scenes as my exhibition.

The day after his last exam, Tom's parents drove up from London to stay the night, before taking him home to begin yet more work experience before he even graduated. They took us out to dinner in the same country house Tom and I stayed in on our anniversary, and over dessert they handed us an envelope with both our names on it.

"What's this?" Tom asked.

"Open it!" laughed Valerie, "Or let Joy open it, and you'll find out."

She and Edward beamed at me as I carefully tore it open and discovered two trans-Europe rail tickets with travel guides and some spending money: a gift that reflected our hard work, they said. Their generosity embarrassed me, but it seemed inappropriate to decline when they were so pleased for us.

"You both deserve a nice break after graduation and you can go anywhere you want. Just so long as you come and join us in Nice for a few days," Valerie insisted, turning to me as she added, "The Riviera is perfect in summer."

Tom was delighted with the gift, less keen on the stipulation of visiting the south of France, having spent many hot Augusts among the hordes of Parisians escaping the overcrowded capital. Every hotel, every restaurant, bar, and sun lounger would be fully occupied, mostly with middle class French, but also with Germans, backpacking Brits, wealthy Russians, and of course groups of Americans, who Tom found particularly irritating.

"They wander around calling everything 'neat', thinking that shouting in English makes them easier to understand," he complained. To him, being cultured meant experiencing 'the real thing', not playing it safe with a multilingual tour guide, visiting the obvious attractions. He sulked briefly after I told him he was a snob, before talking about the places he wanted us to go. Barcelona was top of my list, Lisbon on his. We agreed to do our own research and compare notes, with the plan to leave the week after graduation.

When it was time to return to Wales for the last time, we'd only been apart for a handful of weeks, but I was nervously excited at seeing Tom. His School of Law ceremony took place on a warm July morning the day before mine and I sat with his parents and brother, clapping loudly as he smiled and walked across the stage. He looked handsome and supremely confident in his black gown and, if anyone had asked, at that moment I would have said yes, I am in love with this man, and believed I was telling the truth.

The morning of my ceremony Tom knocked on the door of the bed and breakfast where I was staying. I hadn't seen my parents yet as they had arrived late the night before, with Aunt Vera and Red. My aunt insisted on being there to celebrate "the very first Carter to ever graduate". Would Jenni have been the first? In the silence that followed Aunt

Vera's comment, we probably all wondered the same thing.

Tom was grinning. He had broken the rules and kept his hat and gown overnight so we could have a photo together. I was dismayed.

"What if they think it's stolen and report you? You can't be a lawyer with a criminal record!"

He laughed and called me his "stickler", as he always did when I was terrified a tiny transgression would balloon into a Major Crime. Like the time he borrowed a shopping trolley to transport beer kegs for a party. For months it sat in his garden until I wheeled it back under cover of darkness, breathing a sigh of relief that the Trolley Police would not be coming to take him away.

Or the day he stole a mug from a café because my coffee was over-priced yet gritty, and the heavy pottery mug had my favourite flower – Lily of the Valley – painted on it. I was so fearful of being caught with stolen property I threw it away a few days later and told Tom it had broken.

He might have understood what made me that way if I'd told him about my childhood.

"If I got arrested, it would be my first chance to argue a proper case," he said, unconcerned. "The photo is going on the mantelpiece and when our kids ask why mummy and daddy are wearing those funny dresses, we can tell them the story of how we got together."

I forced a smile when he kissed me and hoped it didn't look strained.

As I checked my watch for the umpteenth time, bile rose up to burn the back of my throat: in a few minutes I would be introducing Tom to my family and he still didn't know about Jenni. I swallowed repeatedly. For more than a year I had waited for the right opportunity but it had never presented itself and now time had run out.

I grabbed his hand and swallowed again.

"There's something I have to tell you before you meet my family."

Unable to meet his gaze, I rushed through the lines I had rehearsed many times, hoping he wouldn't interrupt but most of all hoping he would understand why I had lied by omission for so long.

"I'm not an only child. I have a sister, Jenni. She's older than me and she disappeared one day when I was 11." I was speaking quickly. "We've never found out what happened and we don't talk about it much, but her name might come up so that's who she is."

His eyes widened as I began speaking and his eyebrows remained high after I finished.

"You're kidding. What do you mean you have a sister? Why have you never told me that before? You're kidding," he repeated.

"It's the truth. We don't have time to talk about it now – everyone is waiting to meet you. I'll tell you everything later, I promise."

Admittedly, I had ambushed him, but at least now he knew.

He was so shocked I had to steer him through to the breakfast room where my family stood up as we approached. Then his manners took over and his astonished expression was replaced by the Fitzgerald smile as he shook hands and kissed cheeks.

Red tried a huge hug to make him uncomfortable, but he laughed and lifted her off the floor in return. She beamed her approval at me over his shoulder.

My impulse to vomit had reduced with the relief of finally disclosing the secret I had nearly revealed on so many occasions. Not for the first time, I contemplated why I hadn't told him everything at the beginning of our relationship. It would have been so much easier then. Once I had seen his perfect world it became even harder to talk about my childhood, which felt ugly and broken in comparison.

I was relieved, also, that Tom's parents had left for Surrey before breakfast and would not be meeting my parents or learning about Jenni, for now. Edward and Valerie had made me so welcome, I didn't want them to look at me differently, suspicious at the motives that made me lie for so long.

For the rest of the day I blocked the upcoming conversation from my mind. As I crossed the stage to receive my certificate and handshake, the hall was a blur of faces. Afterwards my classmates and I mingled and drank buck's fizz and talked about our plans for the summer. This was the last time I would see most of the people who had shared their lives with me for three years, and with whom I had shared only part of mine. As our families stood proudly on, we posed for photo after photo, hugged our teachers and thanked them for everything.

Then it was over.

Returning to the bed and breakfast, I was suddenly shy. Reluctant to be alone with Tom, I turned on the shower before he could say anything.

"Hat hair," I said, pointing to the aftermath of a day spent wearing a mortar. I stood under the hot water far longer than necessary, dried my hair slowly, and put on my jeans and blouse for dinner.

When I emerged, Tom was holding a bottle of French Champagne and two glasses.

"Let's celebrate," he said. "And then we can talk."

His voice was tinged with reproach.

We didn't talk that night.

I drank glass after glass of Champagne, followed by wine at the restaurant – the first time my family had been together, other than at funerals, since 1983. I knew ignoring Tom was unfair when he was making an effort to fit in, but with each glass of wine I distracted myself a little more from the conversation we had to have.

Mum and Dad seemed unaware of any tension. Dad was content to sit back and watch the rest of the table, while Mum and Aunt Vera discussed the cute Art History professor and wondered loudly if he painted nudes.

Only Red noticed, counting my refills and suggesting I slow down a bit. Everyone else was in celebratory mood and made Tom and me the centre of their toasts.

"To Tom and Joy and your exciting future in London."

"To Tom and Joy. May your overdrafts be paid off quickly!"

"To you both, please remember your family when you're rich and famous – preferably rich!"

This last toast from Red was heartfelt, although she was happier than I had seen her in a long time. She'd taken a step up from the supermarket and was receptionist in a veterinary practice that cared for family pets, with a farm service for the local community.

It didn't hurt that she'd started dating a mechanic who worked across the road from her, a loud man Aunt Vera was not keen on. Not that she would tell her daughter, but Vera saw characteristics that reminded her of Red's father, and his oil-stained fingernails made her shudder.

By the time we were ready to leave the restaurant, it was late. The buzz had died down and only a couple of tables remained. I'd made sure I was in no fit state for a serious conversation with Tom about anything.

In bed, I was only half aware of him taking off my shoes and watch before I descended into a drunken sleep without a single dream.

13

The deliberate bang of a cup on a bedside table woke me painfully from my sleep.

"What else have you lied about?" Tom demanded the second I opened my eyes. He was dressed and packed up and a glance at the clock told me I had missed breakfast. My body was gripped by the hangover from hell. My head was pounding and stomach so full of acid I doubted even the tea would stay down.

His aggressive tone surprised and irritated me.

"Why would you think there's anything else? And that's not fair: I never actually lied, I just never told you the full story. There didn't seem to be a good time when we were first going out, and how was I to know we'd end up being together so long."

He intentionally misinterpreted my words and suggested I didn't care for him at all, or I would have told him about Jenni before now. A betrayal, he called it, a deceit.

The throbbing in my skull made me antagonistic and we ended up in a fight over a whole range of topics: why he wanted our upcoming trip to include his ex-girlfriend's home town of Bordeaux; why we thought it was a good idea to move to London when we hadn't even lived together at university; and ultimately why we were in a relationship, when he clearly didn't trust me and was displaying a total lack of sympathy for what I'd been through.

"I still see her everywhere, Tom. At the back of the lecture theatre as I'm leaving, in the supermarket queuing at the till. I am exhausted by looking for her face in every single crowd, and thinking I see her on every street corner. I don't even know what I'm looking for! Am I taller than her, or did she keep growing? Has she put on weight or dyed her hair? She would be 24 now and what makes me feel sick each morning is the fear I might walk past her today and not recognise her. I didn't know how to explain all that."

I blew my nose, causing a stabbing pain between my temples so wretched, death would have been a release. Tom was silent.

"My parents divorced because the pressure was too much, and neither of them have ever been the same. I spent more time with my aunt growing up because Mum didn't want to be my mother anymore. Dad refuses to sell the house because if Jenni does turn up one day he doesn't want her to find someone else living there. It was hell for all of us and still is and I just never found the right time to tell you."

After a long pause he said, "I'm sorry."

He scraped his chair towards me and rested one hand on either side of my knees as I sat on the bed.

"You're right, I can't imagine what that would have been like. You still shouldn't have kept it from me, though."

He brushed a wave of hair away from my eyes, a gesture I found futile as it sprung back immediately, so I ducked away.

"C'mon Joy, I said I'm sorry. I'm just shocked you would

keep something so important from me and I know Mum and Dad will be as well."

I let him kiss my cheek, then my lips, then my hands. It seemed our first fight was over. He even made me a fresh cup of tea while I was in the shower, which I vomited into the sink when he went to reception to check out.

Red and Aunt Vera in one car, my parents, Tom and I in another, we drove to Bristol where our plan had been to stop for a cosy pub lunch before dropping Tom at the train station. Mercifully I wasn't the only one with a hangover, my mother and aunt having "cut loose" as they put it, so the pub was abandoned for over-priced, unappetising sandwiches we ate in a service station car park, washed down with cans of cola.

Tom insisted we shouldn't wait with him at the station. My protests were only mild and we parted with a "See you next week" and "Don't forget to start packing".

In the car I pretended to sleep as Mum and Dad made small talk about the ceremony and how lovely the meal was, all of us together like that. Nausea ebbed and flowed as I considered Tom's reaction to my news. Not once had I given him a reason to think I was lying about anything. My indignation convinced me I was in the right and his reaction was callous and unacceptable. This was a side of him I hadn't seen before and I could only hope everything would be fine once we were away and relaxing after a high-pressure year.

~ ~ ~

Our trip began positively enough. The topic of Jenni lurked in the background and I knew it would only be a matter of time before he raised it again but we were exaggerated in our cheerfulness, keen to get off to a good start.

Our *Rough Guides* to France, Spain, and Portugal were well-thumbed and full of scraps to mark places we considered unmissable. We'd agreed on an itinerary over the phone, and it no longer included Bordeaux. I was keen to visit the palace in Monaco and dream I owned one of the glamorous yachts in the harbour, and from there it was only a short train ride to Nice. His parents had bought us the tickets, after all.

We left London Waterloo for Paris on a sunny Thursday, our new backpacks stuffed with t-shirts and shorts. We'd booked a hotel for the first few nights to give our trip a romantic start, even if the Hotel Aurelie – walking distance to the golden dome of Napoleon's Tomb and the Champs-Elysées – was only two stars. After that, the remainder of the trip would be in hostels.

Tom knew Paris well and liked being in charge: he'd been there on holiday with his family for a few occasions – Roland Garros, Bastille Day, New Year – and was keen to share his favourite places with me. It made sense, I thought, since he spoke the language. Things would be different as soon as we were off his 'turf'.

"Paris is better once you get away from the touristy bits. We won't bother with Sacré Coeur. The crowds will be terrible at this time of year and you can't get decent food anywhere nearby. Saint Eustache is better, more sophisticated and not as overcrowded."

I protested, insisting I wanted to be an unsophisticated tourist and see the Moulin Rouge on the way up to the cathedral.

My dream was to visit Monet's garden at Giverny, less than two hours from Paris. I had fallen in love with his Waterlilies the very first time I saw them in a shop window, on a poster I begged my mother for. Although I was never going to follow his style, I was fascinated by his life and story and elated at the thought of walking in the very same garden he had strolled through a hundred years before.

The Church of Saint Eustache was amazing, he was right about that: solid and imposing from the outside then surprisingly light inside with enormously high ceilings and ornate stone and wood carvings. I wasn't interested from a religious perspective. The only time my parents took me to church was for Christmas carols and, as a child, I had pleaded with God to return Jenni to us and decided that his lack of response proved his non-existence.

Tom was also right about the crowds around Sacré Coeur but I was glad I put my foot down because it moved me immensely. The warren of surrounding streets and chaotic, jostling steps leading up to the cathedral was in stark contrast to the tranquillity inside. The air was filled with the universal church perfume of wooden pews, musty books, wax, and cold stone. It took my eyes a few seconds to adjust to the darkness, then I saw hundreds of flickering candles and visitors shuffling quietly along. Their reverence was tangible.

Above us, Jesus loomed with outstretched arms above a cast of mortals and religious men and his gold halo seemed to glow of its own accord.

The perfection of it brought tears to my eyes. For two francs I added my candle to the tiers of light and offered a prayer, just in case. If it weren't for Tom fidgeting beside me, I could have stayed for hours.

After a third long day of walking the beautiful tree-lined streets, our feet were hot and tired so for dinner we picked the bistro nearest our hotel – a lively place with a long red canopy and music spilling outside around the chairs and tables. I couldn't wait for my new-found favourite of *Moules frites* and a cold beer.

The basket of fresh bread was irresistible and I dove in while Tom deliberately held back. The moment I had dreaded was here. He had a right to ask about Jenni but when I thought about describing the agony of not knowing whether she was dead or alive, I knew I would feel that pain all over again. Tom began to speak.

"You still haven't explained why you never told me. You know how important trust and honesty are to me so how could you hide something so big?"

I was perplexed: in my mind I had answered that question. Tom was making this about him when the only person it should have been about was Jenni. Here he was, accusing me again, and my guilt was replaced by irritation. This had nothing to do with deceiving him and everything to do with how painful it was to talk about.

The bread became a dry lump and I reached for my beer to help me swallow it down.

"You know why I didn't tell you. It's not like I told everyone and you were the last to find out. I didn't tell anyone after I left home. I wanted to start somewhere new where people didn't know about my family.

"It was worse than if she had died. At least people can relate to what you're going through. They know you'll eventually be back to a kind of normal and they can break the ice, talk about how difficult it was when they lost someone they loved, and you can sympathise in return.

"This was totally different. No-one knew what to do or say, and neither did we so it was impossible to have a normal conversation. People didn't want to be too cheerful in case it offended us, so they ended up talking about nothing.

"And you can't imagine the gossip, everywhere we went. I hated it. People who we thought were friends wouldn't look us in the eye. Some of them openly said they suspected my parents were involved or suggested Jenni must have brought it on herself."

My mind went back to the occasion when I was 13 and picking out Granny Smith apples in the greengrocer, inhaling the sharp smell I loved. Two women had stopped, one sharing new gossip with the other about a girl who was assaulted on the beach after dark a few miles away.

Mrs Blazey was whispering loudly when she said, "You know what 14-year-old girls are like in this day and age. Let's hope this one isn't another Jenni Carter."

Mrs Elliott was nodding in agreement when she glanced around and saw me.

"Joy, dear, I didn't see you there!"

She had the grace to turn a deep shade of red and stay silent but Mrs Blazey kept going.

"We weren't talking about your sister, you know. Everyone knows she was a good girl. This was another Jenni."

But you said Jenni Carter! I wanted to scream in her face. You think my sister did something wrong and it's her fault she disappeared.

I was too young and too well brought up to be rude to

my elders. Instead I hung my head, dropped the bag of apples and left the shop before they could see me cry. I decided never to speak to Mrs Blazey again, and didn't, not even after her husband, my maths teacher, died the very next Christmas. Uncharitably, I thought that was fitting punishment.

Tom sighed with exasperation. Despite his admission that he couldn't imagine what it had been like, he had not yet asked me how I felt. Instead he told me I was disloyal for withholding a part of me from our relationship. Our food arrived and we ate with minimal conversation. I was angry; Tom probably was, too, but not in a way I considered justified.

As we got into bed, I said I would like to spend the next day visiting Monet's house. On my own.

"Fine," said Tom, and rolled over. He was snoring within minutes while I lay awake infuriated and refusing to consider I had done anything wrong.

~ ~ ~

I am in a hurry. I am walking through a crowded market, trying to get to the other side where I know Jenni is waiting. It must be somewhere foreign because I can hear noises and people talking but nothing makes sense. A man grabs my arm and thrusts a small package at me. I push it away and continue down the tiny alleyways, squeezing past the locals, who glare at the intrusion.

My anxiety grows as people wave their hands at me, talking in a language I can't understand. Were they saying hello or warning me about something? I walk on, trying not to slow down as I pass rolls of coloured cloth, buckets writhing with live fish, and sacks of nuts and lentils spilling onto the ground.

More faces turn towards me and the gap between the stalls is narrower here. I have to use my arms to push past people who are yelling unknown words into my face until I burst through a wall of bodies and find myself in an empty street, the air choked with yellow dust.

I have no idea where I am and don't care; I'm just relieved to have made it through. But the swirling dust is settling and that means I'm too late, I was too slow: the dust was Jenni cycling by, and she has disappeared into the distance without waiting for me.

14

As the train sped north-west out of Paris, I had time to think. I tried to see things from Tom's side and failed.

I wanted him to ask what Jenni was like and whether we were close or squabbled endlessly like he and Ben. I would have told him we were the closest sisters ever and I hardly had a single childhood memory without her. Whenever I was scared by thunder and lightning, she held my hand and whispered she was a little bit scared, too. When I pulled the head off my favourite doll to see what her brain looked like, Jenni gave me her doll until Dad managed to re-attach it. On Saturdays, as soon as we were old enough to ride our bikes alone, we would make sandwiches, pick up Ally down the road, and cycle to the beach four miles away. The sandwiches were usually squashed and warm but there would be ice-cream before we came home.

If he'd shown any interest in my sister, I would have shared with him my hope that one day I'd be an aunt to her children. Not one of those stuffy aunts who doesn't truly know you and gives you birthday presents that look like they were bought for someone else, then complains when your thank-you letter doesn't arrive for ages.

I wanted to be an aunt like Vera.

I didn't want this to ruin our trip. I'd worked too hard and planned too much to waste energy arguing about something neither of us could change. It would be easier to give Tom the apology he needed, even if I did not feel it was entirely merited. All the same, the ugly tone of our conversations left me unsettled.

As the train pulled in to Vernon-Giverny station I pushed thoughts of Tom and Jenni from my mind and followed the throng to the bus that would take us to Monet's home of more than 40 years.

It was every bit as perfect as I had hoped. The village's narrow streets and ivy-covered buildings were too gorgeous even for hundreds of tourists to spoil. In the queue I stood on tiptoe, craning for my first view of the gardens. Once inside, oblivious to the crowds, I drifted through the flowerbeds, my gaze level with bold pink hollyhocks and golden sunflowers surrounded by an orchestra of bees. It was easy to see how Monet had been so inspired by his surroundings. I could only dream that my work might one day move people the way his moved me.

The house itself was quaint, frozen in time with the yellows and blues of the 1920s. As a graduation gift, Mum, Dad, and Aunt Vera clubbed together to give me a good camera, one of the new-style Canons ("It's so quiet, you won't even know you've taken a picture," Aunt Vera assured me), along with a dozen rolls of film. Photos would never do it justice, but I dutifully took plenty, inside and out, as I had promised Mum. A love of Monet was one of the rare things we had in common, and I planned to buy her a waterlily print, small enough so it wouldn't be a pain to drag halfway around Europe.

By the time I reached the water garden, my mind was clear. Breathing in the rich, damp soil in front of the Japanese bridge and waterlilies, I was transported inside Monet's paintings. Low hanging weeping willows were reflected in the still water, the surface only broken by the occasional fish. The brilliance of the different shades of green was astonishing. Three or four times I circled the lake at a snail's pace and each time noticed something new.

Sudden hunger pangs were the reminder that somehow more than five hours had passed. The gardens had been so captivating, I'd run out of time to visit the museum or Monet's grave. If it wasn't for Tom, I would have stayed until the very last bus.

Reluctantly I left the gardens behind and bought a baguette to eat in the sun while I waited for the bus. As I contemplated what mood I would find Tom in, I decided to phone Mum.

In the stifling glass phone box, sweat beaded across my top lip as I lined up my coins, hoping they were enough for an international call. The first francs dropped into the machine as she answered.

"Hi Mum? It's Joy."

For a fleeting second when I heard her voice – "You have to come home, Aunt Vera is dead" – I was elated that this was a reason to escape, until I realised what she was saying and her words landed like a physical blow.

There's been an accident, she told me, her voice high-pitched and wavering. Aunt Vera was coming home from a dinner with friends when a lorry skidded on the road after an unseasonal downpour. It happened late the evening before and – thanks to Tom's meticulous itinerary – they phoned our hotel first thing this morning, only to hear I couldn't be reached.

"You have to come home," she repeated, and I murmured of course I would.

The last of my francs clinked and I set the heavy receiver back in its cradle. My head was pounding from the sun as well as from shock and I spent the next two hours numbly staring at the floor of a bus then a train, thinking only about my beloved aunt and how fast I could get home.

It didn't make sense. I couldn't process what Mum had told me. I'd seen Aunt Vera only days earlier when she organised a lunchtime send-off at her house. She was convinced we would be unable to find proper food over the English Channel so, despite the July weather, she had insisted on preparing a hot three-course lunch. Sitting down with her and Red and my parents for the second time in a week had a different tension to it. After graduation we'd been in a restaurant; now we were seated around the same table where we'd eaten together many times, but not for a decade.

Dad drank a little too much sparkling wine and Mum said she'd drop us home, and we rolled out of Aunt Vera's house in the late afternoon knowing we would not need to eat that night. In the car, I suspected Mum was flirting, the recent thaw both strange and a relief. Dad seemed happy at the attention and invited her in, at which point the chill returned. Since walking out, she had crossed the threshold just once to pick up her belongings. She'd left all the photos, all the childhood memorabilia, cards and gifts we made for her, but had taken Jenni's 6-year-old handprint, immortalised in pottery with a baked yellow glaze.

Back at the Hotel Aurelie, Tom flung open the door as soon as he heard my key and held me while I cried for a woman I adored and who had now left me as well.

This time I was thankful Tom had taken charge. We had seats on the early morning Eurostar back to London, then I would continue on the slow intercity to Cornwall, an eleven-hour trek from hotel to home. We left Paris under appropriately gloomy skies, mindless summer reading now replacing our *Rough Guides*. Tom left me at Waterloo with a kiss and a promise to join me before the funeral.

15

Dad was puffy-eyed and understandably sombre when he met me at the train station that evening. We stood out from the other arrivals, the small groups of laughing families reuniting and European backpackers looking around for a hint of where to go. We hugged briefly, I planted a kiss on his cheek, and then we were helping each other load my rucksack into the boot of the car.

Red had been asleep at home when the police called her, and she called Mum, who called Dad and the three of them rushed to the hospital. Red arrived only minutes after the ambulance as the fire crew took an hour to extract Aunt Vera from her car. By the time Mum, and then Dad, reached the hospital it was clear any hope of 'touch and go' had faded, leaving an ashen-faced Eileen to comfort her distraught niece.

The time of death was recorded as 4.37am, as the sun was beginning to rise, six hours after a white hatchback was crushed almost beyond recognition.

Less than 12 hours after Vera had been boldly, joyously alive, Mum took the paper bag containing her sister's belongings and walked with Red down the beige corridors and out into the sunlight.

Mum's plan was to pick up a few of her own things and take them to Aunt Vera's house. It made sense for her to move in for a few days, she said. The spare bedroom was always made up and she'd need to help Red with the funeral arrangements.

That first evening Dad and I ate in stunned near-silence, letting the television fill long gaps in our conversation. There was plenty for the family to do, he said, with the funeral and the house and the finances. He'd offered to help Red and Mum with anything they needed, sorting out any paperwork they didn't want to think about.

The next day we arrived at Aunt Vera's house to the raised voices of Red and my mother, presenting opposing views on the sort of funeral Vera would have wanted. Not surprisingly, the house was exactly as it had been the previous week, with its hint of rose-tinged perfume. Our arrival interrupted the argument and caused another round of tears as we lamented the injustice of it all.

I had few stories to tell of our trip, cut short so early, but no-one thought to ask.

Her whole life, Vera had not set foot in a church for anything other than weddings and funerals, Red's obligatory school events, and Christmas carols. Yet Mum insisted her sister should have a religious service. It was only decent, only proper.

My thoughts flicked to Jenni, as they had done numerous times in the preceding 48 hours. No doubt Mum was contemplating the funeral she would have given her first child, had the circumstances required it. I grabbed Red's hand and took her into the garden. It was warm with a slight haze in the sky but her hand was cold in mine. I walked us to the very end of the narrow plot where we could sit in the afternoon sun.

Suddenly I felt like the older sister, offering wise words of comfort and with the overwhelming desire to keep everyone happy.

"You know what your Mum was like," I started. "She wouldn't care what happened at her funeral, as long as we all had plenty to eat and drink afterwards. She'd resent paying for an organist but don't you think she'd like the subversion of a vicar offering prayers for someone who didn't believe in God?"

Red gave me a weak smile. "I know. But I'm her daughter, it's supposed to be me taking care of everything. I'm not 12 years old, I'm a grown woman and Aunt Eileen needs to let me do this."

I considered sharing my suspicion that Mum's behaviour was driven as much by thoughts of Jenni as Aunt Vera but didn't want Red to think we weren't all focused on her.

We sat there for a while. In the garden, it was difficult to accept the reality that someone who was there only moments ago was now gone. If I looked up at the kitchen window, I expected Aunt Vera to be there, busying herself at the sink.

I left Red in the sunshine and went inside to talk to Mum. She glanced up from the Yellow Pages as I handed her a mug of tea, appearing at once childishly vulnerable and older than her 46 years.

"You need to let Red look after the arrangements," I said gently. "I know Aunt Vera was your sister, but Red is her daughter. She needs to do this. I'd be the same, if it was me."

Mum lowered her head and a tear dripped off her nose into her lap. My heart ached with unprecedented compassion.

"I'm worried she won't do it right. She's so scatty and disorganised. What would people think if it wasn't done properly?"

I was wrong. This wasn't about Red or Aunt Vera, or even about Jenni. Mum was more concerned with how the floral displays would be compared to those of recently deceased Mrs Tanner and how humbly she would accept compliments from Aunt Vera's friends and neighbours for the amazing afternoon tea she put on after the service, at such a difficult time.

"Just let her do it," came out more harshly than I intended, but I was tired and newly reminded of why I had seen her so infrequently in the past few years. To push my point, I grabbed the phone and the Yellow Pages as I walked back out into the garden.

Red decided on a local funeral director whose daughter she had met and liked. Mr Meneer was around within the hour, respectful yet businesslike, and Red held my hand while she picked cheerful dahlias in oranges and yellows and a white casket, as tears streamed in torrents down our faces.

Neither Dad nor I had eaten since breakfast. Throughout the day, several casseroles had silently materialised on the doorstep, all in carefully labelled Tupperware tubs. I figured Red would need them more than us so when Dad and I left we went to the town's only Chinese restaurant. To my surprise, the staff greeted Dad by name and knew his regular takeaway order.

Two days before the funeral Tom arrived, bearing yellow and white roses for me and sickly-scented lilies for Red. The second part of his graduation present was a car – nothing ostentatious, a second-hand sporty hatch, shiny and black and with 12,000 miles on the clock – and he was eager to try it out on the long run to Cornwall.

Dad awkwardly suggested Tom would be more comfortable in the spare bedroom. I was relieved I wouldn't have to explain why I didn't want him to sleep in Jenni's bed.

Tom was kind and caring towards me and I wondered if he'd sought advice from his parents on how to prevent the first fracture in our relationship from becoming more serious. Perhaps he just felt sorry for me because he knew how much Aunt Vera meant.

He was keen to explore the area where I grew up, since I seldom talked about it.

"Show me your favourite places, I want to see them all. And I want to see family photos, lots of pictures of you as a cute kid."

What sounded like an easy request was anything but. The local park was where Jenni and I loved spinning on the roundabout until we were too dizzy to stand when we jumped off. On the wall behind the community centre we would sit with Ally and spy on the girls taking ballet classes before practising our own clumsy routines in the garden. We always bolted through the overgrown churchyard on our way home from school, scared we would be chased by ghosts if we lingered, but not scared enough to walk the extra half mile around.

After breakfast the day before the funeral, Tom and I left the house. Anxiety made me fidgety as I planned a route that was not charged with painful memories.

I pointed out my primary school, which had been enormous and imposing but had shrunk to its real size as I grew. We stopped briefly at the sports pavilion where Diane and I would sit and watch her Dad play cricket when we were eight or nine and I had my first taste of peppermint cordial. I showed Tom the town's steepest hill, the site of the long-since-fixed pothole that threw me off my bike when I was 10. It had caused the long scar down my left knee he often traced with a finger when we were lying in bed.

Tom liked the town. "I'd expected it to be more run down, being in the country, but it's quite pretty, isn't it?"

Seeing it through someone else's eyes I was amazed to find I agreed, long after I'd last appreciated the beauty of it.

"And now it's time for…" and he tapped a drum roll on the steering wheel, "Random Excursion!" he cried with a flourish. Our game, at university, meant jumping on a random bus service from the town centre for exactly 20 stops. More often than not we'd arrive in the middle of nowhere, save for a small terrace of houses or a farm entrance, and would walk back along quiet roads or a coastal path. Only once did we end up outside a country pub, where we abandoned our plans for a walk when we saw their Sunday carvery – a Welsh lamb roast for only £4.95 including dessert.

"We'll alternate left, then right, then left again to see where it takes us."

Not waiting for my response, he indicated left at once and accelerated hard to start the low-gear climb out of town.

"Stop!"

The voice didn't even sound like me.

The wheels skidded as Tom slammed on the brakes. At the blast of a horn behind us, he steered to the kerb and switched off the engine, turning to me with a frown.

"What the hell?"

"Sorry, I didn't know you were going to go up here. I can't go up this road."

Tom looked up the hill and back at me and I wished his brain would make the connection so I didn't have to say it.

Annoyance was evident on his face.

"If we go up here… this is Jenni's road… we get to the spot where I last saw her."

His frown softened a little as my eyes filled with tears.

"Joy, this is ridiculous. Ever since you told me about Jenni I've been tiptoeing around, waiting for you to open up. Mum told me to be patient and I thought being in your home town might be different but you still haven't explained how she disappeared."

Pushing aside my annoyance that he hadn't asked me about it until now, I picked at my fingernails as I began the story.

I skipped over how I helped Jenni write the addresses on the newspapers and pack them into our faded fluorescent satchels, and how we took the pothole-filled laneway behind the bakery so we could breathe in the delicious smell of the day's first pasties turning golden.

Slowly and matter-of-factly I recited the story of how I lost sight of her when my legs became tired, of finding her bike in the road when I got to the top. As I described Eric pulling up in the van, Tom interrupted me.

"But how is that possible? You must have seen something. People don't just vanish into thin air."

I blinked at him as tears and rage bubbled up inside me, hating him to his very soul for saying what I had heard over and over: "You *must* have seen something" or "You must have seen *something*".

No matter which way people emphasised it, or how many times they asked, the 11-year-old in me always answered a plaintive and impotent "I didn't".

"How can you ask me that, you complete prick? Don't you think I've been asked a thousand times?"

Tom recoiled. Without waiting for an answer, I grabbed my bag and slammed the car door behind me.

To his credit, he didn't try and stop me.

For an instant I wished I'd been like Sandrine and slapped him across his astonished face.

I stormed through the town, heading for a place I knew well. Past the last house, beyond the by-pass and the railway line was a track by the stream, and off the track was a derelict hut. You'd have to know it was there to see it. The tin roof was partially rusted through but a covering of twisted brambles and ivy kept the interior mostly dry. Stones were piled into makeshift seats and an old curtain – originally pink, now brown and tattered – flapped in the empty doorway.

The musky air as I stepped inside took me back to the first time I was here. The sun had been shining when we left home on our bikes but a sudden April shower had Jenni shrieking and running for shelter. It was a coming-of-age scene: the older sister sharing the secret hut on condition that I mustn't tell anyone or go there without her.

That promise was only half kept: I didn't tell my friends but I did go without her to escape our sombre house and sit in semi-meditation listening to the glug and gurgle of the stream.

I closed my eyes and saw Jenni, dashing away from me to escape the rain.

16

Red did her mother proud, even if Eileen did not think so. The room at the crematorium, with its huge window overlooking the valley, was decked in flowers and bright paper streamers that were more flamboyant than funereal.

It was a breezy August afternoon, neither too warm nor too cool. The 100 or so people who crowded into the service had views, past the flower-laden coffin, of mature trees swaying with the wind.

The music was uplifting yet respectful.

The celebrant and Red had woven together the story of Vera's life, punctuated with anecdotes from friends that made us laugh through our sniffles.

In a concession from her niece, Mum had chosen her own reading. For her moment in the spotlight, she started in the Old Testament, receiving reassuring nods from the older mourners as she wove Ecclesiastes ("a time to be born, and a time to die") with Lamentations ("though he brings grief, he will show compassion, so great is his unfailing love"). From there, passages from Matthew and John followed and she spoke as if performing for a paying audience. People were shuffling in their seats by the time she bowed her head solemnly, so Red quickly wrapped up with the invitation that everybody was welcome back at the house.

On cue, *Top of the World* filled the air as the mourners spilled out into the car park. People gave the collective sigh that marks the end of a funeral service, relieved it was over. They were ready to gather in Vera's lounge as they had done many times before, this time recounting memories of the best dinners, the funniest parties, and other times they had spent together.

Fern was there, both to support Dad and because she and my aunt had become friends, catching up occasionally to watch the romantic comedies Dad wasn't interested in and complaining over a glass of wine about the stubbornness of men. Even though Mum hadn't acknowledged to me Fern and Dad's relationship was over, I assumed she was aware.

Tom was on his best behaviour, either taking instructions from Mum who was coordinating food – all served in or on the latest Tupperware, naturally – or ensuring people's glasses or cups were full. Periodically he appeared at my side, quiet and attentive. We had barely spoken since the previous afternoon and I remained angry. This judgemental side of him was not one I liked and left me questioning how much he really cared about me.

Barbra Streisand and more Carpenters were the soundtrack to a wake Aunt Vera would have loved and her daughter was proud to have hosted. Friends wiped away tears as they clasped Red and said how much her Mum would have enjoyed the occasion.

Tom reappeared at my elbow, a small white wine his offering in a crystal tumbler. Aunt Vera always says – used to say, I corrected myself – that even cheap wine tastes better out of good glassware. Around the room were her friends drinking reds, whites, the odd whiskey, all from heavy-bottomed crystal.

A few men around Aunt Vera's age appeared to be on their own, making light conversation with people they had never met before. Were they friends or lovers? I didn't remember any men in my aunt's life. She didn't ever seem lonely, though, so she probably kept that side of her life to herself.

One man was familiar and I had to think hard to place him.

When Red and I were at school – she was 16, I was 13 – Aunt Vera took us to Bath for a weekend treat. It was my first time staying in any sort of hotel, so even the modest guest house felt special. Red and I were in a room with two neat single beds, a washbasin, and white towels edged with embroidered roses. Across the hall, Aunt Vera's double room had its own adjoining toilet, while we shared the large bathroom down the hall with other guests.

After a pre-performance meal in a small Italian restaurant, we joined the shuffling queue of smartly dressed people braving the cold to watch *The Constant Wife* at the Theatre Royal. I felt very sophisticated in my best winter dress with woollen tights and school shoes.

In the interval, Aunt Vera ordered a gin and tonic and two lemonades before introducing us to a very tall, slightly hunched man who smiled incessantly and said he was "charmed" to make our acquaintance. Arthur lived in Bristol and said he and Vera often met up when they were both interested in a performance. He stood close to her but not too close.

We saw him again briefly as people were spilling out

across the pavement after the final curtain, their breath hovering in the cold air. He raised a long-fingered hand and we waved back, politely.

The third time I saw him was the next morning, leaving Aunt Vera's room as I came back from the toilet shortly after dawn. His exaggerated tiptoe as he crept away down the hall gave him a comical air and I was glad he didn't see me.

~ ~ ~

By evening, as the last people were saying their goodbyes to Red, the kitchen was a mess of empty bottles. Tom did his best to clean up along the way and stayed sober to drive Dad and I home.

The last plate had been dried and put away and Red was standing in the hallway with a dejected expression. I felt an ache for her, and for Jenni who should have been here too.

"Come and stay with me and Dad for a few days," I told her. "Tom's driving back to London tomorrow, anyway."

She nodded, her raised brow telling me she noticed how things were between me and Tom.

In the car, I made Dad sit in the front next to Tom – more legroom, I insisted. In reality it was an excuse so I could give in to the tears that started before we even left the driveway and flowed the whole journey home.

Tom understood why I didn't feel able to pick up our trip where we had left off – or he said he did. His disappointment seemed real but an hour later he had arranged to take his old school friend Max instead. The two of them would fly from London directly to Nice to see Tom's parents before continuing as planned. Laughing, he said he hoped the youth hostels had an extra bed so he and Max wouldn't have to snuggle up together. The way he spoke made Aunt Vera's death seem like nothing more than an inconvenient interruption to his summer.

I did my best to be upbeat on our final morning together, two days after the funeral. I told myself I was just tired and overthinking things in my grieving state, that everything was going to be OK once we put all this behind us and moved to London. I desperately wanted to believe it.

Tom seemed quite chipper as he threw his bag into the back of the Golf after lunch. We hadn't spoken about the latest argument and despite my disappointment at leaving so much unsaid I was unwilling to spoil his departure. He was showing no such concerns, as if we hadn't argued at all. Before he left, he held me close and whispered he loved me and would miss me, Max would be a poor substitute. I mumbled I loved him too and wished him a safe trip.

He shook Dad's hand and offered his thanks and condolences again, so well mannered. Dad was impressed at the young man before him, secure in his own skin.

"Hopefully we'll see you back here soon, and under better circumstances next time," Dad said solemnly but warmly.

I waved as the car pulled away, eager for the calm I knew would follow.

Back inside, Dad reboiled the kettle. He'd shown little emotion over the past few days but now, with no-one else around, he appeared to be on the verge of tears.

"It's a sad business. Such a sad business," he said, cradling his cup with both hands as I nodded my agreement.

"She was a marvellous woman, your aunt. She looked after us so well when your Mum left. I was so grateful and I don't know if I ever told her that."

"She knew, Dad, we talked about it loads of times. She didn't need you to say anything. When we lost Jenni she was as helpless as the rest of us so after Mum left, she was glad she could do practical things like shopping and cooking."

We sipped our tea, remembering the weight of the empty house at that time.

"Jenni."

Dad's single word cut the air. When was the last time I'd heard him say her name?

"It's 10 years tomorrow," he said, and his face turned into a gargoyle of grief, his shoulders heaving silently.

My hug was self-conscious and uncomfortable, twisted sideways as Dad was doubled over, head in hands, but it didn't matter. His hair smelled of the same cream he had used since before I was born and the total greyness of it surprised me. Up close, his shirt collar was grubby from his inexpert attempts to take care of himself. The old net curtain – the one with the small rip hidden in the gathers at the top – cast a shabby light over the room and I knew the fabric would leave dust between my fingers if I touched it.

An unfamiliar flood of protectiveness made me hold him tighter.

We stayed like that until he needed to blow his nose. I thought of all the times I had ironed his handkerchiefs over the years, the monogrammed white cotton ones we'd given him for birthdays and the cheaper packs of five he started buying after Mum left.

He was embarrassed at his outburst. Boiling the kettle again to compose himself, he came back in with a packet of biscuits.

"Do you want to talk about Jenni?" I asked. This was the best chance we'd ever had for a meaningful conversation.

He shook his head then opened and closed his mouth.

I waited.

"It's been 10 years," he said again, incredulous. "How is that possible? Where the hell did she go?"

Unlike Tom, Dad was not waiting for a reply. He didn't expect me to have the answer.

"Have you ever been back there?"

"Every single day right after it happened. Even at night until the first Christmas. I drove there over and over and tried to look at it differently each time, in case the police missed something.

"Every possible scenario ran through my mind – murder, kidnapping, a silly accident. Even suicide. I couldn't shake the belief she was out there, maybe scared to come home in case she was in trouble, not sure if we wanted her back. It didn't matter how much time I spent thinking about it, none of the options made any sense."

All I could do was agree. It was as if Dad was able to read my mind and I told him so.

Relief softened his expression. "I was never quite sure what you thought," he said. "I wondered if you thought she was a runaway and it was our fault or were worried we blamed you since you were the last one to see her."

"A bit of both," I admitted. Why had we never said these things before?

I shared how I searched for Jenni in every crowd and on every street and it was Dad's turn to agree.

"It's part of why I stayed here, even after your Mum left," he said. "Some people are amazed we never moved away. When you know nearly everyone you meet, it's less likely you'll be startled by seeing someone you think is Jenni."

I hesitated before asking what I'd wanted to ask for a decade. "Do you think it's possible she's still out there?" I couldn't bring myself to say "alive".

"Statistically," Dad took another deep breath and his chin trembled again. He shook his head. "The police told us years ago she was almost certainly gone." So he wasn't able to use the real words either.

"Of course you never, ever want to accept it. Saying it out loud makes it too real and I could never bring myself to tell you that, in case you thought we'd given up on her. After a while, though, something switches inside you, and you almost, almost don't care one way or the other, you just want to know."

I knew what he meant.

When he stopped talking his whole face deflated, making him older than his years. He'd paid a price for holding on to the hurt and staying in our house just so I would never think he'd given up on Jenni.

He stood up and disappeared briefly, returning with a large storage box that had the name of his bank printed on the side.

"I want you to see something," he said solemnly.

"What is it? A box full of cash I hope!" and he managed a smile before sitting down.

I lifted the lid and knew instantly what the box contained: all the pieces of information I wished I'd gathered so one day I might be able to solve the puzzle.

Flicking through the stack of newspaper clippings, I recognised some of the front pages – a view from a helicopter of the hillside covered in people and an insert of Jenni's school photo next to the bold text, TOWN UNITES IN SEARCH FOR MISSING GIRL. A few editions later, Eric's face stared back at me, cornered and confused, above the caption, IS THIS THE FACE OF A KILLER?. No wonder he left as soon as he was allowed to.

Articles on yellowed paper documented the increasing frequency of child or young adult abduction and decreasing rates of police success in solving them. A few kind letters from well-meaning families with their own missing children sought to give us comfort; several anonymous ones stated we would burn in Hell. Assurances from the police that they were pursuing every avenue of enquiry and would keep us informed. Tarot cards and imploring notes from psychics who promised they could tell where Jenni was – which shallow grave or big city or overseas brothel she had ended up in.

Every article from every newspaper that mentioned Jenni in the first year she vanished, and every new lead and anniversary since.

Dad had stored it all away safely, just in case.

"Your Mum doesn't know I kept all this. After a while, I hardly had a chance to read the headlines before she threw them out, so I had to ask the newsagent to keep copies. At first when I was convinced Jenni had run away, I wanted her to see them, to understand what a huge fuss she'd caused, so she wouldn't do it again. If she was taken against her will, I always assumed I'd have the chance one day to show her how hard we tried to find her."

Poor Dad.

"Mum never thought you were involved though, did she?"

"No! Of course not," he was emphatic. Then, after a pause, "Well, there was one moment, a few weeks after it happened. I refused to let you be hypnotised and your Mum kept asking me why. Several clairvoyants had turned up nothing and the police said in several other cases hypnosis had helped witnesses remember important details. I didn't want to put you through it. You'd told us what you saw, which was nothing, so I couldn't see what gaps there were to fill in.

"We argued about it for days and even though she knew full well I was with her that morning, part of me wondered if she suspected me of something. I assumed she'd let it go until not long before she walked out."

I remembered the argument he didn't know I'd heard. Dad said hypnosis was "brainwashing" and more likely to plant ideas than help me remember anything. Mum said he didn't know anything about it and accused him of not wanting to find Jenni. She even asked if he was afraid of what I might remember. I was in the living room, crying, while they argued loudly in the kitchen. Dad slammed the back door so hard the glass rattled. Mum came in, picked up her book and continued reading without acknowledging me.

"What about now?" I asked. "If you knew we'd still be looking 10 years on, would it have made a difference?"

"Tough question. I was trying to protect you. You were so young and vulnerable that even if I could turn the clock back, I'm not sure I would do anything differently."

I told Dad my plan for marking the anniversary and asked if he would like to come to St Marow with me.

He refused. "I don't need to go there. That's not where Jenni is. I prefer to picture her listening to her Walkman in the garden or playing in the street."

Talking to Dad so openly had relieved some of the anxiety that always accompanied the anniversary. He was right, Jenni was everywhere, but I needed to see the road for real, not just in my nightmares.

We hugged a long, warm hug good night, both of us aware that the balance between us had shifted.

~ ~ ~

I'm lying on a couch much softer than our old sofa at home. A man in a tweed suit is leaning towards me, waving a pocket watch on a chain. He's a hypnotist. I'm on edge, wanting to give in to it, but not at all sleepy or relaxed. He chides me for resisting and asks what I'm afraid of. Nothing, I tell him. I am desperate to remember something that helps find my sister.

Still the silver watch is swinging and its rhythmic tick is the only noise in the room. My eyes follow it back and forth, fully alert, until the hypnotist grows frustrated and slams it into a drawer. The ticking is as loud as before and I realise it's the sound of a bike chain clicking as the wheel spins.

I jump up to see Jenni's bike behind his desk, which means he has her and he's not really trying to hypnotise me. He sees the recognition on my face and launches himself at me so suddenly I throw myself out of bed and wake up with a bang on the floor.

17

The strum of rain against the window the next morning was unexpected; in my memory mid-August was perpetually sunny.

For a millisecond I thought about abandoning my pilgrimage, but I'd spent so long thinking about it, I couldn't back out. I'd go the long way around, make it a proper walk through the town and up the hillside beyond it so I could approach St Marow from the opposite direction. I would stop briefly where it happened and come back down the hill into town, as if we had dropped off our first newspapers and were starting the rest of the round.

Downstairs, Dad was moving around. The jingle of keys would be followed by the quiet click of the front door before he forgot to stop the front gate from slamming. It was a wonder one of the neighbours hadn't offered to fix it years ago.

The faint smell of Tom's aftershave wafted around me as I stripped the sheets from the spare bed but it was not him I was thinking of.

In the fridge, leftovers from the funeral were stacked in plastic tubs. I stuck a few slices of ham and cheese into a bread roll and grabbed a can of lemonade.

Despite the rain, which had eased a little by mid-morning,

shorts and a t-shirt were all I needed under my lightweight cagoule. On my feet were the sandals I had bought for our European trip. Even though they were hideous, the expensive leather moulded perfectly around my feet. Essential for comfort and to avoid blisters getting in the way of our holiday, Tom had insisted.

Tom. Out of sight, and so quickly out of mind.

Packing my Walkman, spare batteries, and my favourite cassettes, I stepped out with purpose.

Traffic was light, and no-one else was out and about on foot. With my hood pulled tightly around my face, I hummed my way through the town, knowing every song equally as well as I knew every inch of the pavements.

By the time I flipped the cassette and waited for the first anguished lines of *Town to be Blamed,* fields had replaced shops. The volume was up as high as my ears would take and, after checking I was alone, I belted out the angry lyrics about tears and dreams and narrow lanes that could have been written about me.

The sun emerged fiercely as I passed the sign announcing my arrival in St Marow village. Suddenly steaming, I stripped off my cagoule and sat in the bus shelter to eat my lunch, overlooking the wet grass of the small village green.

A burgundy car hissed by on the damp road without noticing me, or so I thought. I watched curiously as it did a U-turn in the forecourt of the abandoned Post Office and drew up to where I was sitting. Still the driver's face wasn't visible, the sun blinding me as it bounced off the passenger side window. Someone must be lost.

A man's tanned arm reached across and awkwardly wound down the window.

"Joy?"

Squinting, I peered in. "Eric?"

What were the chances?

A smile lit up his face. "Can I give you a lift somewhere?" he asked.

"Um, no, I'm just walking. Thanks though."

"Ah. I see." And he did see. "It's 10 years, isn't it?"

I nodded.

"And I heard you lost your aunt recently? God, Joy, how are you feeling?"

"I'm fine. I'll be fine," I said, knowing my tone probably gave me away.

"I'm on my way home. Come and sit for a while. D'you want tea? Or something stronger?"

Sandwich crumbs fell off my shorts as I opened the car door. The old Ford was pretty beaten up inside.

Eric did another U-turn and we were at the farm almost immediately.

While he put away the supplies he'd picked up, I moved around the living area, a large, tidy space with the old furniture unchanged since the last time I was there, despite the fact Eric lived there alone.

"I moved Dad into a home two years back. I kept him here as long as possible because he was better when he was around Mum's things, but his memory was gone and he wasn't able to manage without someone looking over him all the time.

"As soon as he stopped knowing who I was, it was time to let someone else take care of him. Deep down he must have known, though: he was only there for a month before he died."

It was the most I'd ever heard Eric speak and his voice was low and calm.

We talked about Aunt Vera and the shock of the accident less than two weeks earlier that already seemed like months ago. I told him I'd been overseas at the time, without mentioning who with. He'd been to Spain on his own the previous year, to Barcelona and Madrid. It was his first holiday abroad and the first time he'd been able to take a break once Harry no longer needed him.

"The travel agent recommended Spain as an easy place to start. It made me realise I've never been totally on my own before, no-one knowing where you are and no-one waiting for you when you get home. It made me feel too mature but young and independent at the same time!"

I wanted him to describe Barcelona but he said he didn't have the words to do it justice.

Ever since one of Miss Robbins's art classes when I was about 12 I'd wanted to visit the city, thanks to her regular slideshows of buildings and artworks around the world to inspire us to "see everything possible in one lifetime". I was mesmerised by the Sagrada Família and imagined growing translucent silver wings so I could fly up and see every breathtaking detail. For years I dreamed of one day walking the warm streets at dusk, then waking at sunrise to set up my easel before anyone else was around.

Eric loved the food, describing in detail Madrid's signature 'Cocido' stew, which made me laugh: apart from the chickpeas, its combination of turnip, cabbage, pork, and beef sounded exactly like the stews we made at home.

Talking to him was easy, natural, and I was drawn in by how kind his green eyes and permanent laughter lines made him appear.

He was young to have lost both parents, who had met

comparatively late in life and produced their only child later still. To his surprise, when he was dealing with his father's estate, he found documentation of an inheritance from his mother to be held in trust until Eric was 28.

"She put money away without telling me. I'm not even sure Dad knew. She must have imagined I'd be settled with a wife and children by now, ready to take over the place and let her and Dad retire to the cottage next door."

Instead he was here alone, wanting to travel more except the farm was hard to leave. He was content, though, and said the money was enough that he could take his time to work out what to do with his life.

"Not quite enough to buy a better car, though?" I teased, and his warm laugh filled the kitchen.

Then he was straight-faced. "I can't believe how much has changed. I'm an old bachelor and here you are with the world at your feet."

He was right, both of us were different since our last encounter. I'd been 16, him 24. Now we were both adults and I was pleased he was treating me that way. Eric had the same quiet manner but a more comfortable confidence had replaced his shyness, without a hint of arrogance, and I realised how attractive that made him.

When he offered me a bottle of beer I accepted. Sitting at his kitchen table, I had no reason to hurry. As for having the world at my feet – I muttered something about things not necessarily being what they seem and he reached out his hand and rested it on mine. His thumb rubbed reassuringly across the back of my hand with the slight roughness of a farmer's skin.

He leant in so slowly that at first I wasn't sure he

intended to kiss me. Maybe he was giving me time to react. Our chairs were too far apart so I had to lean, too. His lips were warm and soft, with a faint prickle from his unshaved top lip. When I kissed him back, he smiled without stopping.

His hand moved up to my hair before settling on my neck, where his thumb continued to caress me. The whole moment – his lips pressed on mine and the sound of our accelerated breathing – felt completely normal.

"Is this OK?" He was the first to speak.

I nodded my reply. He stood up and took my hand, drawing me towards him. The warmth of his fingertips on my lower back and his body against mine filled me with a recklessness that was out of character. For several minutes we stood in the old-fashioned kitchen with its hint of cinnamon, kissing as if we'd waited years for the opportunity.

He pulled away slightly and I knew my cheeks were burning red.

"I want to take you upstairs, but only if you want to."

At this point, I was ready to strip naked and lie on the kitchen table if he suggested it and was astonished at my own behaviour.

"I want to."

He guided me to his bedroom and closed the door in the empty house but let the sun stream in the open window. I forgot my usual reluctance to be seen without clothes in daylight.

Almost without pausing, we lay down and he continued to kiss my lips, my neck, while I moved my arms over his shoulders and smelled grassy fields and fresh linen. As he moved down to my breasts I ran my fingers through his hair and wondered if he could hear how fast my heart was racing.

His fingers were so tanned against my paleness. I watched them as they traced lines down my chest and around my stomach before following the curve of my arched back.

A momentary fumble, the scrape of a drawer, and he was back in front of me. For a second he bit his lip to focus and then we were both impatient, using our hands and laughing at our clumsiness.

At first I watched his face as he watched us moving together, our fingers interlaced. His body on mine felt perfect and I tilted my head back, gripping with my knees as our breathing filled the room. Then I was crying out, digging into his shoulders as if I could pull him even closer. Eric seemed to stop breathing for several seconds before he came noisily, with a long groan. He looked down at me, a ridiculous, gorgeous grin across his face as a giggle welled up from somewhere in my chest. I couldn't hold it back.

"I promise I'm not laughing at you. This is just not how I saw today panning out," I said, as a couple of inexplicable tears escaped.

"Me neither. Not in a million years," he smiled as he said it. "This is definitely better than the afternoon I was expecting!"

We lay side by side. My shyness kicked in so I grabbed the sheet while Eric lay beautiful and naked next to me in an easy silence.

He fell asleep for a few minutes, breathing quietly as I lay looking at him with a feeling of calm flowing through my body.

Tom's face popped into my head, reminding me that I was still lying in another man's bed, however unplanned this was. It was cheating of the worst kind. If I told Tom, he might think I was punishing him for his recent behaviour or would use it to prove I must have lied about other things. He'd never trust me again and I would have ruined any chance of seeing if things would be better once we were in London. As for Eric – I wasn't naïve enough to think this was anything other than opportunistic.

Eric opened his eyes to see a look of disquiet on my face and misinterpreted it as regret.

"I hope you don't feel I took advantage there. That's not what I meant when I offered you a lift."

"No! I would never think that. Let's just take this for what it is – an afternoon neither of us were anticipating when we got out of bed this morning."

I did my best to sound nonchalant; in truth I was glowing. It was weeks since Tom and I had had sex, the mixture of arguments and alcohol and grief making it easy for me to push him away. If I thought hard about it, my relationship seemed changed long before this afternoon.

Eric was only the second man I had slept with. Tom had slept with half a dozen women before me, so I assumed his experience made him a good lover. In one afternoon, another man had proved that to be not entirely correct.

Unlike most of my friends, I had finished university without a single one-night stand. That wasn't what this felt like but I had to work out how to leave. Keen to make Eric think we had no reason for embarrassment, despite how self-conscious I now was, I sat up and pulled on my clothes.

He offered me a lift home. I declined politely, explaining my plan to walk along the lane to where Jenni had been and back into town. Then he offered to come with me and I could have kissed him for being so amazing.

"I pass that spot every day, give or take," He shook his head in disbelief. "I've never stopped thinking about it. About her. And you."

His goodbye kiss was more than a friendly farewell, but there was no talk of "see you soon" or "call me". The relief at not having to make any kind of commitment was accompanied by wanting to stay.

What on earth would Mum say if she knew what I'd just done? From the very first hours after Jenni went missing Mum was convinced Eric was guilty, or at the very least involved. Despite being so young when it happened, I had never wavered from my conviction he had nothing to do with it. Maybe it was easier for her to direct her anger at someone she knew than to stare at everyone she passed on the street, wondering if they knew what had happened. All the same, one day she would have to accept that the evidence she wanted did not exist.

~ ~ ~

As I walked away from the farm, from Eric, the whole day had a surreal air and I approached the bend in the road with trepidation. My desire to be there was waning. I'd come to feel closer to Jenni but the previous night's conversation with Dad made me suddenly sick with the fear that I would know she was gone.

Before I could change my mind, I broke into a run for the last hundred feet, the slap of my sandals on the road drowned out by my noisy breath. I came to a halt. This was it. The twisting pain behind my ribs was even stronger here, like my heart was getting ready to explode into a thousand red shards. In the centre of the road I stood on the exact spot where Jenni's purple bike had lain.

A deafening roar filled my ears and every piece of grief I had ever felt came crashing down, the weight buckling my knees. In the middle of the road I sobbed uncontrollably for several minutes, my tears evaporating quickly on the hot tarmac. I inhaled until my chest hurt, then let out one long, loud bellow, trying to expel all the anger and desperation and fear and loss from my lungs.

I was spent.

18

Tom and I didn't speak while he was enjoying our trip with Max. He sent a postcard from Nice ("It's very Nice! Mum and Dad say hi. Love you" was all he wrote) but he called me the evening he arrived home. His tone was jovial, normal. In his mind, everything was fine between us and I prayed he wouldn't hear anything in my voice that would tell him what I'd done.

It was easy to listen to him talk. He was full of tales of noisy, stuffy youth hostels, drinking competitions, and being caught skinny dipping in the pool of a hotel he wasn't even staying in.

"What was Barcelona like? I want every detail."

"Hot. Crowded. Full of noisy Spanish tourists. But the beer was cold and the food was pretty cheap."

Not quite what I was hoping to hear.

If he'd asked me how the past few weeks had been, I wouldn't have been able to tell him much. After arguing with myself for days, I had decided to push thoughts of the farmhouse to the back of my mind and never mention it to Tom.

I'd had an unexpected phone call from his mother after

Aunt Vera's funeral, a few evenings after Tom left. Uneasily I took the receiver from Dad, not knowing how much Tom would have told his parents.

"I had an aunt growing up," Valerie began. "Millicent was a great-aunt, actually, my grandmother's sister, so she was quite old. I was your age when she died and I missed her so much. I'd always been able to talk to her about the things my mother and I didn't discuss. Tom told me how close you were to your aunt, especially after what happened to your sister" – so he had told her – "and I know this won't be much comfort right now but I'm here if ever you need me."

I was touched. Tom could have told his parents anything – he'd lost trust in me because I'd lied, or I'm not the girl he thought I was – but Valerie was offering support not judgement.

"Thank you, it's so kind of you to say that, and to let us stay in your flat."

"We hope you'll stay there as long as you need. London rents are horrendous and it's such a waste for it to be empty. Edward rarely stays in the city anymore. He does most of his work from home, so he'll only be there one or two nights a month."

When I told her I was looking forward to visiting her and Edward once we were nearby, I meant it.

In that late part of summer, Dad and I spent more time together than I could ever remember. We were both quiet, still grieving, but he booked time off work so we could take day trips to distract ourselves. He even gave me a few driving lessons and paid for an intensive course with a local instructor, so all I'd needed to do in London was take the test.

We joined the tourists on their annual invasion of

Cornwall and crawled for mile after mile behind nervous city drivers along narrow lanes with unforgiving verges. Relaxing in pub gardens or walking through the woods, we enjoyed the ordinariness in contrast to the intensity of the previous few weeks.

After our conversation about Jenni, the transformation happened overnight: Dad behaved as though he had been granted long-awaited permission to talk about Jenni, telling me stories I had never heard before.

"She nearly drowned once, you know. You may not remember but in the summer term she and her friends would go to school before class and use the pool. One morning when she was 10 or 11 they were playing around, seeing who could bounce the highest on the diving board, and she was winded when she hit the water."

I did remember because Jenni had told me I was too young to go with them and I sulked for days.

"Thankfully, Mrs Nancarrow next door went to tell them off for all their shrieking. She had to drag Jenni up off the bottom. Jenni was so scared we couldn't even be angry. The school changed the rules after that and kids weren't allowed in unless an adult was there.

"And then there was the time," he chuckled as he remembered, "she and Red were playing with Aunt Vera's makeup, which they knew was naughty. They were about eight and Vera and your mother had taken you to the market and left them alone for an hour. They couldn't wash the mascara off and they had no idea it was waterproof so they panicked, found nail scissors and cut their eyelashes off instead!"

I hung on every word. The only things I knew about

were the things we had done together. Jenni was a helper and often she would rope me in too, like trying to roast a chicken when Mum had the flu or surprising Dad with a clean car on a Sunday morning.

Not all her efforts were successful, though, like the time we were sitting on the kitchen floor, surrounded by baking trays from the cupboard, when Mum's voice made us freeze.

"What *on earth* are you doing?"

"We're cleaning," Jenni replied, her smile slipping. "Last week you said the trays were sticking so we're making them all shiny again."

Mum grabbed the tray and turned it over.

"I spent ages scrubbing the burnt bits but it was really hard, so I had to use this." In one hand Jenni held a wallpaper scraper. It had taken far more effort than expected but she had been pleased with the result.

The crash of the metal tray on the draining board made us both flinch.

"It's ruined! Can't you tell the difference between burnt food and the non-stick coating? This is useless now, you may as well put it straight in the dustbin."

Looking down at the cake tin I'd made almost no impact on, I was glad Jenni only let me use the kitchen brush.

~ ~ ~

After some prodding from me, Red came to stay for a few days and the two of us sat for hours in the garden, reading books and newspapers and talking.

Aunt Vera had raised her daughter to be independent, which meant being educated enough "to not rely on a man".

While she declared her own business acumen to be more luck than brains, times were changing, she had often told her daughter, and a good education was essential if she wanted to be somebody.

Red didn't know what it meant to be somebody and didn't think that was necessarily what she aspired to. Like her mother, Red was a bit of a free spirit – or at least as free as Vera had been before she became a single mother in a small town.

With Red in our spare bedroom, Mum announced she would go back to Aunt Vera's to start sorting her things, promising at Red's insistence not to throw anything away without asking. She still managed to upset Red, though, by inviting us round to dinner. Red didn't think Aunt Eileen had the right to invite anyone – even family – to her mother's house.

The meal was disjointed and uncomfortable as we struggled for conversation that didn't centre on who was missing. Dad and I had spoken about Aunt Vera, and Red and I talked for hours, but I had exchanged little more than a few words with Mum since her efforts at organising the funeral had annoyed me so much, and Red was still sulking with her.

Unfortunately, that turned the focus to me.

"So, how long until you join Tom in London?" Mum asked.

"A couple of weeks. Edward has a flat Tom and I are using until we get settled, then we'll look for a place we can afford to rent."

Mum thought Tom was "wonderful", probably because she'd caught glimpses of the life she had wished for herself: tennis in the summer, skiing or tropical sunshine in the winter, and taking care of her husband and the household –

with paid help, naturally – to maintain their status in the community. She probably harboured the hope our relationship would give her access to a better part of society or, at the very least, an invitation to the Riviera.

I didn't want my parents to know I'd never told Tom about Jenni. They would have assumed he knew long before this summer and I didn't want to have to explain myself.

Red and I, though, talked about it at length.

"I get it," she'd said a few days earlier as we were stretched out on the grass, sunlight filtering through the leaves onto our freckled legs. "It's so 'big', it affects how people see you. At school, it was bad enough I had no dad at home and a single mum who made a living from Tupperware parties. After Jenni disappeared, it made me even more different from the rest of the girls.

"It was only when I went to university that half of the friends I made had single parents, or gay parents, or were adopted. There wasn't a right way and a wrong way to grow up; everything was normal.

"So I totally understand why you don't tell people. They either bug you for details or they stare like you've grown a second head!"

I hmm'd my agreement.

"Should I be worried, though, about the way Tom's taking it? Like I've done something wrong?" I pushed thoughts of Eric to the back of my mind. "He said it's made him question how much I care for him and whether he can trust me."

Her nose wrinkled as she considered my question. "I thought I'd heard all the worst responses, like 'She probably ran away, which makes you question what was going on at home', or 'It's usually the Dad, isn't it?'. So far, no-one has made me feel bad for not telling them. Maybe Tom has a need to judge people and that's why he wants to be a lawyer, so he helps decide whose behaviour is right and whose is wrong."

Red's response confirmed that my annoyance at Tom was justified. I told her maybe she should have an A Level in psychology instead of me and she laughed. The first time I'd heard her laugh properly since Aunt Vera's death.

"Maybe that's my problem. I studied the wrong subjects and that's why I have no idea what to do with my life."

Our mood turned sombre again. I asked her what she'd do with the house, since she didn't want to live there.

"The mortgage is all paid off, so I'll sell it when my gut tells me it's time. Maybe you and I can take a year off and travel the world and come back stony broke. Or maybe I'll shack up with my mechanic and have babies."

At 24, and with a sudden-if-unwanted inheritance, Red had the means to do whatever she wanted, but I found it hard to think of her settling down yet and told her so.

She sighed. "Jenni and I talked about living in Italy, right before she disappeared. We watched an old black and white Italian film with subtitles and she got all starry-eyed about the lead actor. She thought all Italian men must be romantic if they sounded like that.

"I used to hope she had ridden off on the back of a Vespa with a cute boy whose family owned a vineyard in Tuscany."

"Maybe she would have ended up a designer in Milan."

We all had our dreams for Jenni.

"Sorry to break it to you but we can't travel the world. You have a job and a boyfriend," I reminded her, "and I am moving to London. Although if you're paying, I'll definitely take a trip to Italy with you."

"It's a deal. Can you imagine? You and me in sunglasses and headscarves, zooming through the countryside in a convertible!"

She gave me a Hollywood film star pout and we laughed again. For a second I thought that might solve everything.

"You have a boyfriend too, don't forget!" Red said. Despite our hours of conversation, I had been too ashamed to mention Eric to her, and my actions had further confused my emotions towards Tom. Was it possible to love a person even if you disliked parts of them? Was it possible to love them and cheat on them anyway?

During daylight hours, I told myself one stupid moment of weakness with Eric was not worth ending a relationship over. I reminded myself how I felt when Tom and I were first together, how he made me feel. We both deserved a fresh start in London. But at night, with my eyes closed, I pictured the tan lines I had traced around Eric's neck with my lips and how the muscles in his shoulders felt as they moved under my fingers.

19

"Not making a decision is a decision in itself," Aunt Vera would declare when Red was being indecisive. That's how I came to be on the train to London in September, telling myself the butterflies were from excitement.

I refused any kind of farewell event: we'd had too many family gatherings recently for me to want another, particularly with me at the centre of it.

The train rocked through green hills and forests, then along the red sandy beaches of South Devon, before the sea gave way to the flatness of southern England. As the hours passed, the distance between villages and towns became smaller and smaller until the view merged into one giant colourless sprawl of buildings.

With a judder, the train came to a halt at Paddington. Dragging a case in one hand and my backpack in the other, I stepped down into the unpleasant fug of the station to see Tom bounding along the platform. He picked me up and spun me around, planting a kiss on my lips. The broad smile on his face pushed some of the doubts from my mind and I was relieved at how glad I was to see him.

Like a pro he navigated us round the busy Circle Line,

talking non-stop about all the interesting things we'd do and how much I'd like the area, while I nodded and tried to take it all in.

The flat was on Markham Terrace, an immaculate street of Georgian terraces close to South Kensington Tube and only minutes from the hubbub of Fulham Road. Through a sculpted hedge, the pristine white building had steps leading down to a basement flat and up to a glossy black front door. Climbing to the first floor, Tom grinned at me over his shoulder as he slid the key into the lock. I told myself it was going to be OK. Of course I loved this man, and he loved me and we were starting our new life in a new city.

The bright living area had two sets of glass doors overlooking the quiet street, each with a Juliet balcony. The room was wide, with a large sofa, a well-worn leather wingback chair and an office desk. The compact but modern kitchen was through a door to one side, and down the hall two bedrooms had views of the ground floor's lush garden.

"Wow!" I exclaimed. I'd never been in a hotel this nice, let alone a flat. I unlocked the balcony doors to let in the air, hoping for birdsong and the smell of the trees. Only exhaust fumes and the rumble of traffic reached me.

"Not bad, eh? Max and I used to come here for weekends sometimes when Tottenham were playing. I remember how grown up we felt the first time we had tickets to an away game. Then we got to Highbury and the streets were swarming with bald, overweight Arsenal fans, shouting like they were going to kill us. We were two skinny teenagers in our Spurs strip, terrified we'd get beaten up on our way to the game! We never told our parents in case they didn't let us go again."

Tom had an abundance of stories from his childhood, of hanging out with Max and other friends, trips to the Isle of Wight in a friend's yacht, days at Wimbledon and nights at the Proms, and tropical escapes to make it through the winter. They emphasised his worldliness in comparison to our family holidays of staying with our grandparents and going to country fairs, a beach, or the zoo.

One night at Grandma and Grandfather Carter's, Jenni and I had camped out in an old tent in the garden. I was scared but trying to be brave, until a noise made both of us jump. Frozen with fear that it was a bird or a mouse – and unsure what we would do if it was either – we clutched each other and waited. When the canvas twitched, we ran screaming back into the house and spent a sleepless night squashed into our grandparents' bed.

In the safe light of day, we all went to investigate. Grandfather Carter pulled the tent pegs one by one, as we watched from a safe distance, and dragged the tent away before cursing loudly at the small brown molehill in his otherwise-unblemished lawn.

That first night in London I went to bed early, exhausted from doing nothing on a train for six hours. The disappointment was clear on Tom's face. He'd heated a pie and garlic bread from Waitrose and opened a bottle of Burgundy his parents had brought back the previous week. Two large glasses had made me sleepy and as I worried that the faint noise of cars and aeroplanes would keep me awake, I dropped into a heavy slumber.

~ ~ ~

I am standing with my eyes closed. Then I blink and realise they're not closed; it's so dark my hand is not even visible when I hold it up to my face. The blackness is tangible, a warm fog. The quiet is deafening and I tilt and turn my head, trying to imagine where I could be that is so devoid of light and sound.

I'm scared to reach out in case my hand touches something, and simultaneously scared I'll find nothing.

The first time Jenni says my name it is whisper quiet behind me: "Joy."

I whirl around, seeing nothing, and wonder if I'd really heard her. The second time, she's further away, her sing-song "Jo-oy!" stretching out as she rings her bell a few times, impatient.

I move as only the temporarily blinded do, tapping out with my foot before I commit my weight to the step. I could be in a cave or at the edge of a cliff, surrounded by monsters or about to fall into an abyss.

She's still there; I hear the steady click of the chain as she wheels the bike along. In tiny, cautious steps I move until I know she's right there, so close her breath is warm on my face. But my hands find nothing. To reach her, I have no option but to take another step and I lean too far, one greedy step too many. My right foot touches nothing but air and I'm falling with my arms outstretched, tumbling silently in the darkness.

I wake with a jolt and my confusion is compounded by the new bedroom and my position face-down in my pillow. I hold back a sob until I stumble to the bathroom with Jenni's voice in my ears and an ache from missing her still.

20

The shriek of the alarm at 6.30am made me burrow deeper into the pillow and wish I could sleep for another 10 hours. It was Tom's big day, though, so I forced myself out of bed while he was in the shower to make him tea and toast.

The job he had secured as a paralegal was based on merit, he insisted, and not his father's name above the door. Like everyone, he had to start from the bottom, from where he was hoping to progress rapidly.

I couldn't help wishing I had the family connections and extensive work experience to give me an edge.

The part-time hours would enable him to complete his Legal Practice course within 12 months. The university campus was only a few minutes on foot from his father's offices, and an easy half a dozen Tube stops from South Kensington.

Tom came into the kitchen and did a twirl in his suit, which I had last seen at Aunt Vera's funeral. This time he was all business with a subtle navy and cream tie and white shirt.

"Very nice. You look very ... lawyerly!" I told him proudly and handed him the cup of tea.

"And you look very housewifey!" he replied, looking me

up and down in my short dressing gown and pink slippers.

He dodged my slap and grabbed a slice of toast from the dining table.

"Are you nervous?"

He shook his head. "I've met most of Dad's colleagues before."

"Don't be cocky," his father had advised. "If you keep your head down and make it clear you're there to learn, it won't take long for people to trust and respect you."

Trust and respect. The two most important measures of a man, in Edward's mind.

Tom's busy schedule – four days of study and a day of work that might sometimes run into the evening – meant we wouldn't see much of each other during the week. To lessen my guilt at not having a job, I made Tom breakfast on the mornings he went to university and packed him a sandwich for lunch. In the evenings I made sure something was in the oven or on the stove when he came home. I didn't mind too much; it broke up the days while I was looking for work.

It wasn't easy, searching for a job when all I wanted to be was an artist. A degree from a Welsh university hadn't created the contacts I might have developed at a city university and the chances of being 'discovered' were slim to non-existent. The best starting point seemed to be working in the industry, maybe in an art gallery or museum, so I would be close to people who knew people.

Each morning I began optimistically enough.

With a mug of steaming tea in one hand and a red pen in the other, I would settle down to *The Telegraph* and flick straight to the Situations Vacant, where I scoured every word of every advert, searching for something that inspired me.

The pattern was always the same, though: my heart would begin to sink after I had read everything once, and plummet further as I re-read each tiny advert – as well as the larger ones, even though I knew they were written for people with more experience.

Surely one morning I would stumble across an ad written especially for me:

WANTED: INEXPERIENCED UNKNOWN ARTIST
ARE YOU A RECENT FINE ARTS GRADUATE? DESPERATE FOR CONTACTS TO REACH YOUR DREAM BUT LACKING SKILLS? OUR NICHE GALLERY NEEDS YOU! NO EXPERIENCE NECESSARY. TASKS INCLUDE BASIC ADMIN AND ARTIST LIAISON. WE'LL DISPLAY YOUR WORK FOR FREE, NO COMMISSION. STARTING SALARY £9,000 + BENS.

If only. Before long, I no longer needed to be inspired by the adverts: I was desperate to see anything I was skilled enough to do. Receptionist, waitress, telemarketing … everyone wanted prior experience. I felt I was being punished for spending my holidays trying to become a better artist, picking fruit and vegetables to keep me in paint and brushes rather than thinking about what would look good on a CV.

I spent hours in Chelsea library trawling the Yellow Pages for the names and addresses of businesses that might need someone like me. I started at 'A' *for Artists' Studios and Artists' Supplies*, passed through 'C' for *Crafts and Craft Supplies*, 'G' for *Galleries*, 'H' for *Hobbies and Hobby Shops*, 'M' for *Museums*, and 'P' for *Pictures, Prints and Posters* – a poor second to the real thing, but I couldn't afford to be picky.

"What's your specialist subject?" Magnus Magnussen

would ask me if I found myself on *Mastermind*, seated under a bright spotlight in a black leather chair. "Categories of the *Yellow Pages*, 1992-1993," I would reply.

When the librarians' sympathetic glances turned to downright pity, I looked further afield: first Brompton library, then Kensington Central. I was learning my way around the city by library rather than landmark.

Armed with a list of addresses and a bunch of CVs in my trembling hand, I would push open the front door of each shop or studio without knowing what kind of reception I would get. Older women were usually snooty and dismissive; older men polite and apologetic. Young staff were the least friendly, as if I was there to steal the job they had studied hard and searched even harder to find. I didn't trust them to even pass my CV to the manager or owner, so I became more selective about who I handed it to, to limit how many copies I had to pay for.

In art galleries, I soon discovered that the smarter the décor, the less time they would spend talking to me. If they were willing to stop and chat, it was because no customers were around, and I relished these moments. I'd comment on the work and enquire about the artists' backgrounds but as soon as I asked if they would be interested in my portfolio, their faces closed like a portcullis.

Twice I found myself talking to the artist whose work was on display around us. I was star-struck, without even knowing who they were. They had no idea how much I longed to see someone stop dead and exclaim "This is the one!" in front of a piece I had agonised over for weeks or months. Then it would all be worth it.

I wished I knew how long it would be – or if it would

ever be – before I experienced that.

Weeks passed without a single call in response to my CV. Christmas was coming but no-one was hiring a wannabee artist with no work experience, and the steady flow of first-class stamps were costing me a fortune.

Tom was unsympathetic to my growing frustration and despondency. His view was "something will come along eventually, make the most of not having to work", as if I was enjoying some sort of holiday.

He liked having his breakfast made for him and knowing dinner would be in the oven when he came home. Long after the novelty had worn off, I still did all the shopping and cleaning, planned our menus and cooked, and made sure his shirts were washed and ironed. It was hard to object when I had so much free time, although housework and hunting for paid work certainly felt like a full-time job.

Pushing to one side the voice in my head that sounded like my mother, I decided to sign on for the dole so I wasn't reliant on Tom's small income and the generosity of his parents. The money Dad had given me as a parting gift was gone and I had spent most of the savings left over from my aborted European trip.

The staff at Fulham Job Centre were not sure what to do with me. More than three million people were out of work across the country, many of them with far more to offer than me. No, I had no work experience except fruit picking. No, no car or moped. Actually, no driver's license, although I'd be taking my test soon. No, I can't work nights as I have no way of getting around without public transport. South Kensington? Yes, but it's not my place, I'm not paying any rent, only bills. No, no property, no savings, no inheritance, no family in London. No pets, no disabilities, no dependents. Yes, a degree. In Art History and Fine Art. Painting. And three A Levels in English, Art, and Psychology.

I was eligible for the weekly Unemployment Benefit, which seemed insufficient but would increase when I reached 25. The thought of signing on until I was 25 made me shiver. After the paperwork was done, I sat in a rigid plastic chair for more than an hour before I was passed to someone who connected job seekers with employers.

Marjory – according to her name tag – didn't introduce herself and made no effort to conceal her boredom as she read my details before flicking through index cards with vacancies for delivery driver, cleaner, secretary, and more.

My ears pricked up at the word 'cleaner'. I imagined roaming a gallery after dark with a can of polish in one hand and a soft duster in the other, hoping to casually bump into the owner, or a kind-hearted artist with a desire to mentor someone.

"Um…you said 'cleaner'. Could you tell me a bit more?"

"Cleaner wanted for central London cinema. Must be available from late morning to late evening, variable shifts. Four pounds an hour. Equipment provided. Immediate start."

From her bored tone it was clear she had read it at least a dozen times before.

"I could do that," I said, as much to convince myself as Marjory. A cinema. Not quite a gallery, but film was an art form, wasn't it? And if I was going to keep cleaning, I may as well get paid for it.

One phone call and 15 minutes later I was on my way to Leicester Square, only a stone's throw from the National Portrait Gallery, the National Gallery, and the famous lions of Trafalgar Square. The George VI Cinema had recently re-opened as an independent movie house and the new carpet smell mingled with popcorn.

"It's evenings only on Tuesday and Wednesday, then lunchtimes and evenings Thursday, Friday, and Saturday. Sunday and Monday are your days off."

The manager seemed relieved I was not deterred by the erratic schedule.

"You'll need to be here before the first session to clean up from the previous night – I'm not paying anyone extra to work after midnight. After the lunchtime clean you can do what you like as long as you're back before the early evening film ends."

I nodded my consent, clutching the brief CV he had not even asked for.

"I'm very reliable. I used to pick fruit and vegetables, summer and winter, so I'm not afraid of hard work and I'll do a good job."

He continued as if I hadn't even spoken. "We also have a bar and it gets busy in the evenings. Do you have any experience? I might be able to give you a few shifts."

He wanted me to start at 9am the next morning so he had time to show me around. I didn't ask what had happened to the previous cleaner and he didn't volunteer the information. Before I knew it, I was out on the pavement, squinting in the low November sunshine. I had a job!

I held myself back from skipping through Leicester Square and down to St James's Park. As I passed the Institute of Contemporary Art my heart lifted at the thought I would have money to attend the exhibitions I was itching to see, sign up for artists' talks, and pretend I was the real thing. The roofline of Buckingham Palace was silhouetted against a pink and gold sunset and as I photographed the scene my spirits were the highest they had been since I moved to the city.

For once, I wasn't expected to cook: we ate out whenever Edward was in town. He insisted the restaurants were "nothing fancy" even though they were, because he paid and knew that made me embarrassed.

"When you're rich and famous, you can buy me the best meal in London," he said on more than one occasion.

I leapt up the stairs two at a time, bursting into the flat to share my news. The second I was in the door, I yelled out "I got a job, I got a job, I got a job!" and Tom was there in an instant. He picked me up and swung me around until Edward appeared.

"That's amazing! Where is it? When do you start?"

Edward clapped. "Hold that thought. This calls for a celebration. I've booked a table at *Le Petit Trianon* for 7pm but if we go right now we can start with Champagne at the bar."

I threw on thick black tights and the dark green dress I knew Tom liked and ran a comb through my hair. We were only a few minutes' walk from the restaurant, so I started the story with my trip to the Job Centre.

Tom shuddered. "It sounds awful. All those miserable people out of work. I bet half of them don't even want a job, they only turn up to get their cheque."

Only hours before, I had been one of those miserable people. I chose to ignore his comment.

By the time we were seated at the bar, with Dom Perignon on its way, I was reaching the punchline of where I would be working. Hardly had "George VI Cinema" left my mouth than Edward let out a guffaw.

"I'm so glad you didn't get a job there a few years ago. Quite a reputation it had, and rightly so. Showed all the old pornographic films that weren't available anywhere else. Very popular among the young lawyers, it was!"

"Dad!" Tom grimaced and turned to me. "What sort of place is it? What will you be doing?"

"It's fine, Tom, it's been redeveloped, new owner and everything. It's a proper independent cinema so they can show whatever they like but it's all normal, nothing X-rated. I can even get us cheap tickets."

At that moment our drinks arrived and Edward made a big show of congratulating "the newest employee in London". Cold bubbles tickled my nose as I took a mouthful.

"I'd better go easy. I'm starting at nine tomorrow morning."

"So what's the job, exactly? Cinemas don't open that early, do they?"

"Cleaning," I said, aware before the words came out of my mouth that this wasn't what Tom expected. "But the manager said I could be working in the bar before long, so I'll be getting great experience."

"It's not the right kind of experience, though, is it?" Tom asked, taking the shine off my news.

In the pause that followed, we all looked up hopefully as the waiter glided over.

Edward loved fine food, especially anything French. Tom and his younger brother Ben had grown up in this environment but I found it intimidating. I managed pretty well, putting on my best accent to request the 'pâté' to start, but noticed a glint in the waiter's eye when I ordered 'Boof' as my main course. Tom and Edward both ordered in French, enjoying a quick joke with the waiter that I smiled at politely without understanding.

Then it was mostly legal talk. Tom was always animated when he spoke about how much he was learning, with encouraging nods from his father. Tom was doing well, Edward said. Some of the partners were impressed, suggesting the apple hadn't fallen too far from the tree.

"Well if it had, I'm sure Joy would have cleaned it up for them," Tom said, laughing at his own joke. I stayed silent, instead tucking in to my Bœuf Bourgignon and thinking how nice it was not to be doing the washing up. I quietly wondered if my cooking would ever be this good.

After a rich chocolate tart I was full and sleepy and glad for an excuse not to stay up late.

"That was lovely, thank you Edward. But I should get an early night."

Back at the flat, I left Tom and his father talking about a recent ruling that had caused a headache for one of the senior lawyers.

Mixed with the excitement of what the next day would bring was apprehension about Tom's reaction once he knew the hours I'd be working.

On paper I had it all worked out: I'd be up to make Tom's breakfast and would continue my job search in the mornings. I'd tidy up and do the shopping before leaving for work. If I was organised enough, on the days I had a lunchtime shift I had time to nip back and organise dinner so something was ready and waiting for Tom.

Most evenings he wasn't home much before 7.00pm anyway, so it wouldn't make a huge difference to how much

we saw each other. We'd just have to make the most of
Sundays and Monday evenings. And it wouldn't be the end
of the world, I decided as my eyes grew heavy, if Tom had to
eat beans on toast every now and then because I was at work.

21

The job was easy, if somewhat lonely. I'd gone from spending my days alone in the flat to being the only person in a 300-seat cinema after it emptied out, clearing up the debris of popcorn and fizzy drinks.

I didn't interact much with the staff who took care of tickets, tended bar, and ran the refreshments stand. We had no staff room, and most of the others spent their breaks in the alley out the back, having a cigarette under the awning. I was around people, but not part of anything.

Even with the ceiling lights on full, the two large screening rooms were permanently gloomy. Back of house was a dim rabbit warren of narrow corridors, with stairs up to the projector room. My equipment room was up two flights, so I became expert in how much I could balance in the bucket, leaving a hand free for the mop and long duster pole.

On day one I learned ice in discarded drinks containers melts quickly, and that night I travelled home on the Tube with a sticky stain down my front.

Predictably, Tom was unhappy about my hours.

"So five nights a week I'll be asleep before you get home, and on Saturdays you'll be there during the day as well?

When are we supposed to see each other?"

"Well, Sundays. And Monday evenings. On Saturdays I'm free between 4pm and about 7pm, so I can come back here, or you can come and meet me."

Again, that disappointed face.

"You know it's only until I find something better," I hated the whine in my voice. "I need the money and I'm going crazy stuck here all the time. It'll give you peace and quiet to study and I'm lucky to have a job at all."

His face told me I was right but he was not pleased about the impact on his routine.

"As long as you have enough time to keep looking for a proper job," he said, wrapping his arms around me before adding, "I'll miss you being here when I get home."

~ ~ ~

December started off mild after a wetter-than-normal November until winter pounced with claws like icy daggers.

A few times, on days that were particularly cold or wet or both, I stayed at the cinema between the two sessions and watched the early evening film from the back row. The second the credits began to roll, I would be off to my cleaning cupboard.

It was on one of those days of endless icy rain that I saw one of my housemates from university, Stephanie. We'd written to each other a couple of times since we'd left Wales – she had sent the sweetest card after Aunt Vera died, and we knew we were both living in London – but I hadn't yet had the motivation to suggest we meet.

She was in the early evening session of Damage, seated

a few rows from the back with two other women. As soon as I sat down I noticed her, head and shoulders above the people around her. That gave me the whole film to work out whether to say hi, and whether to tell her I was the cleaner rather than a patron.

"Stephanie!" I called her name as she approached the exit without noticing me.

"Joy? Wow, Joy!" and she hugged me close. "What an amazing coincidence." She took a step back and tutted: "You look pale!"

This had been our standing joke throughout university, where she always said my skin was like her granny's fine china. Her father was born in Jamaica and had arrived in Liverpool as a child, where he eventually married Stephanie's red-haired, blue-eyed mother. Stephanie was a striking woman whose blue eyes stood out in contrast to her warm olive skin and dark hair.

"What are you doing here?"

"I work here." There, I'd admitted it. "I snuck in to watch the film and now it's time to clean up after messy people like you!"

She introduced me to her friends, untroubled by my employment status. "We have to catch up. You have to call me," she said, scribbling her number on a piece of paper. "I work shifts during the week, but I'm free in the evenings and every Sunday. Except not before the New Year. It's too bloody busy and I'm exhausted."

We said goodbye with promises to catch up in January.

A few times Tom had complained my hours made it difficult for us to socialise, not knowing that a bigger problem was my reluctance to spend time with people I didn't know. A few weeks earlier I'd made an effort when he suggested Sunday lunch with Max and his girlfriend in Bexleyheath, an hour east of London. From the stories Tom told, I had a good feeling about meeting Max and was excited to have a day out of the city. I pictured us having lunch in the fresh air on a grassy heath, away from the greyness of London.

It was awful.

Bexleyheath was underwhelming, just another colourless suburb, with hardly a tree between the station and the main street. Lunch was in one of those café chains that claims to be a brasserie but offers basic-yet-overpriced French food served by young and poorly paid staff. Max's girlfriend, Cassandra, was from their home town. At her raised-eyebrow greeting I felt instantly frumpy and by the time she'd finished her second up-and-down assessment her eyes told me I was not worth making friends with.

Instead, she flirted openly with Tom, who loved it and flirted back, while I struggled to add anything to their conversations. When they asked for the dessert menu, I said I was full and wanted to check out the nearby Red House, former home of William Morris whose designs I adored. "Be back for the 3.30 train," Tom reminded me. I was, to find the three of them well on their way to being drunk and planning a ski trip for February I already knew we couldn't afford.

On the return journey Tom was energised, oblivious to how much the conversations about his home town and old friends had excluded me. I tried to sound upbeat as he talked about a repeat outing, in the city next time, maybe in January.

Despite my shyness when it came to meeting people, I thought we'd have new friends by now – neighbours, perhaps, except they were all wealthy middle-aged couples we only saw in passing – or people Tom's age from work. I needed my own friends and my encounter with Stephanie was the first glimmer of hope that my world was becoming a fraction less small.

For Christmas, Tom and I would be visiting his family. Valerie and Edward lived in one of the most sought-after parts of Guildford, where their spacious property had expansive views of the ruins of Guildford Castle in one direction and Pewley Down in the other.

It was easy to explain, for once, why I couldn't make it home to Cornwall. In theory it was my turn to spend Christmas with Mum – a post-divorce practice we'd never officially grown out of – but I knew she would prefer to visit her parents anyway. Dad I was more worried about, until Red said she would take a turkey round there and stay for the night.

Christmas fell on a Friday and by 6pm on Christmas Eve the party had already started for most of the people leaving Waterloo. It was impossible not to feel festive, surrounded by Santa hats and reindeer antlers.

An hour later we were on the platform at Guildford in the embrace of Tom's parents who had been jumping up and down to keep warm. The BBC were forecasting the possibility of snow and I was keeping everything crossed.

For weeks I had fretted about gifts for the Fitzgeralds. I had a brainwave, for Edward at least: on the pretext of wanting to see where Tom worked, I travelled in with him one morning. The building was beautiful – part of a Victorian red brick terrace with decorative cream stone and ornate arched windows. He showed me around, including his father's impressive office on the second floor, and after I left I took several shots of the exterior. A few sketches later, and after another visit to double check the light, I committed paint to paper. The frame was only cheap, but if Edward liked the picture I thought he – or more likely Valerie – would find a better one.

Tom was difficult to buy for. He had so little spare time, books or theatre tickets weren't practical. In the end I bought him a beautiful Cross pen, navy with gold trim, and had it engraved 'Thomas E. Fitzgerald, LLB'. Valerie was easier: I knew her perfume so bought the matching hand cream and body wash set, biting my lip at the cost.

Christmas in the Fitzgerald household was a more lavish affair than anything I had ever seen. A three-metre-high fir tree in the entry hall was overwhelmed with large red bows, red tinsel, and pine cones sprayed gold. A second tree in the main living room was dressed in tiny white lights, white snowflakes, delicate clear glass baubles, and streams of gold tinsel. Underneath this tree were around two dozen wrapped gifts. It was a scene straight off a Christmas card.

The day's agenda, Tom told me, had not changed for many years. Breakfast included sparkling wine with orange juice and sweet, buttery croissants, real strawberry jam, and hot coffee. Tom and Ben bickered like children over the last croissant until Valerie reached across and put half on my plate before she tucked into the other half.

We needed hats and gloves for a stroll into the town and around the old castle grounds. As we puffed up the hill our breath hung in the freezing morning air and Edward warmly shook the hand of almost everyone we passed.

The kitchen was bursting with the smell of roasting

turkey when we returned – it was the biggest I had ever seen and had been in the oven since before breakfast. To feel useful, I offered Valerie my help.

"Before the weekend is over, I want to hear how you're getting along," she said as we prepared vegetables with Bing Crosby crooning in the background. "I remember what it was like when Edward was where Tom is now – nothing but work and study, work and study. It's a lonely time, but it will get better."

Valerie and Edward were already married by the time she was my age. To support her husband she had worked in a chemist and managed the household.

"That first year was tough. I felt like I'd got married for nothing! I scarcely saw my husband, and when he was at home he had essays to write and arguments to memorise. I don't envy what you're going through. And after such a tough year." She tutted and gave my shoulders a quick squeeze, making my eyes prickle with tears.

I tried to keep my voice light. "Tom says it's supposed to be character-building. The only person willing to employ me thinks cleaning is all I'm good for. It's boring, the hours are lousy, and it's light years away from what I want to be doing."

Valerie frowned with sympathy. "Give it time. It's not even six months since you graduated, and the economy is struggling right now. I bet this time next year we're celebrating your success as an artist and welcoming you to the family properly, which will be marvellous."

I was curious at her emphasis: did 'properly' mean 'as a wife'?

Ben tooted on a toy bugle, interrupting my thoughts to announce the next item on the agenda. "Time for presents," he called, and everyone sat down around the tree.

They were a generous family, with each other and with me. I'd begged Tom not to let them go overboard but they showed little restraint. Valerie perhaps thought I couldn't afford make-up because their gift was a large, expanding cosmetics box with a mindboggling number of eye shadows and several lipsticks including one called 'Artist's blush'.

"When I saw that, I knew I had to buy it," she said, smiling as I went to put it on.

Edward was effusive in his praise of my painting, and everyone declared it was only a matter of time before I made it as an artist. Tom knew how much time I would have spent on the detail and his face showed me he was proud.

"Looks like that lipstick was perfect for you!" Valerie laughed as my face grew pink.

After an extravagant lunch, an afternoon of board games, and a light supper with sherry, everyone was yawning and ready to retire, still hopeful the following day would bring snow.

"I got you one more gift," Tom said quietly, reaching under the bed. Earlier, he had given me sparkling stud earrings, apologising for them being zirconium instead of diamonds ("one day these will be real, I promise," he said as he held back my hair) and I wasn't expecting anything else.

The shallow, shiny box weighed next to nothing. It was the kind of box expensive stores use to wrap expensive gifts and rustled when I gave it a gentle shake. Tom was waiting for my reaction.

Layers of tissue paper revealed charcoal material that was soft as a feather under my fingertips.

"It's real silk," Tom said. "Try it on."

At first I thought it was underwear and wondered what exactly it would support. As I lifted it up by its delicate straps, I saw it was nightwear – a silk and lace chemise that would leave nothing to the imagination.

It was beautiful but it certainly wasn't me. "It's beautiful, thank you." I leant forward to kiss him.

"I want you to put it on, so I can take it off," he murmured in my ear. The thought of his brother in the next room and his parents down the hall made me hesitant but I didn't want to miss the moment. Our love life had languished since we moved to London. Tom was tired a lot of the time and complained my job got in the way of lazy mornings in bed and romantic dinners. Other than the occasional quickie before I made breakfast, we'd lacked any real connection. Clearly he wanted that to change.

The chemise fit perfectly and the smooth material made me feel sexy in a way that surprised me. Tom pulled me towards him and slowly let his fingers explore the front before brushing the straps from my shoulders.

"You look gorgeous," he said as I reached away to turn out the light. We kissed each other for a long time, slowly and deeply, with more affection than we had shown each other for months.

~ ~ ~

In my sleep I see Jenni's face in front of me, so close we can nearly rub noses. She's here, smiling at me, and I smile back, unable to look away. I am filled with happiness and we do nothing but stare without moving for several seconds. Her face has a strange pallor and I'm about to ask her why when a frown darkens her eyes and she starts to float away from me.

She's under water, I realise, looking up from beneath the surface. Her face is growing paler and smaller because she's sinking: the purple bike is weighing her down, dragging her towards the invisible bottom.

I plunge my arms into water so cold it burns, ready to grab her, when someone pulls me back. Their grip on my chest makes it a struggle to breathe. If they let go, I'm sure I can still reach her, but I can't break free and she sinks away from me, slowly, until her outstretched fingertips disappear into the blue-black.

Tom was laughing at me as he got out of bed. "You're funny. You had your arms out like you were painting in your sleep." He kissed the top of my head. I lay in bed crying while he took a shower.

After breakfast the boys disappeared to collect more wood for the fire and Valerie and I took our coffees to the warm conservatory.

I had misjudged Valerie, assuming tennis and French lessons were all she did to occupy her time between manicures and lunches. In fact she spent two days each week volunteering in the office of a children's charity, and on Thursdays she worked behind the counter in the town's Cancer Research charity shop.

"It's important to help out where you can. Plus, it keeps me in gossip," she confessed. "I'd have cabin fever if I were at home all day. It's better now Edward is in London so much less. You'll appreciate one day how much effort it takes to run a household when your husband is never there."

I said I'd been looking after everything in London, which was only fair since Tom was working and studying.

"That little shoebox? Wait until you have your own

house. Don't think we're in any hurry for you to move, though. You're welcome to live there as long as you want, although you might have to send Edward to a hotel once you have children. He's terrible without a good night's sleep!"

Children. My sudden sense of unease brought back Tom's casual comment on graduation day about us being 'mummy and daddy' one day. I was 21, approaching 22, and feeling more and more that my life was not my own. Other people seemed to know better than me what I was going to do – first marriage, then babies, while I managed the home, enabling my husband to become the lawyer he'd always planned.

I'd never imagined pushing a pram or playing with toddlers in the park. As an artist, I wanted to be free to set up my easel anytime and anywhere the urge took me. I yearned to create beautiful landscapes people would hang in their homes. Ultimately, I might one day own my own gallery, where I would be able to offer young artists the helping hand I wished I'd had.

Tom – and now his family – had expectations of me that didn't match my own.

Without planning or discussion, we'd set this life in motion at a time when things were simple and now I was on a conveyor belt I was powerless to stop or even slow down. I wasn't sure how we had come this far with such incompatible ideas of the future. One of us would have to sacrifice our dreams; knowing Tom, it would have to be me.

Valerie was still talking, telling me how much she had enjoyed being a young mum of two boys, and I forced myself to focus on the conversation. She had relished motherhood, as she'd expected to.

"I would have loved a girl, though," she said. "There's something special about seeing a reflection of yourself in your daughter and helping her grow into an amazing woman. And of course all the fun stuff you can do, like shopping for party dresses and weeping at soppy films."

I had never done those things with my mum but was unwilling to burst Valerie's bubble. Since Mum moved out, Vera had been the one to take me shopping when I outgrew my clothes. The only time we'd been to the cinema was the first Christmas it was only me.

Valerie sighed loudly. "It tugs at my heart when I see mothers now, holding the hand of their little girl all dressed in pink. So here's to a few granddaughters!" and she chinked her coffee mug against mine.

22

Christmas was over. Tom was too busy with assignments to want a big New Year's Eve, which was fine as I didn't relish the thought of spending the evening with strangers or even acquaintances – particularly not Max and Cassandra.

The conversation with Valerie had left me distracted, pre-occupied with thoughts I didn't know how to share with Tom. At work, I had nothing but time to think as I swept seats, vacuumed floors, and scrubbed toilets on autopilot.

The manager was pleased I had proven to be reliable and thorough. He asked in early January if I would like to earn some extra money in the bar. One of the staff was going on a fortnight's leave while it was quiet, so I wouldn't be under too much pressure.

"I'd love to! But what about cleaning?"

"We can work around that. How about you do an hour in the bar before the first film and the same again before the late session? And if it works out, we can keep you on standby."

More hours and more money – an extra £80 over the fortnight, plus a share of the tips. I didn't tell Tom: I could hear his voice reminding me not to get too settled and to keep up my job search. In reality, no-one was advertising anything in the dead weeks of January and it was an opportunity to add new skills to my CV.

To explain my afternoon absences, I made a few comments about the Institute of Contemporary Art and the exhibition and workshops I was keen to attend. Then I said the second evening film was being pushed back by 30 minutes, to explain my later return.

More lying, made worse by Tom's delight in me making what he called "steps in the right direction" by visiting the institute. It also put pressure on me to do everything else when I wasn't working, in particular real visits to the institute so I'd be able to talk about who and what I had seen if Tom asked, although the likelihood was slim.

I continued to make Tom's breakfast every day and most lunches. For the evenings I prepared large batches of easy-to-reheat dishes so Tom wouldn't have to fend for himself.

Working behind the bar was so much more enjoyable than cleaning. The other barman – a young German named Walter – was friendly and happy to teach me the ropes. Expect a rush 30 minutes before each film, he told me, and don't forget to keep stacking the dishwashers. At the end he'd sort out the takings while I cleaned up the tables.

More cleaning, but I didn't mind. It was a refreshing change to have a conversation with somebody other than Tom. Walter's English was impressive, although his accent made me laugh on occasion.

"My girlfriend and I are going to Edinburgh at Easter," he told me, pronouncing it more like "Eden-berg" and I had to ask him several times to repeat it. "But it says 'Eden-berg'," he protested. Then I wrote down a whole series of English towns – Leominster, Worcester, Beaulieu and Loughborough – until I was clutching my sides as he read them out.

I couldn't remember the last time I'd laughed out loud.

When I told Walter I was a painter his eyes lit up.

"You should ask the manager if you can sell your work in the bar. Why not? If he says no, it's no, he won't sack you."

The next morning I flipped through my small portfolio to see if anything might be of interest. Very few of my paintings had come to London with me since it wasn't practical to store them in the flat. Most of my new pieces were tiny, a way of challenging myself to use watercolour in a smaller format than I ever had before. Although my preferred subjects were natural landscapes with perhaps a glimpse of something man-made, living in a city forced me to try something a bit different. After the success of the piece I painted for Edward – and hoping the family's reaction had been genuine – I practised painting corners of Victorian architecture against wintery blue skies.

I was pleased at the result but knew tourists were unlikely to buy generic pictures that could have come from anywhere. They had to be recognisable.

Inspiration struck the next day on my way to work as I passed souvenir stands bursting with street-name fridge magnets and London Underground stickers: I would paint small London street signs, making them different by showing a bit of the building they were attached to.

The texture of cold-press watercolour paper would work well with the different materials I was trying to capture: Covent Garden on a solid sandstone wall; Abbey Road against the famous red brick; Regent Street on white rendered plaster. Their compact size was perfect for tourists and they were more sophisticated than a Union Jack t-shirt or Buckingham Palace snow globe.

Tom must have known I was painting – it was impossible to clean away the smell completely in an enclosed space – but he didn't ask what I was working on. Rather than get my hopes up, or his, I kept quiet. My hope was that if I showed the cinema manager and offered him 10% of the sale price, he wouldn't be able to turn me down.

I was very nearly right.

"They're better than all the tourist crap out there," the manager said when I took in half a dozen signs and my proposition. I assumed that was a compliment.

"How much are you asking?"

"I was thinking three pounds each. I want them to be affordable but enough to cover the materials, your 10 per cent, and a bit more."

"Ask for five pounds and I don't need a commission. Thicker paper will make them appear more professional, and you'll need clear plastic sleeves or they'll be damaged before they've even been bought. If they don't sell at five pounds you can have a sale and still make money."

I was grateful. Three pounds wouldn't make me much profit – only about 50 pence after everything – but it was hard to value your own work and honestly I was unsure if I'd sell even one.

"Get Walter to put a dozen in the bar. We'll see how they go."

Buoyed at his reaction, I called Stephanie that night. We chatted briefly before organising a time to meet the following Thursday, when my stint in the bar would be over and I would be free between the two films.

~ ~ ~

The cinema was only metres from Chinatown, so Stephanie and I had our pick of cheap restaurants and happy hour beers. It was the first time since arriving in London that I'd eaten out anywhere other than an expensive French restaurant.

Initially I was shy, unsure how the different environment might have changed things between us. Steph, though, was the same as ever, talking like her life depended on it and making me laugh.

She described where she was living, which was over a fish and chip shop on busy Green Lanes.

"It's a bit like being at university, although somehow with even less money and the view is nowhere near as nice. The other women are great – we're all artists of one sort or another, but all of us have day jobs till we 'make it big'."

Stephanie was working at the checkout of a supermarket on Holloway Road.

"It's easy, I can walk to work, which saves me money, and I'm building up my arm strength!" She flexed her skinny arms at me and I made a show of squeezing her tiny bicep.

"I'm hoping to start a Masters of Fine Art in September as nothing good is happening on the job front. I've applied to the Royal College of Art, naturally, although I'll go to whoever gives me an offer. I need to save up some serious cash, so my housemates and I are thinking of having our own exhibition and art sale in the summer. You should join us! Your technique is fabulous, so delicate. Very Turner-esque."

I told her about my plan to sell small pieces at the cinema and she was enthusiastic.

"Brilliant! You'll be a millionaire in no time. What does Tom think of his soon-to-be-rich-and-famous girlfriend? How is Tom, anyway?"

"He's…OK. He's at Law School doing his Legal Practice and working part-time with his Dad. My hours are a bit odd so we don't see much of each other." I tailed off, not knowing what else to add.

"Is that it? No candlelit dinners with a bottle of wine, or romantic walks by the river as the sun goes down?"

"We haven't had time. Once the weather warms up and he's done with this year of study we'll have a chance to enjoy ourselves."

"Hm," she was looking at me intently. "You're young and in love and living in this fabulous city. But you don't seem very happy."

I didn't hesitate before replying, "Happy? I'm not even sure I'm in love."

Stephanie paused with a forkful of noodles as tears blurred my vision. For months I'd kept everything bottled up and my mind was full of unspoken conversations. Red would have listened, but I was reluctant to bother her so soon after losing her mum and then breaking up with her mechanic. So here I was, my first time out with a friend since last summer and I was spoiling it.

Apologising for being such a mess, I explained that life in London was harder than I had anticipated.

She rubbed my arm affectionately. "You've had a tough year, hon. Lots of people are finding it hard after graduation and you're probably missing your aunt, too. It all takes time."

I shook my head. "I'm sad about Aunt Vera, of course I'm sad, but it's more than that. Tom and I … if I think about where we are, and where we're going, I'm questioning whether that's where I want to be. I don't seem to know him as well as I did at uni and … and I don't think he knows me as well as he thought."

I explained then about Jenni, the missing sister I had never spoken to her about, and Tom's reaction when I told him.

"Oh God, you poor, poor love. That is unimaginably horrible and I'm not surprised you didn't tell anyone. I'm amazed you're still standing and I can't believe Tom was so weird about it."

"I know. All I can think is if he really loved me, he'd make some attempt to understand why I kept it a secret for so long. And if I really loved him, I wouldn't be so mad that he doesn't get it. He doesn't seem capable of thinking what it was like – what it's like even now, having that hanging over me. All he cares about is feeling deceived because I didn't tell him sooner.

"It's all so complicated," I sighed loudly. What a relief to be able to talk to someone who was sympathetic and non-judgemental, instead of every conversation about Jenni turning into a battle.

"Well, I'm feeling a whole lot better about my life right now!" Steph laughed, and I was sorry I'd waited this long before catching up with her.

We ran out of time to grab a happy hour pint before I had to go back to work. As we said goodbye, Stephanie bent her knees to look me firmly in the eye. "If you need me for anything, *anything*, I'm here for you. Whether it's for a beer, or a shoulder, or even a bed, just call me."

23

Dad and I have never spoken much on the phone. We never got over our longing for it to ring, while hoping desperately it would not. It also reminded him of his arguments with Mum. Instead, he wrote the occasional letter, usually brief and on the pretext of sending me a local news clipping or the births, deaths, and marriages if he thought I'd know the people mentioned.

So when he called one Saturday morning in January, I was instantly alarmed. He asked if I was sitting down, which struck me as such an old-fashioned thing to say.

"The police called," he began, "because they have a new lead to explore."

He explained that a woman had come forward saying she knew what had happened to Jenni. That her boyfriend at the time – since deceased – had been driving and hit a girl on a bike.

"The girl was killed, according to this woman," Dad said, and his voice cracked even though he had probably rehearsed it a few times. "She said they panicked and buried her in a nearby field. The police expect it to be in tomorrow's newspaper, perhaps even in the national papers, so I didn't want you reading about it before I'd spoken to you."

Dad's tone suggested he accepted what he had been told; I was more questioning.

"Are they sure it was the same day? Was it a purple bike, with flowers on the saddle? How can they have hit her when the bike wasn't damaged?"

My flurry of questions calmed Dad down a bit. He'd taken at face value the likelihood it was Jenni; in fact part of him, like part of me, wanted it to be, however awful the prospect.

"You're right, you're right. It doesn't make sense, does it? The police said they have to follow it up and won't comment until they know more. Maybe it's not Jenni," and I heard a deep sigh. "Maybe she's still out there somewhere." Dead or alive.

"I hope so, Dad. 'No signs of a struggle' that's what the police wrote down, I remember like it was yesterday. I would have heard a car, or the police would have found evidence on the road. Or if they buried her nearby, someone would have noticed if the ground had been … disturbed."

Despite not believing this woman's story, the possibility was making me feel sick and if I continued down this path I might upset Dad further.

We moved on to other topics – the weather, my interminable job search, and Red, who Dad saw fairly frequently. As I placed the handset down, I knew what to expect from here. As with previous 'new leads', we would have days if not weeks of waiting, with snippets of news from Charlie – now a Police Sergeant – if he was able to tell us anything informally. The rush of relief when it turned out to be nothing would be short-lived, replaced by another crashing wave of grief and loss.

I decided not to mention it to Tom and he was too busy to notice the bags under my eyes.

The bleak winter was made bleaker by a series of bombings that made me wish I had never moved to London. In late January I was late for my shift after a small bomb in Knightsbridge shut down the roads and trains. The week after, while I was cleaning the cinema, a device exploded in a passageway at South Kensington Tube Station. The manager came to let me know. Seeing the fear on my face, he suggested I call Tom, and we walked home in silence through dark and foggy streets.

I was scared, I admitted to Tom after Camden Town was also rocked on a Saturday lunchtime. Leaving the flat made me jittery. To reassure me he said there had been dozens of similar incidents over the years, above ground and below ground, so I was "equally safe" in either place. I vaguely remembered BBC headlines over the years about places whose names I didn't recognise and how far they felt from Cornwall.

"Or equally unsafe," I grumbled. Tom's response did not give me any comfort.

News came from Dad: the police had finished their latest investigations. They assured him they were absolutely confident the woman was lying, even though they discovered she and her boyfriend had been in the county in August 1982. She was unable to describe the area, unable to remember where they had supposedly buried the body, and could not explain to the satisfaction of the investigating officer why no-one had discovered any disturbed earth within five miles of where Jenni vanished.

She was just another crazy person with a made-up story, although the police intended to rule out the possibility the accident had happened to someone else's child at a different time and place.

Tom barely glanced up while I said little other than "hm" at intervals while Dad talked. At the end I said I hoped the police could prove she was lying and charge her with wasting their time. My words piqued Tom's interest.

"Wasting police time? What was that all about?"

"Nothing, some stupid woman claimed she had information about Jenni but was lying."

Tom took the opportunity to recite what he knew about false statements and the various penalties "up to and including six months' imprisonment under Section 5 of the *Criminal Law Act 1967*".

His smile was smug and he unmuted the TV without asking me anything further.

~ ~ ~

I swing my legs out of bed. Instead of carpet, cool grass tickles the soles of my bare feet. In the light from the half-moon, I can see my bed is in a field so large the edges are out of sight. Tom is not beside me. A short distance away is the bike, on its side and with its back wheel turning slowly. As I watch, the wheel stops and the words from the police report come back to me: Jenni can't have been gone for more than three minutes.

I break into a run, frantic with the realisation she has been buried next to her bike.

Sure enough, the ground alongside has been dug up: there's no grass, only lumpy earth. I start digging with my bare hands.

At first it's easy to scrape away and I am filled with the adrenaline of hoping this is it. My nails are full of dirt and several fingertips are torn and bleeding from the sharp edges of small stones, but I keep going. Then suddenly they scratch and scrape against an almost-solid surface, the soil compacted as if it has never been disturbed.

Somewhere out of sight across the field, a woman screams with laughter, as if the sight of me digging is the funniest thing she's ever seen. My fingers are useless on the dense soil and anyway it's pointless, this was nothing more than a mad woman's cruel trick.

24

My daily routine was as dull as the cold, grey weather outside. At least Tom had stopped complaining about my hours and rarely checked how my job search was progressing. I was losing hope of ever finding work in a gallery but I kept mailing, phoning, and visiting when it wasn't too wet.

The one shining light was selling 13 of my street-sign paintings in only a few weeks, making me more than £22 profit. In the bar, Walter drew people's attention to the pictures whenever he had the chance and would stretch the truth by telling them the artist was a local girl on the verge of making it big. The most likely to buy a picture? American women, he told me, especially once he started chatting to them with his 'exotic' accent. He'd overheard one or two checking for pictures of Buckingham Palace Road or Knightsbridge, so I was happy to oblige. Sure enough they disappeared after only a few days.

To say thanks, I bought Walter a six-pack of German beer. One dry night while the early film was showing, we climbed up to the roof with a bottle each, carefully climbing over extractor units and railings caked in pigeon poo until we reached the corner bathed in blue from the lights of Leicester Square.

"I come up here when I have the time," Walter said. "I love the feeling of being surrounded by people but invisible. London is great but sometimes it is too much and I miss my home, you know?"

We clinked our bottles and took long swigs as muted noises flowed up around us.

I tried not to think about home so I wouldn't miss it as much – the ragged coastline and wild seas, and the absolute peace you could find simply by turning a corner or climbing over a hedge. London made sense as the place for Tom to be; as for me, it would be worth it if I found work that would help me reach my goal, although I could never imagine getting used to the city or calling it home.

I was lucky, I knew that – Walter and his girlfriend rented a noisy one-bedroom place in an ugly high-rise in Wood Green – but what I wanted more than anything was 'uncomplicated'.

Thank God I had a holiday to look forward to. Tom was disapproving when I came off the phone one night and told him Red was taking me to Italy like she'd promised. Four nights in Rome, then Florence for another four nights.

"What about your job? What about job hunting? How are you going to pay for it?"

Red was paying, I explained. That didn't sit entirely easy with me – after all, Tom and I weren't even paying rent – but when Red whispered on the phone how much she had got from the inheritance, I felt better about it.

"It's only eight days, Tom. Walter's girlfriend is standing in for me, and it's not as if people are lining up, begging me to start work tomorrow. Save all the newspapers and if I see a job I'll apply for it as soon as I'm back, I promise."

I wanted him to be pleased for me. I'd only enjoyed four days of our five-week trip when Aunt Vera died, and being unemployed wasn't exactly a holiday – which he acknowledged, somewhat begrudgingly, once I pointed that out.

All the same, I knew he needed a break as well. He'd spent much of his Christmas holiday doing assignments and getting through what seemed like a never-ending backlog of reading.

The next evening he came home and handed me an envelope. Inside was a small wad of multi-coloured Italian Lira in denominations of 5,000, 2,000, and 1,000.

"It's only about 50 quid but I thought you'd need a bit of cash, even if Red is paying."

"Thank you." I kissed him on the lips. "You know this is as much for Red as it is for me. She deserves a break and hopefully while we're away the recession will miraculously finish and I'll come back to a flood of job offers."

He wasn't convinced, either.

~ ~ ~

Walter's girlfriend Clara was tiny, but strong, and I did my last shift happy in the knowledge she would take good care of the place while I was away. I'd even stocked up my paintings in the bar as the milder weather was bringing a few more patrons through the doors.

In honour of Red staying with us overnight, Tom had attempted to make Cornish pasties, using frozen pastry sheets and minced beef. The result didn't even come close to the real thing but it was the first time he'd cooked, so I was effusive in my praise.

It was great to see Red in the flesh. She looked surprisingly well and acknowledged she'd been drinking a lot less since she and the mechanic broke up. In the house after the funeral he'd drunk far too much and said he had to leave early because "funerals are dull" so she ditched him shortly after.

"It was a bugger to get the car serviced though: I had to drive right across town. And pay for it!"

We shared the wine she brought and did a quick last-minute check as I packed.

"What about your painting stuff?" Red asked.

"This is a holiday, I don't want to be off painting somewhere while you're bored in the hotel bar."

She shrugged. "It's your holiday too. I've brought a stack of cheesy romance novels, so I plan to ignore you at least part of the time!"

My compromise was to take my sketchbook and pencils, which I could work into watercolour later.

The next morning we ate a quick breakfast before jumping on the Tube to Heathrow. Being on the train, full of excited anticipation, reminded me of leaving Waterloo for last year's trip with Tom. It felt like yesterday and so long ago.

Red insisted we have a drink at the bar after checking in, waving away my protests that it was only 10.30am.

"It's Champagne all the way, dahling," she said with an exaggerated drawl.

I ordered half a pint, nervous about taking my first-ever flight, but not wanting to sleep all afternoon.

In fact, both of us dozed on the flight and woke to perfect skies as the plane descended into Rome. Less than an hour later we pulled up to the Hotel Emperor in the centre of the city.

Glass doors swished apart as a porter came to take our bags and the doorman gave us a half-bow. Red and I pulled nervous faces at each other, feeling suddenly shabby and out of our depth. To one side of the enormous lobby, a real person was playing a grand piano. Twinkling chandeliers reflected off the red marble-lined walls.

Other guests walked towards us: a man in a sharp light brown suit, a woman with immaculate make-up and a fitted cream dress to accentuate her tan. Were we in the right place?

The receptionist wasn't much older than Red and frowned in confusion as he checked and rechecked our booking, before confirming we had a deluxe suite with king bed and views onto Via Veneto. Breakfast was included, along with a complimentary spa treatment at any time during our stay. Before I could fully absorb the word 'suite' the porter ushered us to the lifts with our bags on a trolley.

"This is unreal! I have never seen anything like it."

"The second I saw the brochure, that was it. It only has one king size bed, though, so I hope you don't mind my snoring!"

The porter waved us through the double doors to our room. My jaw dropped.

A large entry way opened onto the living area, which was on the corner of the building and had three full-height glass doors, two with Juliet balconies and one with a small table setting overlooking the street.

The walls were covered in what looked like spun gold and were soft to the touch. Underfoot, the bottle green carpet was springy and plush and patterned with flecks of gold. The array of lamps – all lit – and ornate framed mirrors gave it an air of utter luxury.

We padded into the bedroom, where an enormous vase of spring flowers filled the room with fragrance. Here, the walls were lined with dark ruby panelling, edged in gold leaf, and hung with replicas of famous Italian fine art and yet more mirrors. The bed was stunning in its whiteness and was the largest I had ever seen.

We spoke in whispers and tried hard to smother our laughter until the porter left. It was obvious we were not accustomed to this kind of accommodation.

At the soft click of the door closing, Red gave a small shriek and launched herself at the bed, landing on her back.

"Oh my God, the ceiling!"

I clambered up beside her to look. The panelling was even more decorative than the walls and had highlights of red, gold and cream.

"I think Michelangelo has been here!"

"Do you think the chandelier would fit in your suitcase?"

We collapsed into giggles.

"OK, we've got about an hour or so before it gets dark. How about we start exploring?"

"Only after I've seen the bathroom."

We slid off the bed and oohed in unison at the black and white marble décor and spa bathtub.

Outside the air was cool but the sky was blue as we walked down Via Veneto to see the item at the very top of our list.

The Trevi Fountain had a magical air in the afternoon light. We were between the daytime crowds and those who waited for the lights at dusk, so we were able to dip our hands in the cold water, throw a coin over our left shoulder, and admire Salvi's handiwork without too many tourists in the way.

We sat in stillness. I breathed in the scene I'd only seen in books and photos and tried to memorise every curve of the incredible sculpture.

"I have a 'deep and meaningful' question for you," Red said after a few moments.

"Ask away."

"I know we've talked about Jenni and why it's easier not to tell people. What I want to know is how it felt for you at the time she disappeared."

"Oh. That is a deep one," I said.

It was the question I had hoped Tom might ask, but he hadn't. Even so, it was incredibly hard to answer.

"It's strange, you know. I was only 11. It was impossible to process what had happened. Like seeing an optical illusion for the first time, where your brain tells you one thing, but your eyes disagree.

"I felt as if I had 'lost' Jenni – I'd gone out with her in the morning and misplaced her, like you'd lose a teddy bear or a pen. Nothing else has ever given me a feeling like that, not even the loss you feel when someone dies.

"Sometimes I'd leave the house and panic that I'd forgotten something important. Actually, I still do. Tom thinks I'm forgetful because I run back inside, remind myself to breathe, and come out holding my keys or sunglasses or wallet, pretending I'm just scatterbrained."

That made Red laugh. "The ditsy artist! Sorry, continue."

"I know you and your Mum did your best but I was

lonely for a long time. Before, if I was outside having fun, I was usually with Jenni. If I was in trouble with Mum and Dad, she'd be in trouble too and we'd be side-by-side, hanging our heads and accepting the lecture. When she disappeared, I was on my own. I was helpless, literally. I couldn't answer anybody's questions the way they wanted me to, not even my own."

I sighed heavily.

"School was awful. For ages, no-one wanted their kids to walk to school alone but no-one wanted to walk with me. Mum and Dad never said it was my fault, but I felt responsible anyway.

"Did you know Mum wanted me to be hypnotised? Dad said no and she let it go for a while until she started reading about serial killers and how witnesses had recalled amazing details under hypnosis. She must have hoped I'd suddenly be able to recite the car number plate.

"I'd have given anything to be away at boarding school like you so I wasn't reminded of her every single day. I wanted her back so I could scream at her and tell her how much she hurt me. I think I loved her and hated her at the same time."

Even though that thought had been on my mind for years, speaking it out loud was shameful.

Red disagreed.

"Nobody can blame you for feeling that way. And, just so you know, I hated being at boarding school. I was so jealous of how free you and Jenni were, walking to school in the mornings and going to the park with your friends afterwards.

"For seven years I had no control over anything, not

what time I ate my breakfast or did my homework or went to bed or what I watched on TV. Not once did I make a choice of my own. Plus, the other girls made it sound sleazy that my Mum held Tupperware parties. As a boarder I could never escape it: the girls who sneered at me during the day were the same ones who were mean to me in the evenings."

Vera's desire to set her daughter up for life had, even inadvertently, deprived Red of giggly sleepless sleepovers, playing football with the boys in the park, and just being herself.

It had always seemed glamorous but the reality would have been hard, I understood that now.

"All week I was desperate for Friday to come around but then I spent most of the weekend dreading Sunday night. To this day, if I hear a bell that sounds anything like the one at school, I think I'm supposed to be somewhere else.

"Mum thought a private education would pave the way to a good career. Now look at me! Living 10 miles from home and working as a receptionist. Not quite what she had in mind."

"Head receptionist," I reminded her, and she smiled.

"OK, my turn. Can I ask you a personal question?"

"Shoot!" said Red.

"I've never asked you about your Dad. Haven't you ever been curious? I mean, now your Mum is gone, how would you find him, even if you wanted to?"

Red chewed her lip.

"Sometimes when I was younger I was curious. Mum told me bits and pieces, if I asked. She said the divorce was her fault because she knew he didn't want children but took the risk and got pregnant. By that point, she wasn't bothered whether he stayed or left, as long as she got me out of it. She said to me when I was about 12, if I ever wanted to know who and where he was, I only had to ask. By then, I'd decided that if he didn't love Mum, I wasn't interested in knowing who he was. He didn't deserve us.

"I don't think he broke her heart or anything like that, although she said it was hard, raising me on her own. She must have been lonely from time to time and I think that's why she threw so many parties, so she wouldn't have time to notice."

The talk of Vera made both of us go quiet until Red slapped her hand down on the cold flagstone.

"OK, enough melancholy, this trip is supposed to be happy."

"You're right. What's next?"

Red grinned. "Pizza!"

~ ~ ~

Rome was a magnificent, bustling city, so different from the oppressive greyness of London. The history was as rich as the traffic was crazy and I lost count of how many churches and fountains we saw. Nothing could fill me with the awe of Sacré Coeur, I thought, until we were gazing up at the ceiling of the Sistine Chapel.

"Not bad for a sculptor," I sighed. "Maybe I should take up clay modelling – I might find I'm brilliant!"

On our way to dinner that evening, blissfully relaxed after massages for our sore necks, we passed a particularly loud group of young Italians. I wondered out loud how the women were so effortlessly slim and beautiful; after four days of Italian food both of us had loosened our belts a notch. Maybe we should give dessert a miss tonight.

"According to the guidebook this place does the best Tiramisu in all of Rome," Red said and I groaned as she pushed open the door to the cosy restaurant the concierge had booked for us.

She was right.

The next morning, after an early breakfast on our balcony, we let the porter pick up our bags and went to settle the bill. As promised, Red had hired a convertible and we were driving to Florence via Perugia.

"OK, so the car's not Italian, but the sun is shining, the roof is down, and I have headscarves," and she produced them from her bag with a flourish.

With a farewell toot to the bemused staff, she joined the rush-hour traffic – this girl from the country who had only held a license for a few years.

I could scarcely watch. What had seemed entertaining from our balcony an hour earlier was terrifying to be part of. Not half a mile from the hotel Red squealed and I squeezed my eyes shut before she had even slammed on the brakes.

"Mamma mia, how close was that!" and she started laughing and waving at the Italian who was beeping loudly and mouthing what we assumed were obscenities as he gesticulated at us through his windscreen.

"No problem, have a lovely day, thank you very much!" and she nodded and waved until he disappeared.

Unscathed by some miracle, we emerged from the city into a more industrial landscape before we came to picturesque towns, farms and woodland as we criss-crossed the River Tiber.

"Grace Kelly, eat your heart out!" said Red and I pulled out my camera to capture her pose. The radio presenter jabbered away without pausing for breath, between upbeat pop songs we did not understand.

After a couple of hours, Perugia rose up before us. We had lunch and stretched our legs on a stroll through gorgeous cobbled streets.

Passing more quaint towns and villages, we approached Florence in the late afternoon. Along the River Arno I caught my first glimpse of the famous dome of Santa Maria del Fiore cathedral, which I was desperate to see up close.

"It's left here. No, right, I had the map upside down. Hang on, this is no entry. Left!"

I took us across practically every bridge in the city before we finally rounded the corner into the Piazza di Santa Maria Novella. The exquisite charcoal and white basilica made us gasp in unison. Our hotel – the Palazzo – had a more modest façade than the Emperor but its views were perfect.

Only marginally less intimidated than in Rome, we checked in and followed the porter to our suite on the third floor, talking in hushed tones. This time, we remembered the tip.

"Ta da!"

Through the window, beyond the small balcony, the dome and tower of the cathedral were clearly visible above the rooftops. Red had outdone herself.

"What do you think of this?" Red asked. I burst out laughing as I saw where she was pointing: above the four-poster bed, stretching in a massive fresco across the ceiling, were several semi-naked women and a man riding a creature with hooves and a head of snakes.

"Wow. Bit of a passion killer, right over the bed."

"Or perhaps that's how the Italians like it!" Red raised one eyebrow and swung a leg suggestively around the bed post.

"Enough! Or you'll be sleeping in the bath."

We decided on room service and an early night, ready to be up before the crowds in the morning. First, though, the hotel had a rooftop bar with an uninterrupted view of the cathedral and the promise of a breathtaking sunset.

The waiter brought over two fleecy blankets and we settled back into large armchairs.

"We made it here in one piece. This calls for Champagne," Red decided. "Well, prosecco since we're in Italy."

The waiter gave a small bow and returned almost immediately with our bottle and an ice bucket. He made a show of popping the cork, sending it high into the sky before catching it on the way down. We applauded as he began to pour. Red and I clinked glasses. "To us!"

The sky was fading into a dusky pink, turning the cathedral dome redder still. I took a sip, never tiring of the way the bubbles tickled my nose, and decided this was one of life's perfect moments.

Red cleared her throat. "I'm getting married."

"You're what?" Cold prosecco splashed onto my blanket as I sat bolt upright.

Red was grinning from ear to ear, clearly satisfied with the impact of her news. "I'm getting married!"

"You're kidding? You're not kidding! How have you kept that to yourself this whole trip? Um ... who are you marrying?"

"Daniel."

"Daniel? Daniel the vet? Daniel your boss?"

"Yup. He asked, and I said yes!"

"Well, congratulations, of course, that's amazing."

I set my glass down, spilling more in the process, and grabbed her in a huge hug.

"I have so many questions! Tell me everything!"

Still smiling at my astonishment, Red explained: while the proposal was unexpected, they had been in a relationship for several months and their feelings had developed quickly. It had started only a few weeks after Aunt Vera died, not long after she broke up with the mechanic.

Daniel was a young vet and, after university, had returned to Cornwall to join the practice where his father was in charge. A few years on and Daniel's name was now over the door.

Unlike his dad, who seemed to have chosen his vocation because he preferred the company of animals, Daniel was a true people person. He was friendly with all the staff and customers but gradually started finding excuses to spend time in reception whenever Red was working, and hearing her laugh made him smile even when he was in the next room.

Red liked that he always found time for a chat. He was a very tall man with a rich baritone voice whose softness she – and his animal patients – found very calming. She could have listened to him for hours.

One evening they were closing up when an emergency call came in from a nearby farm. Daniel suggested she accompany him to gain a better understanding of the other side of the practice.

As unofficial first dates go, it was terrible. A heavily pregnant cow had slipped on an embankment and was in distress that may or may not have been labour. Daniel was unable to save the calf or the cow and after a gruelling four hours they were back in the clinic, their mood sombre.

Red was good at dealing with distraught pet owners and offering gentle words and tissues; seeing it happen was altogether different.

She'd asked Daniel how he ever came to terms with it.

"He told me he took it so much to heart in the early days he almost gave up. Now he forces himself to switch off at the end of the day knowing he tried his best, and mostly that's good enough and sometimes it isn't."

Seeing how upset Red was, Daniel had given her a comforting hug, which turned into a kiss. Simple as that.

"We didn't want anyone to know, in case it didn't work out. What a cliché – the boss and the receptionist! But we have been sneaking away for weekends since before Christmas and he is absolutely amazing, he makes me so happy.

"You won't believe how much we have in common. He's an only child. His Dad sent him to private school too, which he hated, and we both went to Portsmouth University, although he was there a few years before me.

"We went back to Portsmouth two weekends ago and spent the whole time reminiscing about places we both knew. He said he suddenly realised he wanted to hear everything I'd ever done, and he dropped to one knee and proposed in the street! It wasn't planned, he didn't have a ring or anything, so we went to an antiques shop and he got me this," she waggled her finger. "I love it, but it's only temporary."

I'd assumed the rectangular art deco piece was more of the costume jewellery she often wore.

"We can't see any reason to wait so we've set the date for 15th May."

"But that's not even two months away! You're not…"

"No I am not!" she interrupted, laughing at my horrified face.

Despite my misgivings about the timeline, I was pleased for her. She deserved to be in love and happy after the worst year imaginable, although getting married without her mother there was going to be hard.

"Um," Red began tentatively, "I wanted to ask if you would be my bridesmaid? I only want one, it's not a huge event, but I'd feel funny not having you there with me. And it doesn't mean you have to ask me to be yours when the time comes, I won't be offended. Or you can say no, I won't be offended at that either. There's no pressure. If you say 'no thanks', I can decide if I want to ask anyone else."

I put my hand out to stop her rambling. "I would love to. Nothing would stop me. Unless you ask me to wear pink taffeta, and then I would have to kill you!"

Red studied me silently.

"I wasn't sure how you'd feel – you and Tom have been together for ages and I assumed you'd be married first."

I was absolutely fine, I assured her.

"I understand why you're in a hurry," I said. "You're practically an old maid, time's running out! And who's to say Tom and I will even get married?"

"Of course you will. I bet he's waiting until he's finished studying so he can do it properly. You'll be perfectly respectable and move to Surrey and have exactly 2.4 children and a golden retriever."

She was mocking me kindly. She liked Tom and had

been relieved that I moved to London despite our rocky patch in the summer. I hadn't spoken to her about the problems since then.

"I don't know. I don't think I'm the marrying kind. I'm happy for you, I just never pictured myself walking down the aisle."

"What does Tom want?"

"The way he talks about the future sometimes, he's assuming we'll get married and have kids. It makes my insides freeze. That's not the response you're supposed to have, is it?"

"If you love him, it will all work out. You're only 22, not an old maid like me," she said with a playful elbow to my ribs. "You don't have to make a decision now, not when he hasn't even asked you yet."

I shared then what had happened 12 months earlier, how my heart stopped at the same moment as my insides did a backflip when I thought Tom was proposing.

She burst out laughing. "You must have freaked. I wish I'd seen your face!"

I had to agree it was funny, looking back. My feelings hadn't changed, though, and the more time passed, the more I worried about where our relationship was going.

Tom always said he liked how different I was from the girls he'd grown up around, girls who had been so indulged they grew up expecting to be treated like princesses. He found them dull for the most part, blonde and boring and not given to thinking independently. Once they inevitably married, they would happily give up work for the chance to support their husbands' careers, raise children, and join various organising committees.

"So why would he want me to become one of them and pop out a couple of kids as soon as he puts a ring on my finger?"

"I don't know. Maybe he's been with enough women to know what he wants. Not like you – and this isn't a criticism, but I can't imagine being married to someone without knowing what it's like to sleep with another man."

I sighed and weighed up whether or not to tell her.

"Actually … I slept with someone else."

"What? Since you've been with Tom?"

"Last year. Not long after your Mum died, when Tom and I were having issues. I still can't believe I did it. I felt terrible but once I was in London it was easy to pretend it never happened."

Red frowned with concentration as she calculated the timeline.

"So it was before you left Cornwall. I was with you for more than a week and I think I might have noticed a strange man in the house, so it must have been right after Mum's funeral, or right before you packed up your bags. What happened – did you have a wild night in the pub and meet up with an old boyfriend?"

"No. You won't believe it when I tell you."

I told her and she didn't believe me.

"Eric Tremayne? The farmer the police thought might have murdered your sister? Well, you do know how to pick them!"

"That's totally unfair," I was indignant at Red's simplistic description. "I know for certain he didn't do anything. I bet he's wished a thousand times he never stopped his van. All he did was try to help, and for that he was treated like a criminal.

"The police turned their farm upside down, and assumed he was guilty only because they had no other explanation. The fact that no-one found any evidence didn't stop them, or the newspapers. He had to move away to get some peace.

"He runs the whole farm on his own now, although I get the sense he doesn't want to, now that his parents have both died. He's keen to travel more and we talked about Barcelona and architecture and how he wants to learn to cook. Promise me you won't tell anyone. Mum and Dad would have kittens and I don't want it to get back to Tom somehow."

Red threw her hands up in defence.

"OK, I'm sorry. Whatever makes you happy. God knows, I don't have the best track record. If you say he's alright, then he's fine with me. It's our secret, I promise. How was he in the sack?"

"You don't deserve to know. But he was great." And we giggled like schoolgirls as Red refilled our glasses.

She didn't mention him again, so neither did I, not wanting her to think it was a big deal, although our conversation brought back memories I had done my best to suppress.

The next morning, our feet rested after a day in the car, we set out early to see Santa Maria del Fiore and climb the bell tower. The mixture of colours on the exterior should have been garish but the soft pink and so many different textures and patterns changed every few steps as I walked towards it.

We puffed and panted our way up the narrow staircase, cursing each other and our love of pasta. Our reward was crystal-clear views of the Duomo. Beyond the city, low, wispy clouds grazed the hills.

The simplicity of the dome against the complexity of so many tiny terracotta rooftops framed by green hills would make an incredible painting. In an effort to capture the scene, I took multiple photos, not convinced I would ever do it justice with my brush.

Florence was much more relaxed than Rome, although the main tourist areas were busy and the Ponte Vecchio was a throng of tourists. We were happy to wander through the streets, stopping for coffee or gelato when our feet were tired.

On our final morning, I wandered back to the cathedral to start my sketches while Red shopped for handmade leather shoes. I asked what she needed them for, working in a vet's practice in a small country town.

"You never know. Anyway, need doesn't come into it. Mum said every woman deserves at least one pair of ridiculously expensive Italian shoes in her lifetime."

The end of our trip came too quickly and in the airport bar I looked at Red over my lager, glad my cousin was such a wonderful person.

"I have never had so much fun in my life. Thank you for an amazing holiday. It's insane to think you're getting married in less than two months! I'm sorry I'm not there to help."

"I know, it's going to be a rush but I want your opinion on everything though. When I find things in magazines I'll call you and you can sneak into the newsagent and help me decide."

The prospect of being caught reading magazines I had no intention of buying made me nervous. I could already hear the voice behind me asking, "are you going to buy that, or stare at it all day so nobody else can?" and blushed with humiliation.

At Heathrow, squally rain lashed the glass wall of the

terminal, almost drowning out our tearful goodbye.

"Back to reality, hey?"

"See you in a few weeks."

I'd left Tom enough food to survive the week but empty Waitrose bags on the kitchen benchtop indicated Edward had taken his son food shopping – something I never let happen. If we couldn't afford to feed ourselves while living rent-free, we weren't cut out for living in one of the world's most expensive cities.

Tom was out, giving me time to unpack, put the washing machine on, and check the newspapers he had helpfully left in a neat stack on my side of the sofa.

Ninety minutes and seven newspapers later, I was as dejected as before my holiday: the cinema would not be losing its cleaner any time soon. Perhaps I should take on any full-time position I could find, even if it was still only cleaning. A nine-to-five job would leave me with less time to paint but at least Tom wouldn't be able to complain about never seeing me. He'd made it clear his goal was to be independent from his parents once he finished his year of study, and my part-time salary was not enough to get us there. Would he still expect dinner to be waiting when he came home?

I had no choice but to keep cleaning and keep searching – and not give up painting while I waited for a miracle.

~ ~ ~

Using all my weight, I push open a heavy and elaborately carved wooden door and find myself at the back of a theatre, squinting at a stage in the far distance. The whole place is empty; I am an audience of one. Then I notice someone on stage under a dim spotlight. As I draw nearer I see it's two people: a woman sitting statue-like on a chair, bowed over a child on her lap.

From the clothes the child is wearing, even from a distance, it has to be Jenni: she's wearing the burgundy dress with large white polka dots that matches my green one. These were 'good clothes', saved for when we had company, and Mum would slap at our hands as we fiddled and stroked the velvet trim.

Closer still, I see the woman is Aunt Vera, which makes my throat catch. The backdrop has been painted to resemble a country road with high hedgerows that curve into the distance. This scene can't end well but I continue, my feet silent on the thick carpet.

At the halfway point I strain to identify a faint noise. Only when I'm almost at the stage are my aunt's quiet sobs audible, and I see she's not motionless, her shoulders are gently shaking.

She lifts her head when she hears me and the sight breaks my heart. Her eyes are red from crying and black mascara has pooled below her lashes. She stares right at me and shakes her head with sorrow because the girl is not Jenni.

Aunt Vera's tears convey what I feel: we just want to know. If she's dead, let us bury her and lay flowers on her grave.

25

Two days before Red's wedding, Tom and I drove down for the rehearsal dinner. It was my first chance to suss out the man my cousin was committing herself to for the rest of her life.

I liked Daniel instantly. His manner was warm and easy and he looked at Red when she was talking as if she were the only person in the room.

The celebrant was one of Daniel's oldest friends and he walked our small group – Mum and Dad, Daniel's parents and his best man – through the order of activities in the back room of a pub where we were all having dinner. Using plastic figurines of the bride and groom, he showed where they would be standing and made us all laugh with his falsetto impression of Red saying "I do" and Daniel going in for a kiss.

Mum and Dad, neither of them a parent of the bride, played a slightly different role: Dad would be walking Red down the aisle; Mum was one of the witnesses who would sign the register.

During the meal I was quiet as everyone else chatted. Daniel's parents quizzed Tom on what it was like being in

London in the midst of all the bombings, the most recent of which – the massive Bishopsgate explosion three weeks earlier – had shaken the city and made me question how much longer I could bear living there.

Instead of joining the conversation, I was imagining what might have been. I was eight or nine, I remembered, when Mum came back from the shops to discover Jenni and I making wedding dresses out of toilet rolls – streams of which lay all over the floor. With sticky tape and pins, I had followed Jenni's direction to fashion her a dress with long sleeves and a flowing train. The net curtain from the living room made the perfect veil, until I stepped on it and tore a hole that was still visible, if you knew where to look. One day, Jenni said, she would design her own wedding dress. I was bouncing up and down, "my turn, my turn!" when the front door opened. We knew before "What on earth…" even came out of Mum's mouth that we were in trouble.

The thought I would never get to see Jenni standing next to a man she loved, and the fact that it should have been Aunt Vera walking Red down the aisle, left me feeling glum.

~ ~ ~

On Tuesday – Red's wedding day – the big puffy clouds were expected to blow away before the 2.00pm ceremony. Red had arrived the previous night with several bags and a carefully wrapped wedding dress, given Dad a grateful kiss for offering her his spare bedroom so she wouldn't wake up alone, and immediately commandeered most of bathroom as well.

The four of us ate a hearty breakfast, expecting we would

be too jittery to focus on anything much for lunch. Red dove in like a starving dog, piling egg onto fried bread and eating bacon with her fingers.

"After all that pasta in Italy I haven't touched anything bad for weeks. This is heaven!" she said.

She disappeared upstairs with her plate, singing, to begin the long process of getting ready. Tom was keeping well out of the way and I was in my bathrobe with time to kill.

Inside the musty sideboard I delved under old magazines until I found the padded photo album from my parents' wedding, which Mum hadn't taken and Dad probably hadn't opened since she left.

The tracing paper covering each leaf was pristine.

The guests' clothing made me smile – bad over-the-ear haircuts and wide-bottomed trousers for the men, kohl-lined eyes and micro mini-dresses for the women. Except my mother. Her dress was a cross between a lace tablecloth and a demure night gown. In the black and white photos she appeared to be even younger than her 21 years, but formal at the same time.

Long sleeves covered her arms and the full skirt of semi-sheer lace, adorned with daisies, roses, and other flowers, brushed the floor.

The vigorous ringing of the doorbell interrupted me, announcing the arrival of Red's stylist – a short, round ball of energy, who needed two trips to the car to collect the materials she needed to take upstairs.

Most of the guests I recognised from the photos were people we hadn't seen in years – Uncle Allan and Aunt Sue (divorced), Dave and Sonia, the family friends who became my sister's godparents (divorced). Dad's old school friend,

Malcolm, who I was sure ended up in prison for something fairly bad.

It was hard to imagine Mum and Dad were ever the two smiling people captured in time and I wondered if all marriages end up being a disappointment.

Dad sat down next to me – at ease in the stiff morning dress with its high-collared shirt and a rose in his buttonhole – and groaned when he saw the album on my lap.

"You'll be next," he said with a wry smile.

"Don't count on it!" I laughed off his comment but he looked at me curiously.

"Maybe I don't need to get married. Society has changed, you know."

"Surely you and Tom want a wedding? Marriage is still the respectable thing to do, especially before you have children."

I was non-committal in my response. "Think of all the money you'll save!"

"You mustn't let that put you off. I always assumed I'd be walking you girls," he immediately corrected himself, "walking you down the aisle one day. We can help, your mother and I. We've talked about it."

I told him he was sweet and when the time came he'd be the first to find out.

The high whine of a hairdryer competing with the thump of a disco beat through the ceiling was my cue to escape.

"I'd better go and shower. It'll take a while to get this mop under control," I gestured at my hair.

I wasn't excited about the day. The Red I grew up with was smart, unconcerned with convention, and comfortable in her own skin – exactly like her mother. So I was surprised and a little disappointed at how willingly she'd been swallowed up in the circus of a wedding.

I'd pictured her and Daniel on a clifftop overlooking the Atlantic, exchanging vows in front of a handful of people as seabirds floated on the warm air currents above. Instead, the past few weeks had been a flurry of phone conversations about peonies and anemones or roses, white shoes or silver, a floral headband or a tiara.

I did my very best to sound interested and as the weeks passed I dutifully searched out all the pictures in all the magazines Red wanted my views on. A few times I bought the magazines to avert any accusations of loitering, but quickly tired of the inevitable exchange at the till: "Oh, you're getting married?" followed by "No, I'm just the bridesmaid."

My scowl usually discouraged further conversation.

Showered, and with damp strands escaping from the towel around my hair, I knocked and opened the bedroom door to see how Red was getting on. My nostrils flared involuntarily. The bride's bouquet – she had settled on simple crimson and fragrant white roses – competed with the stylist's own perfume and the styling mousse she'd used on Red. The fog of hairspray caught in the back of my throat.

Red pivoted to see who was invading the room, making the stylist, with the last clip in her mouth, wobble on her chair. A cumbersome frame of plastic hoops and net swayed from side to side as Red jiggled to Ce Ce Peniston's Finally.

"Ready?" she asked and I thought I caught a whiff of alcohol.

"I can do my own hair, honestly," I said feebly, eyeing the array of brushes, rollers, and cannisters spread out across the chest of drawers, "All I need is some decent mousse."

The stylist assessed the challenge before her.

"Don't worry, my love, I'll have you fixed up in no time."

Dad wiped away a tear when Red stepped daintily down the stairs to show everyone the finished product. Somewhere under all that satin and netting and make-up was my cousin, glowing at the reaction she was causing.

"Well, don't you look beautiful," Dad stated. "Both of you," he added quickly, reaching out to bring us close. The stylist had pinned Red's hair off her face so it cascaded in large waves to her shoulders, accentuating the bareness of her back. I wondered if her head hurt as much as mine, clips jabbing my scalp in several places to hold up what was somewhere between a chignon and a beehive.

A silver Rolls Royce conveyed Dad, Red, and me to Roach's Lane Registry Office – which was nicer than the name suggested – while Tom, Mum, and Daniel's parents followed in an identical car. The plain Georgian frontage gave way to a wide, light hallway with polished black and white floor tiles and an ornate ceiling. Excited chatter came from the ceremony room down the hall.

Crouching, I puffed out Red's skirt to its perfect fullness and we were ready.

As the speakers crackled with the first notes of The *Bridal Chorus*, the room fell silent and three dozen people turned towards the door. Today, I reminded myself and my churning insides, was not about me. It was not me in my crimson bridesmaid's dress, gripping a small posy, and trying to walk slowly in heels without clenching my teeth, that made their faces shine with anticipation.

The room would have been quite dark in its day but a thoughtful modification had replaced a back wall with glass bi-fold doors that opened into a lush internal courtyard with a tinkling water feature. Daniel was standing at the front, hands clasped nervously but with a smile of pure happiness as he peered past me at Red and my Dad walking in.

I sank into my seat.

Every pair of eyes was glued on the bride and groom as they began their vows. There were giggles as the celebrant took Red and Daniel through the relaxed and very personal ceremony. Red spoke of her intent to trust Daniel and love and support him and warm his toes, even in the middle of a freezing winter's night if someone called with an emergency. He said he would cherish her every day of her life and promised to settle every argument with the flip of a coin and a kiss. It was adorable, I had to admit, but the way Tom kept squeezing my hand was distracting.

Weeks of fretting and agonising were over in what felt like seconds as they became husband and wife, a pronouncement sealed with a passionate kiss and a roar of approval and applause. Outside, confetti fluttered around us as we gathered in the street. Several beautifully restored old farm trucks were waiting with white ribbons across their bonnets and open-top trailers fitted with bench seating.

Daniel had taken charge of arranging the reception venue and sworn the guests to secrecy so it would be a surprise for Red.

"It had better not be in his clinic. Or a hay shed," she joked.

We were driven out of town and along increasingly narrow and rough tracks, laughing and jostling as we bounced around, holding on to our seats. Tom chatted easily with someone's parents as I caught up with Red's university friends I'd met at Aunt Vera's funeral.

The venue – a former hunting lodge, now a restaurant with two luxurious bedroom suites – stood on a rocky patch near the bottom of a wide valley. A long stretch of the woodland, cleared decades earlier, provided stunning views along the river that ran only metres from the lodge and cut the valley in two. It made for a beautiful backdrop as the happy couple posed at the centre of their guests. When the photographer was finished with the group, he whisked away the bride and groom for some more intimate shots.

From the narrow windows and deep granite walls, I expected the inside to be cool and damp but bare stone walls were softened with tapestries, and a small fire was burning in the hearth, despite the mild May afternoon. Through the windows the hawthorn trees were still in blossom, standing out against the vibrant green of the valley.

To one side, a table of early arrivals had escaped the photographs. A fair-haired couple and another man were engrossed in conversation, heads bowed, until they all leant back and roared with laughter and I realised the blond man was Eric. A flush crept up my face. I glanced at Tom, who was taking two glasses of sparkling wine from a waiter's tray, before reminding myself that of course he wouldn't think anything of it.

Tom mingled easily as he always did and I stayed at his side until it was time to eat. The string quartet became barely audible against forks clinking against china plates and overlapping conversations.

Between the starter and main course, Red and I found ourselves alone in the ladies' toilet and I chided her for not warning me Eric would be among the guests. She blinked at me with eyelashes laden with mascara before remembering why it might be an issue.

"Daniel invited him. He knows all the local farmers and asked a few to the reception, as we didn't have room for everyone at the Registry Office."

She gave me a nudge and a wink. "Play your cards right and you could be going home with two blokes tonight!"

I was not impressed and told her so. "Anyway, he's brought a 'plus one', his girlfriend I expect."

Red hadn't met her before and, from her accent, knew she wasn't local.

"Does it bother you? I thought you two had a one-off thing and that was it?"

"Of course it doesn't bother me, he can bring who he likes." My protests were mild in case they raised Red's suspicions. "I was more concerned about how Mum would react to him being invited. I'm surprised she hasn't caused a scene yet, thrown her drink over him, and accused him of God-knows-what."

Red assured me she had warned Aunt Eileen to behave and had seated her as far away from Eric as possible.

"I admit, I was a bit uncertain myself when Daniel added Eric to the guest list. But it made sense, what you said in Italy, about there being no evidence. So I told Aunt Eileen that Daniel wanted him here and made her promise to ignore him."

I spent the remainder of the meal lost in my own thoughts, debating whether to say hello to Eric and his girlfriend or keep Tom and me at a distance. Tom, thankfully, was engrossed in conversation with Daniel's father about the ethical and legal rights of vets versus doctors when it came to euthanasia and didn't notice how distracted I was.

Empty plates were cleared and the speeches began as waiters topped up our glasses. Dad faced the unenviable task of representing the father of the bride and had been whispering his speech under his breath for days. He hadn't let me read it, so I was as keen as anyone to hear what he had prepared.

He started by talking about Red as a child, painting a picture of a joyful and mischievous girl, full of energy and spirit, like her mother, and a much-loved part of our family. Naturally he had to include Aunt Vera. Everybody knew it was coming; still there wasn't a dry eye in the room.

"Vera would have been incredibly happy", Dad told the room as his voice wavered, "to see her daughter surrounded by so much love. Daniel would undoubtedly have met with her approval, although she would have given him a hard time, to test what he was made of."

He summed Vera up beautifully as a lioness, fiercely protective of her sole offspring, but intensely proud to see her grow into an independent woman, choosing her own path. He wished them every happiness and I saw Mum wipe away a tear as we raised our glasses in a toast.

Daniel's thanks were sincere and heart-warming as he addressed Dad. "I know it means a great deal to Red that you were here for her on what I hope is the happiest day of her life. Although I never had the good fortune of meeting Vera, it's clear that she would have been a wonderful mother-in-law." He turned to Red, whose eyes were shining. "And I would probably never have needed the syringe of horse sedative I always carry with me, just in case."

Once the laughter died down, he turned again, his glass raised in a toast to me as the lone bridesmaid, and again my cheeks reddened.

"Every bride needs someone special to share her day and I know Red feels incredibly lucky to have your love and support."

"Hear, hear," Tom nudged me and joined the applause.

The best man's speech did not disappoint either. Daniel was described with great affection as a loyal, caring man who saw his purpose in life as making all creatures great and small as happy as they could be. And then he shared stories of the young vet-in-waiting at university, his romantic disasters only surpassed by his culinary catastrophes. It was the pick-me-up the room needed.

Dessert followed, then coffee, the cutting of the cake, and more wine as the musicians made way for the evening's DJ.

Daniel and Red – the new Mr and Mrs Pascoe – took to the floor for their first dance to the soft drumbeat of *Show Me Heaven*. They stood, touching, oblivious to anyone else and kissing gently. There was that look again, the 'we are the only two people in the world' gaze I'd seen at the rehearsal. Had I ever looked at Tom that way? And had he ever done the same to me?

After cheers and a few lewd tips on how Daniel might really show Red heaven later on, everybody was up on their feet. Daniel's grandparents had the whole room in stitches when they attempted to *Vogue* with everyone else.

I was beginning to relax: the day was coming to an end, I'd survived, and – most importantly – Red had enjoyed the amazing day she deserved. I picked at my cake, happy to watch other people dancing and trying not to seek out Eric between the bodies.

The tempo changed again and Tom led me to the dancefloor where we swayed inexpertly to a soaring saxophone solo. Pubs and loud, lively nightclubs had been more our scene and this was the first time we'd ever danced close and slow.

He'd bought me a beautiful silver necklace the previous week and presented it to me with breakfast in bed. In the run-up to the wedding, when Red and I were on the phone every other evening, our anniversary had slipped my mind.

In my heels, my ear was level with Tom's chin as we moved to the music.

"I guess we'd better start talking about our own plans soon," he said, matter-of-factly.

I waited for him to elaborate as my insides began to tighten. I'd always had a sense of something missing in me, like when I heard other girls at school talk of marrying their tall, dark, and handsome man, or saw them playing games to find out their compatibility score with boys they fancied. My bottom drawer contained paint-smeared overalls, not magazine cuttings of bouquets and the perfect three-tiered cake.

Tom continued: "I mean, it's been two years. We're happy, we know what we want. And it won't be long before I need to look the part at work."

"Do we have to talk about this tonight?" I didn't want a scene but now was not the time.

"I spoke to your Dad about it last night, actually. It's a bit old-fashioned to ask, I know, but I thought he'd appreciate it."

So that was behind Dad's comment. This was beginning to sound like a conspiracy.

"It's been a massive day. I'm tired and my feet are hurting. Let's leave it until tomorrow." I gave him a kiss to shut down the discussion without an argument.

The second the song ended, I asked him to get me a drink, needing a moment to compose myself. I turned back to our table and suddenly Eric was there, touching my elbow. His smile was tentative and I hoped my face wasn't visibly beetroot under the party lights. Wearing a brilliant white shirt with a green tie that nearly matched his eyes, he looked even better than I remembered.

"I was going to say hi earlier but you had a lot going on, being bridesmaid. You look lovely, by the way. Beautiful."

I couldn't help but smile and thank him, feeling a glow.

"Is that your boyfriend?" his head tilted towards the bar.

I nodded. "That's Tom. And your girlfriend?"

"Oh no, Rachel's only a friend. I've known her for years – she lives in Kent, next door to my cousin's farm, and we dated a bit, way back. She's more like a sister."

I realised I was still nodding and his hand was still cradling my elbow. It was ridiculous to feel pleased that Rachel wasn't his date, when I was here with my partner.

Tom returned with my Southern Comfort and lemonade and a whiskey for himself.

Eric put out his hand and introduced himself as an old friend of the family, the two of us sharing a glance that acknowledged the inaccuracy of the description.

"That's quite a handshake! I'm Tom, I'm Joy's boyfriend," then with a conspiratorial wink, "Soon to be more, I hope."

"Oh, I didn't know. Great, really great. Well, we're off now. Unfortunately the cows don't care if I was up late, they'll be awake by 5am. Nice to meet you Tom. It's good to see you again Joy."

He kissed me swiftly on the cheek and, before I could

say anything, Dad was at the microphone calling for "all the single ladies" to catch the bouquet. Tom pushed me forward and Dad gave me a nod and a smile as single friends and relatives jostled for position. Thankfully I didn't even have to pretend, as the flowers flew straight to shrieking second cousin Tracy while her boyfriend received sympathetic pats on the back.

Red and Daniel were spending a romantic night at the lodge to end their day, as honeymoon plans were on hold until after the busy foaling season. To a chorus of cheers and a few coarse comments, they disappeared up the worn granite stairs with a wave.

Guests began to drift away, a few of them, like Eric, expecting an early start. A line of minibuses were on hand to ferry us back into town and Mum asked if our driver could drop her off on our way home. It was a strange foursome: my divorced parents in the back – Mum chatting away amicably to Dad – while I sat glumly in the front seat and stared out at the starry sky; Tom was silent and I didn't know if he was tired or thinking about the conversation he was planning to have. Maybe I didn't know him at all.

26

Spears of sunlight poked through a gap between the curtains, brightening the backs of my eyelids. I stared up at the Artex-covered ceiling and traced the curling grooves as I had done thousands of times before.

Jenni and I used to squabble, over and over, about who was in charge of the curtains being open or closed. Her bed was nearer – she could reach out and pull back one half – but my bed was the one illuminated in the orange of the street light or the rising sun. Sometimes when I was sleeping she would tug the curtain deliberately if she was bored and eager to talk.

I got up and scraped back Jenni's side of the curtain, then lay with the sun warming my pillow. Until the light knock at the door, I hadn't thought about Tom.

He bent down to kiss me before lifting the quilt. He always looked irritatingly good in the mornings, as if he hadn't moved at all during the night, while my hair suggested I had been wrangling wildebeest in my sleep. Not this morning, though: I thought I'd removed all the pins but my hairdo was miraculously intact.

"This takes me back to university!" he said, hopping under the quilt as I shuffled over. "I was glad I only had a single bed so I had an excuse to squeeze up against you."

He propped himself up on one elbow.

"I enjoyed myself yesterday. Everyone I spoke to was so nice and they all said what an amazing job you did as bridesmaid. I did want to talk to you last night but you were right, it wasn't our moment."

Tom raised a finger as I opened my mouth to speak.

"No, let me say this. I've been practising for days."

He took a deep breath.

"I know things have been difficult for you in London but I have confidence in you, I know you'll get a proper job soon and I want to be there to help you.

"Mum and Dad love you and can't wait for you to be part of our family. They've been exactly where we are right now, with all the same pressures we're going through. They're also aware that the Partners will be discussing who has the stability and maturity to take the next step at work.

"I want to be that person, and I want you by my side, raising our own family until we grow old and grey together.

"So," and he fumbled under the quilt for the small cream box I hadn't seen him bring in, "will you marry me?"

The pop of the lid made me flinch. Suddenly my nose was inches away from two oval diamonds either side of a large, deep-blue gemstone – aquamarine? sapphire? – framed with more than a dozen small diamonds, all set in a gold band.

It was grotesque.

Tom continued nervously, filling the void as he extracted the ring. "It belonged to my great-grandmother on Dad's side, and it's been in our family for more than a century. Dad gave it to Mum when he proposed. Now it's my turn to give it to you."

Tears sprang to my eyes, which Tom naturally interpreted as delight. He beamed at me and, without waiting for my answer, reached for my hand.

I was temporarily paralysed, until the cold metal touching my fingertip made me jerk my hand away as if I'd been burned.

"Wait!"

Tom was frozen in an ungainly half-lean, confusion across his face and the ring hovering in mid-air.

"Wait a minute," I said, more gently. "Can we talk about this? I know you've talked about it, several times – about getting married and having babies. But you've never asked if that's what I want.

"You have it all worked out, you always have. You grew up in a happy household with your brother, plenty of money, holidays abroad, parents who still love each other. I understand why you want that for yourself.

"My childhood was completely different. Even before Jenni disappeared," and here Tom unconsciously rolled his eyes, "even before our family fell apart," I glared at him. "I never pictured myself getting married. And Mum and Dad's divorce proved their vows were a waste of time, so why would I make the same commitment when it obviously doesn't mean anything?

"I can't even stand the idea of being a bride. Being a bridesmaid was hard enough, I don't want any of that fuss for myself. It doesn't mean I don't love you," although I suspected it did, "it means I don't want to marry you. Or anyone. I don't want to get married at all."

I finished my unrehearsed speech. Like a child whose parent has told them their best drawing of a rocket ship is no good, Tom's lower lip trembled.

Trying to squeeze a tear out to show Tom I was not saying this lightly, I waited for a reaction I could not predict.

What was it he'd said, early in our relationship when I was nervous about meeting his family, scared I wasn't good enough? He'd assured me he wasn't interested in the types of girls he had grown up with. Perhaps if he had stuck with one of them he would be in bed with a tearfully jubilant fiancée right now.

"I don't know what to say." His voice was soft, astonished. "We have talked about this. Last year, you remember? I asked if you would marry me and you said you would, so what's changed? I know it's been hard for you, I'm acknowledging that, but I thought everything was fine between us."

"Everything is fine, that's not the point," and also not true, but that was another conversation. "The point is, it can carry on being fine without me standing up there like a specimen under a microscope, pledging to love, honour, and obey you. What's wrong with carrying on the way we are?". Although I knew that would be delaying the inevitable.

"What's wrong, Joy, is that *this is what people do*." Scorn filled Tom's voice. "This is what adults do when they love each other and want to commit to each other and build a life together. I don't want to introduce you to my colleagues as my girlfriend. I don't want our children to grow up with parents who are 'common-law'. How will that look?"

"It won't 'look' like anything because I'm not having children." As the words tumbled out I was aware it wasn't the right way – and not the best time – to share this news; that didn't stop the wave of relief as I voiced something I'd held back for so long.

"Of course you'll have children. I'm not saying let's start tomorrow, but one day."

"Listen to me, Tom: *I don't want children.* If you'd ever thought to ask, I would have told you. I never mentioned it when we were first together because I wasn't thinking that far ahead but after two years my feelings haven't changed.

"I know I could never risk losing them or leaving a child without a brother or sister," I said, and glowered as Tom muttered "that's ridiculous" not quite under his breath. "But I also know I don't want to be stuck at home for years, up to my knees in nappies. I'm not that kind of person."

"How can you make such a massive decision now? You're only 22, you could change your mind in 10 years and it wouldn't be too late."

"What happens if I never change my mind? What if we spend the next decade together and all the time you're waiting for the day I tell you I'm ready to start a family, and I never do? I don't want that kind of pressure and I don't want to end up disappointing you."

I was holding back tears. Tom had never cried in front of me and went to the window where he was a silhouette against the bright sunlight.

"Yesterday when I saw how happy Red and Daniel were, I was thinking how much I wished it was us. Now what?"

I assumed it was rhetorical and stayed quiet.

Tom turned to face me. "I asked you a question. What do we do now?"

"What do you want to do?"

"For once, will you give me a straight answer? You're holding all the cards here. I ask you to marry me and in five minutes I find out more about you than I learned in two years. I need to know what you want."

"Well, that's a first," I snapped, and felt like a bitch as soon as the words left my mouth. "I'm sorry but you can't deny that everything we've done is because of what you want. We're in London because that's where you have to be. We're living off your parents because it means you can finish your studies quicker. I get it. But I'm trying to be a landscape artist, and I'm living in one of the biggest cities in the world, working in a crappy job just so I don't feel like I'm taking advantage.

"You like my art but you treat it like a hobby, something to keep me busy until I find a real career. You're going to be a brilliant lawyer and I have done my best to support you but I can't change what I've wanted since I was little."

Tom's expression was one I had never seen before and I resisted the urge to break the silence, concentrating instead on the dust motes floating around his head.

"I'll go back to London today."

I nodded. "Okay, we can do that."

"No. I need time to think on my own."

So he wasn't willing to talk. I wasn't sure which was stronger: the relief I'd been honest with him at last or the shock I may have just scuppered our relationship.

He left to pack up his things and drove away while I was in the shower. He didn't even say goodbye.

I scanned the room, relieved the small velvet box was nowhere in sight.

Dad's face was full of anticipation when he appeared at the breakfast table.

"Well?" he asked.

"Well, what?"

"Do you have anything to tell me?"

"Tom has gone back to London," I broke down, "and I think we're splitting up because I don't want to get married and have babies. And the ring was foul!"

Not the news Dad was expecting. Regardless, he opened his arms and held me while I sobbed into his dressing gown.

"So he did propose? Why on earth would you say no? He's a terrific young man, so mature and responsible, and he knows exactly what he wants to do with his life."

"That's the problem. It turns out that what he wants and what I want are totally different."

Dad opened his mouth, perhaps to contradict me, to tell me it might appear that way now, but we'd make it work. Instead he said I was welcome to stay as long as I wanted, maybe musing over his own failed marriage. For better or worse.

I asked him not to mention anything to Mum or Red. I wasn't ready for a barrage of questions, and Red deserved to bask in the glow of newly married life without worrying about me.

The next day I was on the train, spending money I didn't have on a ticket and returning to the city that wasn't home. The knot of apprehension was like moving to London the first time, only worse because this time I knew what was waiting.

The long journey gave me time to run through every potential scenario in my mind:

Tom is devastated and has gone away for a few days, most likely to seek his parents' advice on how to bring me round to his way of thinking.

Tom is furious at my rejection and has already packed up my belongings.

Tom loves me so much, he is waiting to tell me he's changed his mind about marriage and kids, he's satisfied with me as I am.

Tom, Tom, Tom. I was so caught up in worrying about his feelings, I hadn't thought about myself.

What did I want? I would have traded anything to wind back the clock and change the course of my whole life. If only I'd called out to Jenni the second she disappeared from view that day or cycled harder to keep up with her. If only I'd remembered my mother's advice and paid better attention, I might have noticed something useful. Maybe Mum would never have left and my views on marriage and children would be different. Maybe one tiny change could have saved Jenni – and the rest of us – from what followed.

To stop the tears that were threatening, I closed my eyes and drifted off to the noise of the rails.

~ ~ ~

I'm on a busy train, swaying gently from side to side. The train picks up speed and starts to shake, the 'clack, clack, clack' too loud and too fast. When I open my eyes I'm alone in the carriage.

Through the glass door towards the front all I can see are parallel tracks stretching into the distance. Turning to the back, it's the same view. This single carriage is hurtling along at high speed, even without an engine. I press my face to the glass and in the distance I see a shape on the track, growing closer.

We're travelling so fast I don't have time to process that it's Jenni's bike before we're on top of it, crushing it until it becomes stuck under an iron wheel. The screech of metal on metal is like the fingernails of the devil scraping down a blackboard.

27

No Tom waiting for me at Paddington this time, helping me with my luggage and talking about all the things we might do – none of which we had.

By the time I got back to South Kensington station it was almost 5pm and I was hungry. I hadn't phoned Tom to let him know I was coming, and he wasn't necessarily expecting me because our plan had been to stay another night and return after lunch on Friday.

On impulse, I walked up to the telephone box outside the station and pulled my notebook from my bag.

"Hello, Stephanie? It's Joy. I need a bed."

Less than an hour later Stephanie opened her front door, brandishing an open bottle of red. "Come in, come in, I've ordered pizza."

One of her housemates was away so I took her bed, squeezing in between an easel and paints, a trestle table, and a stack of canvasses that made me feel right at home. We sat on the living room floor, on an old navy carpet that needed a good clean, drinking wine, and dissecting every word of my conversation with Tom. Stephanie refused to accept I had anything to be sorry for.

"You haven't said it's over. You've said you don't need a wedding ring to stay together, which is not the same thing at all."

"For him, the two things seem to be the same. I don't understand why he proposed in the first place when I've never dropped any hints, not like his last girlfriend. It's only ever been him who's brought it up."

"So he's an old romantic from an old-fashioned family. Lots of girls would kill for a big shiny engagement ring but you shouldn't feel bad for not being one of them. He fell in love with you, so he shouldn't want to change the person you are or try and change your mind about marriage."

She was right but it left the issue of children. If he was so sure he wanted them and I was so sure I didn't, where did that leave us?

I remembered what he'd asked me the day I finally told him about Jenni, when he was hurt at my comment that I hadn't known we'd stay together: "When was it you first cared enough about me to think our relationship would be long term?"

At the time I thought what a great prosecutor he'd make, pacing the courtroom in front of a jury. I hadn't replied then and I wasn't sure, almost a year on, that I knew how to reply now. Growing up, planning for the future had never been important. All my family cared about was whether today was the day we found Jenni.

I took another large sip of Rioja.

"I didn't come right out and say it's over but I made it clear we want different things. It's probably good this has happened now, before ... well, before we drift on for a few more years and he's even more disappointed at how much time he wasted with me."

Stephanie frowned.

"And what about you?"

"What about me?"

"What do you want?"

I laughed sharply. "Tom asked the exact same question. I don't know. What I want is for someone else to make the decision. It seems crazy to break up with someone who loves me so much he wants to marry me, for God's sake."

"But does he love you enough not to marry you, that's the question. Getting married is only about a ring and a fancy party. If he can't see that your feelings are just as important as his, maybe he doesn't love you as much as he should. Or let's think about this another way: if you wanted to be with him enough, you'd get over this wedding phobia of yours and get back to the business of being together."

I sighed. "You're right, you're completely right. I think he should love me enough to do what I want, and he thinks exactly the same about me. It's checkmate."

Stephanie clambered over on all fours to give me a hug. "It'll be OK, one way or another. In the meantime, you can stay here as long as you need."

I lay awake in bed for a long time, my mind racing and my heart thumping from too much red wine. Plus, the traffic noise, the swoosh of double decker buses only metres from the window, kept jolting me back to my surroundings.

When I woke up the hum outside hadn't changed; only the sound of dustbins being emptied told me it was morning. Stephanie's offer was kind but I would never be able to sleep here. I thought about my soft bed in South Kensington and knew I didn't want to stay there, either.

I told her over toast and marmalade. It was only fair to

face Tom, and at least we had a spare bedroom.

I stayed until late afternoon, not wanting Tom to know I'd spent the night with a friend. This way it would seem I'd arrived straight from the train. Ironically, Tom's lack of trust was causing me to lie more.

All was silent when I opened the front door – Tom must have gone to work, I assumed – so it was a surprise to see him on the sofa with one of his huge law books open in his lap. He looked at me, expressionless, and I took a seat in the wingback chair normally reserved for Edward.

"Your Mum called last night to check you got back safely and to say she's happy to pay for your copies of the photos from the wedding. I had to lie and tell her you'd gone to bed early. Where were you?"

His voice was cold, deadpan. Again, the accusation, as if I'd deceived him, when all I'd done – all we'd both done – was taken time to think.

"At Stephanie's place. She had a spare bed and you said you wanted time to think." I remembered Steph's question, 'what about you?'. "And I needed some time alone, too."

"Alone? You were with Stephanie. I hope the two of you had a good laugh."

So he was angry. Somehow that seemed easier to deal with than disappointment.

"I needed someone to talk to, another perspective. No-one's laughing at you for proposing. I wish it was what I wanted but I can't change the fact that it's not. I wish things could stay the way they were."

Another lie. I'd ignored all the times Tom's casual comments had left me unsettled and had chosen not to see this coming.

We sat without speaking for a while. If Tom was expecting me to say something else, I had no idea what that might be. A loud growl from my empty stomach took me to the kitchen and I put two servings of lasagne in the microwave to defrost.

His eyes were fixed on me. "Are you going to move out?"

"Do you want me to move out?"

"Stop it, for God's sake just stop it. You keep answering a question with a question and all I want to know is how you feel about me. I can't believe I'm asking this but are we done, or do you want to try and make this work?"

He had a point. He knew my feelings about marriage and kids, weddings, London, and becoming an artist, but not how I felt about him.

If he needed to hear it, then I had to be honest. "I think we're done. I don't want the things you want and it's crazy to think we've gone this long without either of us realising that. Or maybe I knew and didn't want to admit it because I loved you."

"You don't love me anymore." A statement, not a question.

Tell him the truth or protect his feelings?

"What I've realised is I don't love you enough to sacrifice what I want."

He stood up and walked straight out of the door without a word. From the window I watched him turn right and march in long strides towards Fulham Road.

The microwave pinged. My appetite gone, I turned on the Six O'Clock News to hear the newsreader talk in optimistic tones about Britain's budding economic recovery. I speculated on what that might mean for my employment prospects.

Tom didn't come home that night and he didn't call. I suspected he was punishing me for my night at Steph's so I tried not to care and drank the best bottle of red in the wine cupboard – one of Edward's specials, a Châteauneuf-du-Pape the same age as me – then ate both portions of lasagne and fell into a stupor on the couch.

The harsh ring of the telephone shocked me awake. The room was too bright for the amount of wine I'd consumed and the mantelpiece clock only came into focus when I squinted: 9.47am.

"Hello?" My voice was raspy.

"Joy. It's Valerie."

Of course, Tom ran home to Valerie and Edward. I braced myself for questions.

"Is Tom there?"

Why was she asking me that? My head hurt and through it passed a flash of worry about where he was.

"He hasn't turned up for work so Edward asked me to call in case you'd slept in."

I couldn't lie, even though I knew she'd worry. "I'm not sure where he is. We had an argument last night and he left around seven and didn't come back. I thought you were calling to tell me he was there."

I heard her fingers strumming anxiously on the cabinet in their hallway and pictured the immaculate nail varnish and gold jewellery. The memory of seeing her wearing the ring Tom had tried to give me sent a shudder of nausea through my body.

"Where might he have gone? Who does he know in London?" Her voice was elevated with concern.

Who did he know? My mind was a complete blank. He

occasionally mentioned other students when he worked on group assignments, none of whom came to mind.

"Um, he could be with Max?"

"Why would he not come home?" She hesitated, knowing the answer even before she asked, "Did something happen?"

"Yes, something happened. It's a bit complicated and I should be talking to Tom about it."

Hinting that she was aware, Valerie simply said, "You know he loves you, he wants you to have a good life together," as if that was enough.

Out of the corner of my eye I caught a movement and shrieked with alarm before I realised it was Tom.

"He's here Valerie, it's OK, he was in the other bedroom. I have to go." Without waiting for a response, I hung up.

Tom looked and sounded as bad as I did, nothing like his usual early-morning self. He said he'd gone to a pub on Fulham Road, intending to come back at closing time. Instead, he kept walking, climbed over a locked gate into a private park and sat under a tree until the sky began to lighten. He hadn't noticed me asleep on the couch so slept in the spare bedroom to avoid disturbing me.

"Can we talk?"

I gestured at Edward's chair and he sat down carefully.

"I've been thinking about this all night, trying to work out what's going through your mind, and none of it makes sense." He sounded calm but deflated. "I thought we were happy and I don't know how I read things so wrong. Last night, you said 'we're done'. What if I hadn't proposed? Would we be having this conversation right now?"

I pondered his question.

"Maybe not right now, but it seems inevitable we'd

reach this point eventually. I meant what I said last night. I didn't want to admit things weren't right and haven't been for a while. Everything was so much easier when we were studying. All we had to worry about was meeting assignment deadlines and paying the rent." Not that Tom had ever worried about that.

"We were focused on the same things. After we graduated, that changed and I realised how little I think about the future and how clearly mapped out your life is. You say you want to support me but I'm not sure you understand how hard it's been. How do you think I feel, knowing I'm not good enough for anyone to employ in a decent job and the only reason I can live here is because your parents are paying for it?"

Tom had no answer because he'd never thought about it.

"Every decision I make, it's not only the financial impact I'm thinking of. I'm questioning whether it will get in the way of you becoming the lawyer you want to be.

"Even all this," I waved around the living room. "I shop and cook and clean and make sure you don't have to worry about breakfast, lunch, or dinner. I want to be equal in a relationship. A partner, not a housekeeper. You accept it because it's what you're used to and you like it that way.

"What would happen if I found a full-time job with normal hours and wanted to keep painting? Would you still expect me to take care of everything?"

I stood up, needing coffee to wash the stale wine taste from my mouth. Tom stood up too and reached for my hands.

"We can fix this. I'll stop talking about marriage – forget I even proposed. In a few weeks I'll have finished studying so I can do more around here and we can take a proper break.

Why don't we go to Nice? Mum and Dad have said we can use the house any time we like and all it will cost us are the flights."

"You're not listening to me!" I was practically shouting, even though he was right there.

"This isn't about 'now' or getting through the next couple of months. You shouldn't have to give up what you want any more than I should. And if I want to live in a tiny cottage in the middle of nowhere and do nothing except paint, even if it never makes me any money, then I should be able to, without the fear of ruining someone else's life because in reality what you want is children and grandchildren."

The phrase 'irreconcilable differences' popped into my mind.

I was imploring: "The more I think about it, the less I can imagine either of us being happy if we stay together. Can you?"

Tom dropped into the chair, comprehension beginning to set in to his face. Sadness filled my whole body. I'd never set out to hurt him, yet here we both were.

"All Sandrine ever wanted was a ring," he sighed.

It took me a second to remember who Sandrine was. Where was this going?

"She was determined to be married and in the end it didn't matter who to, as long as she became Mrs Somebody and had a man to take care of her.

"She said she cheated on me to be sure she loved me, to be absolutely certain I was 'the one'. She made it sound as if I should be flattered that she chose me over the other guys she slept with while we were dating."

My stomach did an anxious flip at the word 'cheat'.

He gave a half laugh. "She would kill to be where you

are, right now."

I went into the kitchen and made the coffee I so badly needed, pouring one for Tom out of habit. The toast popped up and I buttered his slices thickly, the way he liked it.

It seemed we had reached an agreement: we were over. No tears, no screaming, no unforgiveable accusations neither of us could take back. It all felt very mature and very sad.

Tom didn't expect me to move out straightaway. He said, somewhat pointedly, that I was rarely at home during the week anyway so the spare room was mine until I sorted myself out. I was grateful. It would help to stay until the following weekend, however awkward it might be, so I didn't have to take any more time off work.

~ ~ ~

I arrived early for my shift, keen to be out of the flat and on friendlier ground. On my walk through Green Park I practised telling the manager I either needed more hours – bar work, selling tickets and popcorn, anything at all – or I had no choice but to find a job with more hours somewhere else.

In his office, he listened without interrupting while I explained my situation. For an instant I thought I was going to be fired.

He remained silent after I finished, putting me through a torturous sixty seconds while he examined a chart of staff, scribbled on a pad, and then spoke.

"If you come in a bit earlier to clean – and you're quick anyway – I can give you full shifts on tickets or refreshments. You won't get tips but the hourly rate is more than bar work. I charge a deposit for the uniform, so take care of it."

He turned the pad towards me and all I noticed was the circled figure of £151.25, £25 more than the two weeks I'd spent working in the bar, and close to double my current salary.

I smiled at him gratefully.

"Thank you so much. I'll come in early to learn how everything works and you won't even have to pay me for that."

"I know," he replied, and I swear he almost smiled.

28

By Sunday everything was packed. I had accumulated remarkably little in eight months apart from canvasses and a box of painting paraphernalia, which I'd already dropped off at work, ready to take to Stephanie's.

I would be moving into a bedroom at the rear of the building where it was quieter. Two of the women had been dating for a few months and were using my arrival to officially move into one room, which brought the cost down for everyone.

Even after paying rent, I would be better off financially than in South Kensington.

Tom and I only saw each other in passing during that final week. I was grateful for my irregular hours and stayed at the cinema all day now I no longer needed to take care of housework between films.

As we passed in the kitchen early on Thursday morning, I said I'd be moving out on Sunday, to give him time to arrange to be elsewhere if he wanted. On the contrary: he said he would be there and when Sunday morning came he made a show of tidying the flat. An odd time to start sharing the load, I thought, until the doorbell chimed and he pressed the security buzzer.

"Mum and Dad wanted to see you," he said, at least having the grace to look shamefaced at the ambush.

I was pissed off. Talking to Valerie on the phone was one thing but having her and Edward – two people I was fond of – present while I deserted their son was not going to make this any easier.

Valerie floated in on a cloud of expensive vanilla, with Edward close behind.

"Dear Joy," she clasped my head to her chest like a child. "What a sad day this is, for all of us. Edward and I are devastated at the news," she said, as if someone had died.

She released me and we sat down, while the men stood to attention over us.

"I'm sure you have your reasons, and we all know it's been such a difficult year," she dabbed away a sincere tear. "Even so, we all wish you'd take more time to consider what you're doing."

I imagined what my mother's response would be once I told her. She'd cry too at losing her ticket to the life she'd always wanted and the prospect of sipping French wine while watching the sun set over the Riviera.

To my surprise I was sad but not devastated at the end of my first relationship, my first love. My only tears had been the previous week when I told Dad I thought it was over. Once Tom accepted what I was saying, the heaviness that had become so familiar in recent months had lifted.

The finality of moving out, though, and the realisation Tom and I weren't the only ones affected by my decision, hit home. It wasn't an ambush; they were here to wish me well. Edward put his hand on Valerie's shoulder while she cried, and handed me his monogrammed handkerchief as my nose began to run.

"I'm sorry, I really am," I sniffled. "I wish things were different. Tom is going to make someone a great husband one day. Just not me."

"We'll really miss you, we all will. If ever you need anything…" and Valerie dissolved into her tissue.

Leaning over to give her a kiss, I thought I might miss them more than I would miss Tom.

"I'll invite you both to the opening of my first exhibition," I promised, which at least made her smile.

I declined Edward's offer to drive me to Steph's, unwilling to prolong my departure, and instead thanked him and Valerie for everything – and meant it.

Tom helped me downstairs with my case and at the bottom of the front steps we hesitated awkwardly before a simple hug. I tried not to inhale the aftershave I loved, then handed him my key and hoisted the rucksack onto my shoulders.

There was something cathartic about dragging my belongings through the streets and underground stations of London, trying to avoid tangling up in pram wheels or taking out small children with my rucksack.

At Finsbury Park, 13 stops and a million miles from South Kensington, I jumped on the bus that would drop me off opposite Stephanie's flat.

Loud footsteps thudded down the stairs almost before I'd finished ringing the bell and the door burst open.

"You're here!" Steph's emphatic hug nearly knocked me over. Several smiling faces were peering over the bannister.

"Hello!", "Hi!", "Welcome!". I'd only met two of them

the week before, and only briefly even then, so we sat down to proper introductions. All of them were artists of one sort or another: Fatima was a portrait artist; Deb painted abstracts in bold and dark oils that varied between ominous and refined; the couple, Vi and Dawn, both had degrees in textile design.

By day, though, they worked in an office, hospitality, retail, and teaching respectively.

Although Steph was also a painter, our styles were poles apart. She favoured the colourful abstracts of Kandinsky and Kupka and worked with acrylics on canvasses almost the same height as her that were impossible for one person to lift. They were hard to sell as the photos in her portfolio in no way conveyed their full impact. I admired her for staying true to what she wanted to paint but was quietly grateful my street signs were so easy to carry.

The household was like a creative community where the residents' work hung proudly on the walls and all the reading material was about different forms of art and artists. Once a week everyone pitched in to collectively scour the saved-up newspapers and circle any jobs that might be of interest to one of the group.

This approach was so caring and so different from what I was used to. It struck me that Tom had never helped me look for work: not once had he offered to check the papers, read over an application, or even buy a postage stamp. I felt cheated at the amount of support he enjoyed from me while he gave very little in return.

In Finsbury Park, everything was shared; shopping, cleaning, and even cooking evening meals were all done on a roster. The others embraced my odd working hours, sending me off each day with leftovers from the night before for a nutritious dinner while the early evening film was showing. We ate incredibly well, thanks mostly to Fatima's love of chilli and fresh spices and her knowledge of the best markets.

My ever-dependable lasagne was an instant hit.

I didn't think about Tom as often as I expected to, even in the first few weeks. If he did come to mind it was more often because something triggered it – like receiving a job rejection letter forwarded from South Kensington – than because I was mulling over what happened. Occasionally, I allowed myself to wonder if things would be different if our trip had not been cut short last year. We might have talked about Jenni more and maybe he would have apologised for his initial reaction. Maybe I would have come to understand why he felt so deceived. All that was irrelevant, though, when I reminded myself he still expected we would marry and give his parents the grandchildren they wanted so badly. It was hard to see our break-up as anything but inevitable.

Barely a month after leaving South Kensington, life felt surprisingly normal. Perhaps it was the increasingly summery June weather making me smile every day or perhaps it was my new-found independence. Only having myself to worry about was liberating and Steph was right, sharing a flat with these woman was like being at university. The added benefit was that they all understood the struggles of trying to become a professional artist and all had advice on how to avoid falling into a pit of despair.

When I moved in, they were making plans for their own art exhibition and sale, the one Steph had mentioned over dinner in Chinatown. They were enthusiastic about including my work in the list of items on offer.

The plan was to hire a nearby community hall and turn

it into a gallery space for the day. Vi worked in the gift shop at the Victoria and Albert Museum, hoping it would be a foot in the door for her as a graduate of textile design. After three years she hadn't yet broken into a more fitting role but was able to borrow all the display tables and stands we needed. From what I saw in the print samples and screen-printed t-shirts draped around the flat, her talent was amazing and I couldn't understand why no-one had taken her on.

Over a lunch of homemade dips and toasted pita bread one Sunday at the start of June, we held a brainstorming session about how to tackle the event.

Stephanie turned to me. "You remember the module we did in our last year on how to promote yourself as an artist?"

"Professional Practice?"

"That's the one. Can you remember anything from it that might be useful?"

"Let me think: Don't hold an exhibition in a remote part of the country and expect lots of people to turn up. Invite everyone you can think of to make up numbers, including your dentist and the woman with blue hair from the shop you buy candles in. And always, always check for spelling mistakes to ensure your artist's profile doesn't say you have 'a degree in Fine Ars'."

We cackled at the memory of our brilliant but unfortunate classmate. "Poor Andy. Even if his work ends up in the Tate, he will never live that down!"

Vi was the most knowledgeable and wrote a plan for creating leaflets, free listings in tourism and events brochures, plus a tiny paid advert in the local newspaper. Fatima said she would paint a portrait of each of us for individual flyers with our biography and contact details.

Steph, Vi, and Deb had previously sat as models for her portfolio so she was confident she had time to paint me and Dawn by early August.

We agreed to each chip in £60 for promotional materials. If anyone made no sales at all, or not enough to cover those costs, the others would ensure everyone broke even, at least.

Given our location, we would be catering to the local audience more than to tourists so, with enthusiastic support from my housemates, I expanded my street signs to include nearby landmarks. I set aside two days and travelled all over north London, camera and well-worn *A to Z* in hand. On the first day I took photos of Holloway and Seven Sisters roads before heading to Highbury, across to Stoke Newington Park, and back in a loop via Upper Street.

The second day, I walked up to Archway, enjoying panoramic views of the city until the traffic fumes drove me down a side street. This part of London was unknown to me, so I wandered until a long brick wall blocked my path: Highgate Cemetery. Not a great idea for a street sign. Still, I was drawn by the greenness beyond the wall and walked until I found a gate. Immediately the air was cooler. It was peaceful. The trees, in full leaf, were alive with birds having conversations with each other, turning the traffic into nothing more than a background hum.

Apart from my grandfather's funeral, this was the first time I'd been to a cemetery since I was a child. I'd been brave enough to run through the scary churchyard on the way to and from school when I had my sister by my side. Later, when it was me and Ally, or me on my own, I chose the longer route to avoid the way my heart leapt at every sound.

I had thought about death more than most people of

my age. From talking to Dad, I knew I wasn't the only one to experience guilt when I thought how relieved I'd be to know Jenni was definitely dead. In a wooden box under the damp, heavy earth she would be safe, forever. We would know where she was when we spoke to her. We would stop searching for her face in every crowd and stop needing answers to our questions. On her birthday we would leave pink and white chrysanthemums in a glass jar on her grave.

Aunt Vera always insisted she'd be buried "over my dead body!" to make us laugh. Her ashes were packed away in a neat white box at the back of a cupboard in Red's house while she waited for the right time to scatter them.

In the oldest part of the Eastern Cemetery, the path was so untrodden moss ran down the middle. Trees curved their branches protectively overhead and gravestones leant gently against one another, as if giving comfort. Many of the names and inscriptions were obscured by ivy or worn away by the weather.

I liked the idea of having a place to go to mark Jenni's existence. Not a graveyard, though, not until we knew.

The thought that some people had no-one to visit them, to untangle the weeds, and scrub away the lichen, made me melancholy. If I stayed any longer I knew I would find it hard to shake my mood so I took a few quick photos and set off for home with enough to get me started.

Raucous laughter as I climbed the stairs to the flat made me glad the others were there.

Fatima leapt up when I walked in.

"It's time!" she threatened, with a smile. My portrait was the last she had to tackle. I was dreading being photographed almost as much as I was dreading being immortalised in paint, even if her work was amazing.

Her portfolio showed her ability to capture people even more realistically than a camera could, as if she saw through their features at what was inside, and that was what ended up on the canvas.

Each piece was named after what she observed when she studied her subject. 'STEPHANIE : MELLOW' and 'DEB : DARKNESS' both fitted perfectly.

Seeing my discomfort, Fatima assured me she only needed a couple of shots, as long as I posed in person for the final details.

~ ~ ~

With the exhibition fast approaching, the flat was abuzz with caffeine-fuelled artists before 6am most mornings. At work, I began taking short naps during the early evening film.

The smell of paints, inks, and cleaning fluids filled the air. Only half-joking, we said we'd have to stick a NO NAKED FLAMES sign on the front door. If I closed my eyes, I was transported back to Miss Robbins' art room, which was tidied at the end of each day but never lost that smell of dried and drying paints and fixative sprays, mingled with raw clay.

I declined Fatima's offer to see myself in progress so, when the unveiling came, I had no idea what to expect. Nervously I picked paint from under my nails.

"You were a tough one," she said. "Normally, a word leaps out early on and I think 'Yes, that's it!', and it shapes the tones and the background. You were mysterious, guarded even, and I waited and waited for the right description to come to me."

She moved towards her easel. "And your name is perfect because I ended up with the most amazing contrast."

With a small flourish she flipped the easel and I was standing opposite what was obviously me, above the title:

JOY : LOSS

Sorrow dripped from the canvas. My hand went to my mouth as my eyes filled with tears. She had captured an elegance I had never seen in myself, and eyes that were sad and searching. The jade and lime greens of the background contrasted beautifully with my hair and gave the painting an ethereal effect, as if I was at the edge of a forest, about to run away.

"It's … me," was all I managed.

"So you like it?" she asked nervously. "People don't necessarily like what I see if they have never seen it in themselves, but I guess you know if you've had a loss your face can't hide. This painting is one of the best I've ever done. I burst into tears and that's when I knew it was ready."

I nodded, unable to speak, and Fatima stroked my back while I blew my nose.

"Punters will take one look at your face and buy something out of pity," Deb announced when Fatima presented the portrait to everyone else. I loved her bluntness and hoped she was right. All of us were hoping for a lot out of this exhibition, from recouping our money to making useful contacts.

Dawn and Vi declared it "brilliant", while Steph kept switching from me to the painting and back, smiling and nodding. "You look incredible. Amazing," she said and I fumbled for words.

We sent written invitations to dozens of gallery owners.

We dropped leaflets into every café and small business within two miles of the venue, and into the letterboxes of all the nicer houses in the area. We phoned everyone we knew and asked them to phone everyone they knew.

Our landlord, the fish and chip shop owner, proudly told his customers he had artists living upstairs. He handed out flyers as well as sticking leaflets up on his wall. I wasn't optimistic about art dealers stopping by for battered cod, but it couldn't hurt.

At work, Walter's enthusiasm was endearing and he handed customers a flyer with every drink, until I reminded him to focus on locals only: our budget was spent and the tourists wouldn't be around for long enough. I was in the middle of a painting, a memento for him to take home to Germany. Despite being named after a monarch from the 1930s, the cinema itself was an ugly early 60s building that had never come back into fashion, so instead I painted the street outside – a typical London yellow-brick terrace of shops with flats above, with a glimpse of the cinema off to one side.

In the flat, we were high on anticipation as we rushed to get everything ready in time. The only blemish on our positivity was the day Stephanie received a letter from the Royal College of Art, rejecting her application – the last of all the places she was waiting to hear about. "I didn't even get an interview," she said. "I was sure I would, and I'm impossible to resist once people have met me!"

We sympathised and said they didn't know what they were missing, they'd be sorry when our exhibition propelled her to fame and fortune.

"There's always next year," she sighed.

29

We were up with the sun on exhibition day, running on adrenaline and ready to start our creative convoy through the streets to the community centre. I don't know what we would have done if it had been raining.

Stephanie had mounted her two favourite canvasses, enormous pieces that each needed a person at either end to lift them. A few early morning joggers and shopkeepers setting up on the pavement gawked at the spectacle as we passed.

By 8am when we opened the doors – flanked by Steph's oversized paintings to create a dramatic entry – everything was in place. The lighting wasn't perfect but we'd filled the space well and created a u-shaped path so visitors could inspect things left and right and not be intimidated by our eyes boring into them while they perused our work.

To bring in passers-by, we had a colourful homemade board – a giant arrow on a stick directing people to "Local artists' exhibition and sales, one day only" – and took turns standing on the corner of busy Blackstock Road only metres away. That was my least favourite part of the day as everyone stared, which was exactly the point.

All of us were familiar with how professional galleries did things and, despite our nerves, we knew we had to talk to anyone who paused longer than normal. They might be hoping for a nice picture to hang in their living room, or they might represent a gallery or auction house or be a private dealer hoping to make a discovery. We'd briefed each other on our work so anyone could jump in and make a sale if the artist was busy with another customer or outside waving the arrow.

By ten past eight we were anxious and strumming our fingers. Every 30 seconds one of us peered out the door in case anyone seemed lost. When the first people, a young couple with a Jack Russell, walked in at 8.25am it took all our willpower not to squeal with relief. If not for Dawn's idea of playing soft classical music in the background, they would have heard our hearts beating. Although they didn't buy anything, they murmured nice things as they browsed and smiled at us as we grinned back.

I wouldn't say the floodgates opened but for the next few hours a steady trickle of people came through. Some popped in out of curiosity from the park across the road with small children in tow and three of them bought Dawn's cute floral-print t-shirts. Others had a flyer in their hands and were more seriously interested.

Several of my local street signs had gone, along with two small pieces I had painted from sketches in Florence.

Not that it was a competition, but by lunchtime, Fatima was winning. She had sold two pictures and taken a deposit from a man who wanted her to paint his wife's portrait as a birthday present. He'd given her a hundred pounds up front, with another hundred due on completion.

This area was home to greengrocers, off-licences, halal kebab shops, and Afro-Caribbean hairdressers, surrounded by Council-run high-rises, not affluent homeowners looking for original artworks. I thought suddenly of Tom and how he would have turned his nose up at me exhibiting in a community centre. Unlike him, I felt more at home here than in the sanitised streets of South Kensington, where I always expected someone to walk up and ask me what I was doing there.

Vi came to relieve me of the arrow and I went inside to see Steph jiggling triumphantly.

"I sold a big one!" she whispered. "This bloke came in, he's an accountant with an office down the road, and he wanted something eye-catching for the wall everyone sees when they walk in. He said it's tax deductible so he didn't even haggle. Two hundred and seventy-five pounds, just like that!" and she clicked her fingers. "He was cute, too. Said he wants me to put my phone number on the back so he can prove it's mine when it's worth half a million."

Our excitement levels rose with every sale. By mid-afternoon a dozen pieces displayed red Sold! signs on them and Vi and Dawn were running low on t-shirts. People were kind and encouraging, wishing us luck even if they didn't buy anything. Stephanie only had to chase out one group of loud teenage boys who threatened to slash the painting she had sold.

Every piece I had painted since arriving in London was on display. The ones I was most proud of were where I had balanced greenery, architecture and water in recognisable scenes around the city. My paintings of St James's Park Lake and Hyde Park's Italian Water Gardens I sold to the same person, a white-haired Londoner who had lived his whole life on the north side of the river and said he loved the lightness of my style. I gave him a discount, partly out of gratitude and partly because he said he was going home to fetch his neighbour, who he thought might like my work too.

Dawn and Vi had a long discussion with a woman interested in items to sell at her stall at Camden market. She suggested they turn some of their designs into scarves and shawls, even placemats and coasters, which she would sell for a small commission.

Deb – to everyone's surprise, including her own – sold most of her abstract pieces.

"Just proves there's no accounting for taste," Deb said, blasé but clearly satisfied as she folded banknotes into her pocket. The technical skill of her work was evident but to me the paintings resembled science fiction posters or were just plain ominous. The local audience liked them, though, which was all that mattered.

Steph bargained successfully with a couple of people, also local business owners, to sell two other canvasses. One buyer said she displayed local artists' work in her café and had space for other – smaller – pieces if Stephanie wanted to get in touch.

By the time we closed the doors I had sold 17 street signs and taken orders for several one-offs. Three of my Italy landscapes had sold, along with five London cityscapes.

The second we got everything back to the flat we emptied our pockets into the middle of the floor: £2443.35. No-one knew where the 35p was from, but we didn't care, we were delirious. Each of us came away with a profit, far beyond our expectations. Best of all, we'd made useful connections that might lead to future work.

Exhausted but buoyant, we walked down the road to The Castle, intent on celebrating.

The pub landlord, Mark, asked how the day had gone as he poured our pints. He pointed to an empty part of the wall with a rectangle that was less yellowed than the surrounding wallpaper.

"Remember the photo of the pub when it first opened? Some scumbag stole it right off the wall last week. How much would you charge for a painting to replace it?"

I took a quick guess at the size. "If I frame it, I can do it for £225. If you frame it, £190."

He rubbed his chin and considered the six of us. "£150, unframed, and you get a free Sunday roast and a pint."

"Each?"

He chuckled. "Of course each!"

"Done!" and I shook his hand solemnly. The girls cheered.

All day Sunday we lay about on the living room floor and the sofas, tired but basking in our success.

"We've all worked bloody hard and we deserve a proper celebration," Vi said. "What about bowling? Or a posh restaurant, or a picnic?"

"My vote is a picnic in the park next Sunday," Stephanie announced, "with fancy bread from Waitrose and their how-much-can-you-squeeze-into-one-tub salads. And beer."

"Mmmm, Waitrose salads."

"A picnic it is, then."

I was hesitant: Sunday was Jenni's anniversary. Everyone else thought it sounded perfect so I muttered my agreement, knowing I had a few days to decide.

For much of that week I was lost in thought. Not wanting to bring the others down off their high, I kept myself away, sitting in the park for hours in the long, light evenings and window shopping during the day when I wasn't at work.

My emotions seesawed. I was happier living with Steph than I had been at any time since I arrived in London but I still didn't like the city and had not found my feet in the way I'd hoped. In positive moments, I told myself my work was good enough to sell – the exhibition proved that. At other times I questioned whether anything would come of it, or whether I was destined to be a cleaner for life, only selling my art in bars and community centres.

On my mind, too, were thoughts of Aunt Vera. In the run up to the exhibition I had given little thought to the fact it was 12 months since she'd died. In the days after, I gave in to my desire to wallow and I wished I had gone home to be with Red. Except she had Daniel now and probably didn't need me.

And now Jenni's anniversary was here. The feeling of this year being a turning point was inescapable. Jenni had been gone for half my life. I had only five, maybe six years' worth of memories of being her little sister.

By the end of the week, when I'd been late for work twice and given people the wrong change in the bar almost every night, it dawned on me that my sadness was more than grief: it was homesickness for Cornwall, the place I had been desperate to get away from for so long. Despite the voice of logic telling me Jenni was gone for good, a little piece of me believed she was still there, and – whatever it meant – I wanted to be near her.

30

Heavy rain overnight left the ground damp and my hair frizzy. We spread out plastic bags and blankets and flopped down in the shade of a huge elm tree, watching cyclists whizz along the footpaths ignoring the No Cycling signs.

"Who's hungry?" Fatima had taken charge of the food and spent Sunday morning shooing us out of the kitchen while she filled the flat with smells that left us salivating.

Dish after dish emerged from layers of foil. Beef kofta with mint yoghurt, herby lamb meatballs, hummus to go with the crispy falafel, and a large tub of tabouleh. "That one's from Waitrose," Fatima admitted. "You were all so excited about their salads, I couldn't bear to disappoint you. There's potato salad, too."

Dawn cracked open a six-pack as we filled our plates and before long the only sounds were chewing and exclamations over the food.

Steph noticed my mood and shuffled over. "You're quiet today, hon."

"Yeah. Bit of a sad anniversary today. You know. Jenni."

"Oh. Ah." She nodded knowingly and patted my leg. "I'm glad you're here with us, then."

We took quiet sips of our beers.

After a few moments, I said: "I think I need to go home."

"Whatever you need. You can go home, or you can sit here and be sad and get totally pissed if you want. We'll carry you up the stairs if you're too drunk to walk, I promise."

"No, I mean home home. Cornwall." Saying the words out loud, it felt like the right decision even if I hadn't known for sure until just then.

Stephanie's wail made the others whip around. "She's leaving us! You can't go!" and she wrestled me to the grass until I tickled her.

"Not right now! I mean in a few weeks, when summer's over and I've saved a bit more. I just don't think this is where I'm supposed to be."

She looked forlorn. "I get it, I do. I grew up in a city but still feel like I've been chewed up and spat out sometimes. It's not easy, this whole 'being an artist' thing."

The others said they'd miss me and the conversation turned to people's home towns and homelands and the possibility of organising an artists' retreat in the country, with proper cream teas and walks on the beach.

That night I phoned Red. Her immediate response was "You can move in with us". I loved her for that, but said I had no intention of cramping her style as a newlywed and I'd ask Dad if it was OK for me to move home until I found a job.

"Well, you'll have to come over for a meal every week, then. Don't worry, Daniel's a better cook than me, much better than his best man's speech suggested."

"In that case, you're on!"

Dad sounded delighted and said I was welcome for as

long as I wanted. It made sense even though I dreaded being back in my childhood bedroom – more than ever now I had the new memory of the disastrous proposal. My intention was to rent somewhere cheap as soon as possible, assuming I found paid work.

The decision inspired me to tackle the half-done paintings stacked in my room, as I knew I would never finish them otherwise and they might make money. Steph asked if there was anywhere I wanted to go back to, somewhere to remember London by. No, nowhere, I told her, wanting to revisit Highgate Cemetery on my own. It seemed ironic that the place I felt most at peace in the city was full of dead people.

The cinema manager seemed genuinely sorry to lose me and wished me luck with an extra £40 in my final pay. Straight-faced, but with a glint in his eye, he said he didn't want to see me again unless he was at my gallery opening.

Walter used my impending departure to tell bar patrons my paintings were limited editions by an artist who was now exhibiting elsewhere. Not exactly true, but the tourists lapped it up. On his last day at work before he and Clara went home I presented him with my gift and he broke into what I hoped was enthusiastic German before remembering himself and thanking me, over and over, as he kissed me on both cheeks.

I took my mounted painting to The Castle, pleased with the way the sepia wash had given it an aged appearance, more like the stolen picture than the present day.

Mark whistled. "This is great. Better than a photo!"

He promised this picture would be firmly attached.

Tying up loose ends was satisfying and made my final weeks fly by. When I reflected on the past few months, I was proud of myself for remaining in London after Tom and I broke up. I hadn't given up and run away, I'd tried living a more normal life away from the manicured gardens and French restaurants of Kensington and was still sure it wasn't the place for me. A few doubts broke through when I thought about how hard it might be, finding work in Cornwall out of tourist season, but if I could work as a cleaner, I could work anywhere.

"Will you see Tom before you go?" Steph asked.

I waved an envelope at her. "I can't see any point. Remind me to post this the day I leave so he has my forwarding address. I don't want him to know in advance. What would I say? 'Sorry for choosing the life of a pauper over being the wife of a famous lawyer?'," I giggled. "Maybe I should send him the portrait Fatima painted so he can throw darts at it."

The girls held a dinner on my last night. They had a gift: Fatima had painted us all lounging on a bench in the park where we took our beers on warm evenings. The way she had added me made it seem as if I had been sitting there with them.

"This is amazing," I cried. "I am going to miss you all so much!"

"You're amazing," Steph said. "We want you to remember, every time you see this, that we all believe in you. You're going to make it as an artist. You already are an artist, so you should call yourself that and feel proud. And," she was welling up now, too, "if you ever decide Cornwall is too clean and green and crime-free for you, we will welcome you back to this dirty old city with open arms."

We ate and drank until late. I promised I would visit,

and they promised they would escape to the country for an artists' retreat sometime soon.

Walter had put me in touch with three friends who were driving from London to the ferry in Plymouth and had room in their van for me and all my luggage. Sharing the cost of petrol was cheaper and easier than travelling by train and they were happy to take a detour into Cornwall on their way to picking grapes in France.

In broken English, and despite me knowing no German at all, they decided to teach me the German lyrics to *99 Red Balloons*. When that proved too much of a challenge, they taught me as many swear words as they could think of, growing more and more raucous as they gave me ruder and ruder phrases to pronounce. I told them my favourite, for the way it sounded, was "verfickter Scheißdreck", but I ducked out of sight as they wound down their windows at traffic lights and yelled it in unison to bemused motorists.

~ ~ ~

In the middle of the night I push the front door shut behind me. It's my house, even though I don't entirely recognise it. A few steps in, the door creaks as it begins to slowly open again and I'm hit by a freezing wave of fear. This nightmare is not new; I am well acquainted with its rules. I want to flee, to reach the solid door at the end of the long, long hallway before whatever is behind me catches up.

I start moving with feet made of lead. The silence is threatening because I know what's coming but suddenly Jenni is beside me. She's on her bike and she lifts me onto the saddle rack and starts peddling, fast, because our lives depend on it. With her I feel braver, stronger. This time I'll make it, we'll both make it, beyond the white door.

We reach the door – I've never made it this far before – and Jenni turns the handle and wheels us through. We should be safe but we can't budge the rusty bolt that has never been used. In the corner of the room is a small, low bed and Jenni shoves me underneath. My protector. I don't want to leave her but she pushes me harder and I lie there petrified, staring sideways at the bike wheels and her feet, waiting for the inevitable.

Usually I wake up halfway down the hallway as the thing is about to catch me. This time it's going to get Jenni unless I can save her so I scramble out and try one last time to lock the door. With a bang that makes my ears sing, the bolt shoots across into the keep. We are safe! I turn to Jenni in delight but the room is empty. For once, though, I know I have kept the monster at bay.

31

Autumn had been Aunt Vera's favourite season. Spring was when she "defrosted and dieted", she said, and summer was too busy to stop and enjoy. Autumn, after the last of the straggling tourists had left, was sweet and golden as the leaves turned and the sun grew lower. And winter? "Apart from Christmas, it's best left to hearty casseroles and red wine by the fire," she told me once.

The trees were half bare and the remaining leaves were every imaginable shade of red and ochre when I took my easel out to the valley. I had plenty of pictures from the wedding to recreate the May-time greenery around the lodge and was more interested in capturing the stonework accurately.

Daniel suggested they hang an enlarged wedding photo in his waiting room for everyone to see. Red, in an uncharacteristically coy moment, said it felt weird bringing their love life into work. She asked my opinion and I had to agree.

It gave me the idea of giving them a painting of their reception venue as a gift. Most people would simply see a lovely Cornish valley; Red and Daniel would be reminded of their special day every time they passed it.

The weather was perfect. Everything was damp after an early mist, making the autumnal tones even richer against the now-blue sky, and my paint would dry slowly in the cool air to give me the finish I wanted.

Painting in public made me self-conscious and I disliked interruptions when I was immersed in my work so I was pleased to have the valley to myself. Miss Robbins had told me it was a sign of my potential that, even at 12 or 13, I was able to shut out all distractions while my classmates were busy flicking paintbrushes at each other when her back was turned.

I was so absorbed, the appearance of a wet Springer Spaniel startled me. It dropped a stick and stood panting up at me, tongue out and stumpy tail wagging so frantically its whole body jiggled.

"Hello there. Who are you? Do you want me to throw that for you?"

Its head was damp and warm as I gave it a pat and scanned the valley. On the opposite bank of the river a grey-haired couple were walking along, holding hands. The man gave a wave, and I waved back. At the shout of "Otto!", the dog took off with his stick, launching himself into the river with a splash, tail still wagging crazily.

Maybe that's what I need, I thought. Long walks through the woods with a dog in tow – or towing me – so I had some company without the effort of having to make conversation.

All day I painted in the fresh air, the lack of pressure so different from the hectic weeks before our exhibition. The river provided relaxing background music and fresh water to clean my brushes. By late afternoon, as the light was fading, I was pretty much done. Almost as an afterthought, I added two people in the distance: the dash of white next to a figure in black would have meaning to those who knew.

That night, I went to a pub with Mum and Dad. Dinner for the three of us had been Mum's idea, a casual suggestion that it would be "nice for us to go out as a family", which made Dad uncomfortable and me suspicious. During conversations about who'd got married, had a baby, or moved since I was at home in May, Mum was clearly itching to say something else.

She held on until we'd cleared our plates and settled back in our chairs, then glanced at Dad and shifted in her seat.

"Did you see Tom before you left?" she asked.

Earlier in the year, when I let her know Tom and I had broken up and I was moving in with Stephanie, she had expressed motherly concern until I explained what had happened. Her sympathy changed to disbelief and from her comments it was clear she considered my decision to be selfish and ungrateful.

Was that a generational thing, or just my mother? Even at Aunt Vera's funeral I had overheard her crowing, to people who didn't care, that "Joy has landed herself a marvellous man, a young lawyer who is going to be a big London barrister one day". How relieved she must have been when Red stopped dating the mechanic and married a vet instead.

"No. Why would I? We broke up months ago, you know that."

"No reason. It's such a shame, that's all. We liked him a lot," and she nudged my father who had clearly been briefed but gave a neutral "hmph", so she continued. "I thought if you saw him again you might wonder if you'd made the right decision. His family seemed *so* nice."

I changed the subject and told them my plans, to pre-empt any lectures or questions about how I planned to support myself. While the autumn weather was mild and the roads quiet, I'd travel around to the main tourist sites and begin my local portfolio. Based on the success of my street signs, I decided to try something similar by painting Cornish signposts, from the distinctive cast-iron posts to granite milestone markers. These would be easy to transport and leave on a sale-or-return basis with shops that sold local arts and crafts. Materials were a little cheaper so I would make money even if I charged less than I had in London, assuming any commissions weren't too high.

The enthusiasm from the pub landlord in Finsbury Park gave me another idea: Cornwall was full of picturesque inns and I could ask publicans if they were interested in a painting of theirs – or miniatures tourists might buy.

"How long will you be living with your father?" Mum waited until he'd gone to the toilet to ask. Was she put out that I hadn't asked to move in with her?

"Not long. A few weeks, maybe less. It depends on whether I sell a couple more of the pieces I painted in London or have to wait until I find a steady job."

I decided not to mention I had an appointment coming up at the Job Centre, planning to sign on for the dole if my fledgling CV didn't land me any work soon.

Dinner the night after with Red and Daniel was much easier. Their house was a warm and relaxed mess of their combined belongings, in stark contrast to the spotless clinic.

Red was wholeheartedly supportive when I told her my plans over homemade rabbit cacciatore. Daniel was, indeed, an excellent cook.

"You don't have to put all your eggs in one basket. Try a few different things and go with what works. If you can sell stuff at this time of year, think how well you'll do, come summer. And in the meantime, the dole is there until you find something steady."

She and Daniel were "overwhelmed" when I presented them with the painting.

"I heard you were good, but this looks like a professional artist painted it," Daniel exclaimed.

"She is a professional artist," Red replied. "Or she will be once someone gives her a chance. In fact," her face lit up with the sudden idea, "why don't we turn the reception area into a mini gallery? It'll brighten up the place and give Joy plenty of exposure."

Daniel nodded. "I'm happy with that, as long as the prices don't make people think we're trying to be too fancy."

Red leaned over to give him an appreciative kiss and I pushed away a jab of envy.

She was animated as she thought it through. "We can let people know she's available if they want to commission something specific. And we can have a launch party!"

"It's an incredible offer," I said, "but I'm not sure everyone around here will see my name as a positive selling point."

"Stuff 'em," said Red. "If people are like me, when they see a picture they either like it or not. Unless it's a Picasso or something, they don't care whose signature is in the corner."

Even so, I thought it would be sensible to replace my

usual squiggle with "J.A.C." and on the back write "J. Agnes Carter" so it wasn't as obvious.

~ ~ ~

The sudden opportunity to display my work had me out of bed early each morning plotting routes to the places that would have most appeal. Driving to locations that had been photographed by a million tourists before me, it was hard not to feel like I was on holiday: Gunwalloe cove with its tiny church nestled on the edge of the sand; the old tin mine at St Agnes perched implausibly close to the edge of the heather-covered cliff.

At Perranporth, the beach carpark – overflowing in the summer months – was empty except for the cars of a few hardy surfers. The tide was at its lowest point, hardly visible beyond the expanse of golden sand. Through the middle, a snaking stream ran all the way to the sea and glistened in the sunlight while a stiff, cool breeze brought me the smell of salty seaweed.

This was home.

True to her word, Red invited me to dinner with her and Daniel every week. Quite casually over roast chicken one night she said, "Eric Tremayne came in to the practice today," and took a forkful of food that she chewed deliberately slowly to watch my response.

I casually replied "Oh?" and continued eating. I didn't want to be the first to speak.

"He's got himself a puppy and she needed her vaccinations. Cute little thing she is, shaggy and blond, just like Eric. They look adorable together. He saw our new painting and said how good it was so I told him the artist was a very talented local woman and he should commission a painting of his farmhouse. He's seriously considering it."

She was smirking as she spoke. Daniel watched our odd exchange. "What am I missing here?"

"Nothing at all," I hoped my shrug conveyed indifference. "Next time you see him, tell him he can book me in any time. I'd be glad to have the money."

I went back to my food, quietly elated that he admired my work, and wondering about our odd and undefined connection. True to her word, Red had kept my secret even from Daniel so this teasing was for my benefit only. I hadn't contacted Eric since I'd been home in case he misinterpreted it; all our other meetings had been pure coincidence so a phone call would be out of character and anyway I wasn't sure what I'd say.

Daniel asked if I was still thinking of getting a dog, something I'd mentioned after my encounter with the spaniel.

"I'd love to but I'm not sure I can right now – food, vet's bills – the sensible thing would be to wait until I have a job."

"I have the perfect solution," he said. "I have a wonderful client, Mary, who's been coming to us for years. She urgently needs someone to take care of her dog for a few months and I said I'd try and help. Her Mum had a stroke last week so she's moving to Bristol to take care of her when she comes out of hospital. There won't be room for Bruno. He's a Boxer, about to turn two, and he's very good natured. He'll need a good walk once or twice a day but he won't give you any trouble."

Bruno sounded like a perfect option. House-trained, not too big and wouldn't leave fur everywhere. Plus, if things didn't work out between us, his owner would be back in a few months. It would force me out of the house, come rain, wind or shine, and give me an opportunity to try my skills at painting animals, if he sat still long enough.

"Come to think of it, she might let you rent her house while she's away. It's pretty small but there's a large garden and it's near the woods so it would be less disruption for Bruno."

I had been past the place a few times: a tiny white cottage standing on its own at the end of a narrow drive, halfway between the woods and the cliffs.

"That sounds amazing. Would she do that? I don't even know her."

"I reckon she would. We can vouch for you and I'm sure she'd be happy knowing Bruno was able to stay at home."

Less than a day later, it was all arranged. Over a cup of tea with Mary on the Sunday afternoon I met Bruno, who was gorgeous. "Named after Frank Bruno because I love watching him box," she told me with a grin, "and they are both big brown-eyed softies."

Bruno leant into my legs as I scratched his ears while Mary and I chatted. She didn't want any money for rent as she'd been expecting to leave the place empty, given she was disappearing in such a hurry. As long as I took care of the bills, that was fine; she was grateful for this favour. She'd stock up with plenty of food for Bruno before she left and Daniel would know what to do if he needed the vet for anything.

It was too good to be true. The cottage was thick-walled and incredibly quiet with an open fire in the deep granite hearth and an Aga in the kitchen. When I said I was trying to be an artist, Mary threw her hands up, "Aha!", and led me to an outbuilding, a converted stable not visible from the front of the house.

"This is where I work," she said, opening the door to a sizeable space with bookshelves covering an entire wall and a large wooden desk. "I'm a bit of a writer, poetry mostly, and this is where I spend my days. The phone works and there's a sink in the corner. The heating isn't great when it's freezing outside but you'll be fine with a blanket. I'll find you an old sheet to throw over the desk and you can turn it into your studio."

I wanted to throw my arms around her and tell her she was the one doing me a huge favour. No doubt my face made it obvious.

"You'll love it here. There's something special about going for a walk along the clifftop on a blustery day when no-one else is around, then coming back and hiding yourself away with a big mug of hot chocolate. People think I'm a bit weird," she chuckled. "Cornwall in the summer is beautiful but I much prefer it in the winter."

I had found my kindred spirit. The best days were during the colder months when the surf was smashing against the cliffs or crashing onto the shingle, days when the onshore wind was blowing so hard you could lean against it without falling over, watching giant waves roll in like thunder.

As he helped load my bags into the back of his car, Dad said he was disappointed I was moving out so soon, but I sensed he was also a little bit pleased to go back to his routine.

"I've left you a heap of meals in the freezer and you can

always come over for dinner," I told him. "Mary is lending me her moped, so you can't get rid of me completely."

He knew Mary's cottage well.

"You were too young to remember but we used to go to the woods sometimes to walk Wally. We lost sight of you one day when you were only two or three. We were calling and calling and your mother was starting to go frantic. It was Wally who found you, not more than fifty feet from where we were. You must have heard us but were so absorbed in whatever you were doing, you ignored us."

My mother's irritated voice rang in my head: "Pay attention, Joy!"

32

In the drab brick building I'd only ever driven past, I approached the front counter at the Job Centre with trepidation. As soon as she saw me, Fern's face lit up and she ran around the desk, arms open wide.

"As soon as I saw your name, I made sure you were on my appointments pile. How are you? When did you get back? How is everyone?"

She talked nineteen to the dozen as we moved through to the busy appointment area.

Thank God it was her. I'd been fearing a lecture about leaving paid work to be unemployed in Cornwall, combined with a disregard for my hope of becoming a professional artist.

As soon as she stopped for breath, I asked why she hadn't come to Red's wedding, despite receiving an invitation. I had been surprised, and I knew Red was hurt by her absence. Instantly her face lost its sparkle and she was hesitant before I pushed her to tell me.

At Aunt Vera's funeral, in the living room after the service, Mum had spoken to Fern briefly, but clearly: Len was off limits, Eileen said. If Fern hadn't butted in five years ago, Len and Mum would have reconciled, and she would appreciate having that opportunity again without Fern around. Out of affection for Dad, rather than stand in the way of his potential happiness, Fern had chosen to disappoint Red and miss the wedding.

Suddenly Mum's recent behaviour made sense.

"Don't you think if Dad were interested they would have gotten back together by now? You and he stopped seeing each other 18 months ago. How much longer does she want!"

"I suppose. I don't know if anything would be different a second time around, though. He was stuck in the past back then, and I want to be with someone who's fully with me now. I'm not asking him to forget Jenni – God knows, I'll never stop thinking about Molly – but that house is not a healthy place for us to be."

She was right. Dad deserved to be with someone who made him happy and if that meant selling the house, he would have to let it go.

Fern checked her watch: "Alright, down to business before we run out of time," she said as she read through my CV.

"Hm, hm, not bad. It's good to see your manager gave you more responsibility. You're obviously not afraid to get your hands dirty and you've got experience handling money and dealing with customers. So what sort of job are you looking for?"

That was the problem. The work didn't matter as long as I had enough money to pay the bills and enough time and space to paint.

Fern said that made it easy and hard. "I don't want to put you forward for anything too basic because people assume you'll leave as soon as a better option comes along, which is a safe bet."

I told her the kinds of jobs I had applied for in London – everything from packing art supplies in a warehouse to the British Museum gift shop.

"I don't have anything right now but shops or supermarkets would be a good option: the hours are regular and you have the opportunity to work your way up to supervisor, if that's what you want."

It wasn't what I wanted but it might be the means to an end. I asked her what else my degree might make me suitable for and mentioned the career options our tutors had suggested – television, conservation, or graphic design.

"Well, we don't have too many TV stars down this way! You'd need to be in Plymouth or Bristol. Here's a thought: you used to like writing, didn't you?"

I nodded.

"Well, if you're out and about visiting galleries anyway, why not write reviews of their exhibitions and submit them to the local paper? Since the new Tate Gallery opened in St Ives, the whole county seems to have developed an interest in art, so it might open a few doors, even if the money isn't much."

I'd drawn up a list of galleries to contact, some of which I knew had regular exhibitions of local and occasionally national painters and sculptors. Being paid for my opinion on their work sounded almost too easy.

As the appointment came to its end, I told Fern I'd love it if she came for lunch at the cottage. She scribbled her phone number on a scrap of paper and said she'd be delighted.

Her advice, and the absence of any immediate job opportunities ("Temporary positions won't come in until closer to Christmas"), inspired me to jump on the moped and visit a few galleries.

Time to push some boundaries, I thought, and started with an exhibition of oils, *Art and the Human Body*, which I found only slightly less distasteful than a butcher's shop window. Even armed with a notebook and pen, I doubted if anyone would mistake me for a proper critic and I prayed no-one would walk up and demand to know what I was doing.

My comparison of the 'fantasy meets still life' series to Gaugin's oil paintings of food was truly awful and I crumpled it up the moment I finished writing it.

The next two reviews were more mainstream – a small independent ceramics gallery hidden away near Truro cathedral and a new watercolour exhibition of Cornwall in winter – and I mailed them to the local paper with my CV and a covering letter. To my amazement, the editor called with the news he wanted to publish my exhibition review. They weren't hiring anyone permanently, but their rate for casual work was £25 for quarter of a page and they would be happy to receive more pieces.

I was ecstatic. Despite the meagre money it was a start; another way to try and edge my way into the industry and build up my CV.

~ ~ ~

The phone rang while I was in the studio, engrossed in painting. I let the answering machine pick it up while I perfected the veins of a leaf with a brush so fine each individual strand was visible. The name Clare Robbins meant nothing to me and I assumed she was a friend of Mary's.

"I was reading about the new watercolour exhibition in

The Packet this morning and nearly spat out my coffee when I saw your name. I had to find out how things are and your Dad gave me your number. Let me know if you have time to catch up."

Clare Robbins. Of course, *Miss* Robbins. I had never thought of her by her first name. At least I knew one person had read my review.

"I have thought about you often," she told me over hot chocolate a few days later. "Not just when headlines pop up about your sister. I was curious to know where you'd ended up after university and whether I'd see your name up in lights one day. Then, hey presto, you dropped onto my doormat!"

I told her she was too kind and summarised my disastrous year in London.

"Don't think of it as a disaster. Everything can be a learning opportunity and nothing – well, hardly anything – is ever a waste. Take the cleaning job, for example: if it wasn't for that, you might never have started painting street signs and it sounds like they turned out pretty well. And holding your own exhibition is no mean feat!"

She hadn't lost her ability to make me feel better.

"I did something similar to you after I graduated. I packed up and moved to Stoke-on-Trent purely because it was the centre of the ceramics industry. I hated it!" she laughed. "It was not at all what I expected. No-one cared about a naïve young potter, however deserving I thought I was. The whole area was overloaded with amazing potters of every style who'd been working for years to build up a name for themselves.

"I was utterly miserable. I only lasted eight months before deciding to go back and train as a teacher, so I could share my love of what I do and have time to develop my own work. I never knew I'd enjoy it so much. It's an amazing feeling to help young people discover their own creativity."

"I never thanked you," I said, "for what you did, how you helped me, after Jenni. The art room was my sanctuary. I have no idea where I would have gone if it weren't for you."

"I know," she said simply, and smiled at me.

She asked if I had a portfolio she could see. I had taken to carrying an A4 folder around with copies, in case I ever needed it.

"These are all older pieces," I explained, "mostly from London and a few from Italy earlier this year. Since I came home I've been working on local landscapes and signposts, and my plan is to have them ready for the tourist season. So if you can think of anyone who might want to display them…"

"Joy, these are amazing," she cut me off as she flicked through the folder. "Your technique has developed so much since school – and I was impressed with it then. Like this one," and she held up a Piccadilly Circus sign. "The way you've granulated the colour for the stonework is exceptional and I love how you've been able to lift out the details here. I knew it! You have serious talent."

A warm flush spread across my cheeks as I saw pride and delight in her face.

"I might have a business proposition for you. I make a bit of money selling my pottery in a few places that want to support local artists, and not only with work aimed at tourists. If you can put together a bigger portfolio of pieces you've painted since you've been back, I can speak to a few people, show them your work and ask what they think."

I was lost for words.

"Miss Robbins, I…"

"Call me Clare!" she burst out laughing, "I'm only 38!"

"Clare, sorry! That's so kind of you but please don't feel obligated. I have a list of ideas to try and places that might be interested."

"Let me help you. There's nothing wrong with using your contacts – in fact, it makes the most sense to start with people who know you. I can't promise anything but I know it's hard to find good landscapes; everyone tells me they are up to their ears in fishing harbours and lighthouses. And there's nothing to stop you working on your other ideas at the same time."

Since moving home I'd been lent a house, a dog, and a moped. My paintings were hanging in a local vet's clinic and Dad's bank, and now I had an offer of help to put my work in front of people who might sell it.

"That would be amazing. Incredible. Thank you!" I couldn't express how much I appreciated her offer.

We parted with a promise from me that I would have the first pieces ready in a couple of weeks. Straightaway I called Dad, animated to share my news, and to invite him over for a home-cooked lunch.

~ ~ ~

Dad rapped on the cottage door the following Sunday.

"Come in, it's open!" I called from the kitchen. The final fresh herbs from Mary's greenhouse were going into the beef and carrot stew that had been bubbling slowly in the Aga all morning, and green beans simmered in a pan.

"Hi Dad." I gave him a kiss. "Lunch won't be long."

He sat at the dining table set for two, complete with tablecloth, an unlit candle, and a small glass of Cornish daisies.

"This is very cosy. Were you expecting someone better looking?" His jovial disposition made me happy.

"No Dad, you'll do perfectly."

At the knock on the door, he turned towards me, eyebrows raised.

"Could you get it?" I asked him. "The beans need draining."

Fern had seen Dad's car before she knocked; I was relieved she came in anyway. She told me Dad's face was an absolute picture as it dawned on him he'd been set up, in the nicest possible way.

"Hi Fern! Everything is keeping warm on top of the oven. You'll find a green salad in the fridge and there's ice cream in the freezer if you have room for dessert. Dad – don't forget to light the candle. I'll be back around 5pm," and I kissed them both on my way out before jumping on the moped and disappearing up the drive.

Red and I had concocted the plan after I shared what Fern had told me at the Job Centre.

"If he sold the house, I'm certain they would have a shot."

"Yep. Life's too short, and Uncle Len needs all the help he can get!"

33

"I've had enough of miserable Christmases," Red announced one dreary afternoon when the street lights had flickered on at 4.00pm to highlight the rain coming in sideways. "It's Daniel's favourite time of the year and our first Christmas living together so I want it to be special. Are you in?"

"Can I bring a date?" I asked.

"A date? Of course you can. Who is he?"

"You'll love him. He's very friendly and cheerful and he's got the most beautiful brown eyes. Plus he will clean up anything you spill on the floor."

"Bruno!"

"Who else would it be!"

"Well, I was beginning to wonder. You have been on your own for a while now. It must be time we set you up on a date."

"Thanks but I'm fine. I like the quiet life, just the two of us."

"What will you do when Mary gets back?"

I was trying not to think about that. I was enjoying living someone else's life but eventually Mary would be back. I could possibly afford to rent another cottage somewhere but I would miss Bruno enormously. Despite his lack of conversation, he was a great listener and walks were much more fun when I had someone to throw sticks for.

The gloomy weather did not dampen my creativity. For days at a time I shut myself away in the studio, lost in the emeralds and viridians of the woods and fields I was painting. My favourite pieces were in the portfolio I'd given Clare, who rang me weekly with updates on who had seen it and what they thought. Fern was right – the new Tate had generated an influx of art-loving visitors even at this intemperate time of year.

The phone call I had been waiting for came the same day I had failed to secure a cashier job in the lead-up to Christmas. My conversation that morning with the toy shop owner had lasted less than 15 minutes and I didn't need to wait for her letter to know I'd been unsuccessful. So my mood was despondent and I considered letting the call go to voicemail before scooping up the receiver at the last moment.

"Hello?"

"Joy? It's Clare. I have news!" Her voice sounded jubilant and I quickly sloshed my brush before wiping it on my overalls so I could concentrate.

"A place in Newlyn sells all sorts of arts and crafts including my ceramics, and the owner thinks your work is great. He doesn't have anything quite like it right now, so..." and I held my breath as she paused for effect, "so he wants to sell your paintings!"

From our simultaneous squeals, I guessed she was also jumping up and down in jubilation.

"Oh my God. I'm going to be an artist!" I yelled at a confused Bruno who started barking with excitement.

When we'd all calmed down, she explained how it

would work. "He'll take each piece on consignment so you only receive payment once it sells, but he's got a great place down by the harbour and a solid reputation. He's been selling my stuff for years."

Clare filled me in on the next steps, talking about contracts and commissions, although I was barely listening. A painting I created was going to be on display in a shop and – eventually, I hoped – in the house of someone who loved it.

Adrenaline was making my hands shake too much to finish what I was working on. Instead, I took Bruno for a long walk along the clifftop, neither of us feeling the cold rain through our coats.

~ ~ ~

On Christmas morning I awoke to the weight of a warm dog pressing against my right side. "Happy Christmas, Bruno." I nuzzled his soft head and stroked his velvety ears. "You'll have to wait for your walk but I promise you'll have fun."

The weather gave the impression of being undecided so I dressed in multiple layers to be ready for anything. I was feeling positive about the day ahead. This year was about making the newlyweds' first Christmas special and I hoped Mum would be on her best behaviour with Red's in-laws and refrain from flirting – either with Ray Pascoe or with Dad – after two or three glasses of wine.

Dad and I pulled up to Daniel and Red's house, both of us stifling laughter at the illuminated reindeer and cottonwool-covered bushes in their front garden. Outside, the house was merrily ablaze with coloured lights; inside, the unmistakeable smell of pine needles took me back to the previous year with Tom and his family.

I hadn't bothered with decorations in the cottage but Daniel and Red had enough for all of us. Cards were strung on ribbons all around the living room walls, and colourful paper chains dangled from corner to corner. On the over-sized tree, in between long ropes of gold and silver tinsel, fairy lights reflected off baubles of every colour and shape and a large star scraped the ceiling. It was over the top and wonderful.

Everyone was in fine spirits as we sat down to open our presents. Red and Daniel bought me a stuffed toy dog resembling Bruno so I would have someone to keep me company once Mary returned. We exchanged books, scarves, and the latest cassettes while Radio 1 played 40 years of Christmas music in the background. Red reminded me so much of Jenni as she handed out gifts with pure happiness written on her face; it hurt to look at her. I distracted myself by working Bruno into a frenzy with discarded wrapping paper.

One glance at the ominous clouds darkening the north coast sent us south to a beach we knew would be sheltered. We were not alone, and Bruno danced around my legs, desperate to be released. "Off you go!" He bolted the second I unclipped his lead.

We strolled along the damp sand, wishing everyone we passed a "Merry Christmas".

I was rubbing the belly of a friendly terrier, watching two wetsuit-clad swimmers splashing in the surf, when I heard Mum's voice, "Oh no. It's that man. Get Bruno away from him."

"Eileen," Dad's voice had a warning tone to it. "Leave it alone."

Bruno and a young golden retriever were playing tug-of-war with a piece of seaweed as thick as a rope; the man was Eric.

"You've always been so naïve, Len. I don't care what anyone else thinks, he's guilty. I know it in my heart."

"You can't still believe that, can you Mum?"

She turned with a face like thunder. "Who else could it have been? It was written all over his face from the second I saw him. No wonder he ran off to the other side of England. I wish he'd never come back. I don't imagine his poor parents ever recovered from the shame of it all."

She was almost spitting in Eric's direction and I knew contradicting her would be pointless. He was too far away to hear, I hoped.

I called Bruno, who was having far too much fun to obey me, so I walked over in their direction.

"Merry Christmas! I heard you were back," Eric smiled, peering over my shoulder at my mother, who glared as Dad pulled her away.

"I'm afraid your Mum doesn't like me very much."

"I wouldn't worry. She doesn't like many people," I said, liking the way the light wind was ruffling his hair.

"I didn't know you had a dog."

"Bruno's not mine. Do you know Mary Inglesby? I'm house-sitting for her for a while."

He knew her.

"This is Bonnie, after *Bonnie and Clyde*, because she hasn't stopped stealing things since the day I brought her home. She's lucky I'm a pushover and don't mind wearing odd socks. Bruno seems to like her. We should have a double date!"

He looked embarrassed as soon as he'd spoken. "I mean,

a play date. A date in the park." His face turned pinker.

"I think they would enjoy that," I kept my tone non-committal.

"Great. Um…how about Tuesday? Three o'clock? I know Mary's place; Bonnie loves it in those woods."

I hadn't expected an actual time, assuming it was just one of those things people say, but it was a date. At least for the dogs.

"Three o'clock. Great," I said, feeling my own cheeks start to burn.

"See you then. Happy Christmas!" and he backed away, whistling to Bonnie, who ignored him.

I grabbed Bruno, avoided Mum's piercing stare, and started towards the car park with an unwilling Boxer tugging at my arm.

Back at the house, mugs of spicy mulled wine warmed us up while Red assigned tasks for preparing lunch. Each time she and Daniel passed each other he stole a quick kiss and I was unable to stifle the envy I felt, even though Red's happiness meant everything to me.

As she handed me the napkins to help set the table, she asked quietly, "How was Eric?"

"Fine. I'm surprised I haven't bumped into him in the woods as he's been taking Bonnie there for weeks, he said. You're right, she is adorable."

"What I said is they look adorable. She's totally got the upper hand but he doesn't seem to mind at all."

Red struck a match and lit the fat white candles down the centre of the table.

"It's OK, you know," she continued, lining up the placemats.
"What's OK?"

"If you like him."

The teasing smile I was expecting didn't materialise. What would she think if she knew I was seeing him again in a few days? I stayed quiet; it was only for the dogs, after all.

She stood back and admired her work.

"Done! Please be seated, everyone!"

Dad began the convoy of dishes from the kitchen to the table, laughing as his glasses fogged up from the bowl of vegetables. Once the gravy and cranberry sauce were in place, Red appeared, a broad smile on her face as she carried aloft the roast turkey for Daniel to carve. We groaned at the terrible jokes in our Christmas crackers, swapped cheap plastic trinkets, and piled our plates with food.

It was the best Christmas any of us had had in years.

~ ~ ~

The ground is hard but dusty, like a playing field at the end of summer when the grass has worn to dry earth. Powder rises gently when I scrape the tip of my shoe along the surface.

I'm standing in a queue that curves back and forth in both directions like a giant snake, making it impossible to count how many people are ahead of me, or behind,

No-one seems familiar but I feel oddly at ease, surrounded by strangers and waiting for goodness-knows-what. As we start to advance, different faces appear and disappear in the zigzagging line of bodies and suddenly I see her: I would recognise the back of Jenni's head anywhere.

With all my might I will her to turn around, and she does, her face lighting up like she's been given the best present in the world. Through blurry eyes, I grin back at her and wipe away tears of sadness mixed with relief that she's OK. Jenni is crying through her smile, too, and nodding gently to let me know she is thinking the same.

She turns this way and that to avoid losing sight of me as the queue weaves along. Even though I can't touch her, the love she is sending towards me wraps me up like a blanket and I feel like we're the only two people here. We wave a few times and smile some more while everyone else continues in small steps. They haven't noticed us, two sisters communicating without words.

For once, I am filled with gratitude that these few moments with Jenni have left me with a sense of peace.

34

After a wet Tuesday morning, the weather had cheered up, if not warmed up, by mid-afternoon. When Eric knocked at the door at exactly 3 o'clock, I had been ready for half an hour and was close to overheating in my hat and scarf and woollen socks.

All day I'd darted back and forth in the small house, dusting shelves and sweeping corners for cobwebs that weren't there and checking and re-checking that the front porch was tidy. I wasn't particularly messy, but I was full of nervous energy and wondered if he might expect to come in for a cup of tea when we got back and what I would feel if he did.

We walked down the driveway to the road, Bruno straining at his leash because he knew where we were going and Bonnie because she was keen to play.

It hadn't occurred to me on the beach to ask where he spent Christmas Day, given he had no family nearby.

"There's a few of us waifs and strays about, so we generally get together at the pub for a turkey roast and a few beers and stories. They have a nice log fire and all the old Christmas songs playing. It's good fun."

We talked about what I'd been up to since I came back. I assumed he knew the situation with Tom but didn't want to mention it. I said how lucky I'd been to find the cottage and Bruno, even if it was only temporary. Having the time and space to paint without any interruptions was blissful and I shared the news I was now 'for sale' in a Newlyn gallery, thanks to Clare.

"Congratulations! That's quite an achievement considering you've only been back a few weeks. You must be very good." Eric's words were encouraging.

In the woods, we strolled along muddy paths while the dogs ran back and forth, madly chasing each other until we distracted them with sticks. Mostly it was Eric with questions and me with answers – so different from the previous summer. He asked how my parents were – despite Mum's reaction on the beach – what it was like having Christmas with both of them for the first time since the divorce, and how Red and Daniel were settling into married life. The conversation felt easy and the nerves I'd had all weekend were dissolving.

"How come you're not wearing a ring?"

Instinctively I checked my left hand, as if surprised it was bare.

"Why would I be wearing a ring?" I remembered how much my habit of answering a question with a question used to annoy Tom.

"Well, when I saw you at Daniel and Red's wedding, it sounded like your boyfriend wanted to get married."

"He did. I didn't." My statement came out harsher than I intended and I didn't want Eric to think I was annoyed at him. "We broke up a while back. It took me a while to acknowledge we wanted different things out of life, too different to compromise on."

"Like getting married?"

"That was part of it. I'm not into all the fuss and attention and marriage doesn't mean a whole lot to me. It's only a piece of paper, not a magic spell. I prefer to think people can stay together because they want to, not because they have spent a ridiculous amount of money on a wedding and don't want to admit it was a waste."

"I had no idea you were such a romantic!" Eric was mocking me.

I gave him a half-offended shove.

"It wasn't the only issue, though. He expected his future to revolve around London and I could never see it feeling like home. And," I may as well say it. "and I don't want to have children, whereas he always assumed we would."

Eric didn't appear to be horrified: "That would be pretty hard to compromise on, for sure."

We walked in silence for a few minutes, navigating fallen branches and muddy puddles. I hoped he wasn't judging me. Somewhere in the undergrowth the dogs were crashing about as dusk crept in and I hoped they'd come when we called.

"All the 'fuss and attention', you said. Is that because of what happened after Jenni disappeared?"

I gave it some thought. "I'm sure it's connected. I hated being the centre of attention then, and I still hate it. I don't remember being that way as a child. In fact, Dad says I was a bit of a performer, a show-off, until... after. All those hours and hours of questions. I couldn't have made anything up if I'd tried but could never be sure that the police – or anybody, for that matter – truly believed me."

Talking about it took me right back there, to the sickening sense of being a rabbit in the headlights. All eyes in the room boring into me to make sure I was telling the truth.

"Sometimes I would get so nervous and confused I'd struggle to remember whether I was telling them what I knew or what they wanted to hear."

"Yeah, I know how that feels," Eric was the only one who could empathise. "I guess the difference is they were trying to help you. With me, they tried everything to catch me out, to prove I had motive as well as opportunity. They twisted my words until I even doubted myself. It's not a time I like to remember."

I apologised.

"It's OK, I'm the one who brought it up," said Eric. "I've never had anyone to talk to about this. Mum and Dad never for one second suspected I'd done anything wrong, but they were so upset by what they read and heard they couldn't bring themselves to discuss it with me, ever. When Dad suggested I take off to his brother's place in Kent for a while it was a relief for all of us, even though I was afraid I'd seem guiltier and Dad would find it tough to manage the farm on his own.

"My friends never doubted me, but they didn't understand what it was like to be involved in something so awful. You're the only person who gets it. I can't imagine what your Mum would do to me if she knew I was talking to you."

I shook my head. "I'm sure she doesn't really think it was you," although my tone was unconvincing. "We haven't talked about it much. Until recently, none of us have talked about it much," and I relayed Tom's reaction and the arguments that followed.

"It's not for me to criticise someone I don't know, but he doesn't sound very sympathetic. You kept a secret because it was painful to talk about it. Just because his ex-girlfriend wasn't trustworthy, he can't assume you're the same as her."

"Well, it turns out he was right ... about being able to trust me."

My words hung awkwardly in the air and I wished instantly that I hadn't spoken.

"About last year," Eric made a face. "I hope I didn't make things difficult between you."

I assured him it would never have worked out with Tom anyway.

"I wish I'd realised it sooner and not kept going for two years. It was harder for him as he didn't see it coming whereas I'd been ignoring the signs things weren't right."

The cottage glimmered ghostly white in the gloom as we approached. Both dogs had run out of energy and I decided I'd talked enough about Tom. Eric hesitated, as if he didn't want to go.

"Could I see some of your paintings? I'd really like to, if that's OK?"

I ummed and aahed for a few seconds then let the dogs into the house – where they instantly flopped on the rug – and grabbed the keys from the hook by the front door.

"It's all out here. Mary let me turn her writing studio into my own space so it's a bit of a mess. Most of it is in progress and I'm trying some new stuff so you don't have to pretend you like it." I was in danger of babbling.

"Red told me you liked the painting I did for them at the vet's, though?"

"That's yours?" He was genuinely surprised. "It's amazing. Red told me it was a local artist but didn't say it was you. She said I should commission a painting of the farmhouse but personally I can't see the point of looking at a picture of a house when you're sitting in it."

I stifled a laugh; that wasn't quite how Red told it.

Trying not to stare, I stole glances at Eric as he moved from piece to piece propped around the room, examining paintings of local coves, beaches, and hillsides. He made admiring sounds and murmured names, recognising many of them or asking where something was. He flicked through my stack of London street signs and the new signposts I had done for Land's End, St Michael's Mount, and Frenchman's Creek.

"I love these. I mean, I don't know anything about art, but I think they would be nice on a wall."

"That's all I ever wanted: to paint something people liked enough to hang in their homes. Even if it's in the toilet!"

"Well, if you paint me a signpost for Tremayne Farm, I promise I'll hang it in my toilet. The indoors one!"

Apart from Miss Robbins, he was the first person to see my new work. I'd kept Red and Dad away, shy about letting anyone see it until I'd decided it was good enough. Eric was complimentary without it sounding fake.

I wanted him to stay longer and tried to picture what was in my fridge. "Would you like to stay for dinner?"

He didn't hesitate. "I would, thank you. Bruno may have to share his with Bonnie, though, she'll be starving by now."

We went back into the house and I fed the dogs while Eric resurrected the fire.

To my relief, the fridge contained the ingredients for a spaghetti carbonara.

"Sounds great, I love Italian food," Eric said, "and I can't remember the last time someone cooked for me."

Was that a confession he hadn't dated anyone for a while? I wasn't brave enough to ask yet.

Over the pasta and red wine in front of the hearth – he enjoyed the occasional glass, he said, even though he was normally a beer drinker – we talked about my trip to Italy and the ridiculously fancy hotels Red had booked us into.

"We were so out of our depth and the staff knew it. When people held out their hand we didn't know whether to shake it or give them a tip!"

After his trip to Spain, Eric was keen to do more travelling. "Italy is right at the top of my list – and not only because I would happily eat pasta every day for the rest of my life." I made a mental note to make a lasagne for the freezer. "I love how different it all is. The food, the language, and all the ancient buildings that somehow haven't fallen down yet."

The roaring fire and two glasses of red gave me the courage to get a little personal.

"So, you know all about me. Now it's my turn: why aren't you married?"

Eric shrugged, unperturbed by my question. "I never found anybody I wanted to ask. I haven't been out with heaps of women and none of them developed into anything serious. Except my last relationship two years ago: she suggested we move in together, and that's what made me realise I didn't like her enough to say yes.

"Mum and Dad hoped I would meet a nice girl at a

Young Farmers' Dance, marry her, and have a couple of kids who would inherit the farm. It worried them because they were so much older than everyone else's parents. They didn't want me to be on my own.

"I don't mind my own company, especially now I have Bonnie. This is nice, though," he gestured to the empty plates.

He was hard to read. Maybe Bonnie was all he needed and this was no more than a date for her and Bruno.

"I'm a bit like you I think," he continued. "If you have the right relationship to begin with, the marriage bit shouldn't change anything."

We sat quietly for a while, and this time it was comfortable, although my mind was trying to work out what it meant that Eric was on the rug next to me, a sleeping dog on either side of us. He didn't mind being alone but that didn't mean he wanted to be.

His eyes were fixed on the fire so I jumped slightly when he spoke. "You and Bruno will have to come over to the farm. I know you only go to St Marow every five years or so," and his smile was soft, "but I'd like it if you were there more often."

I admitted I hadn't been there since I'd seen him the previous year, although it was never far from my thoughts.

"In a way it becomes harder the more time goes past. I can't bear the place and yet I'm drawn to it, which starts an enormous build-up as soon as I think about going."

He said he understood, and I knew he did. "I'm so glad I bumped into you on the beach as I've been thinking about something since I heard you'd moved back. I had the idea of putting up a sign, a sort of plaque, where Jenni disappeared. Not a memorial, not saying she's died or anything. Something that shows we haven't forgotten.

"Only if you want to, though. She wasn't my sister and it's not as if I even knew her but in a strange way she's been part of my life ever since that day. You all have."

"That is …" and I struggled for the right words while the lump in my throat threatened to prevent me from speaking altogether, "that is the most thoughtful and meaningful thing anyone has ever done for us. I don't know if it will make it easier to be there but it's worth a try. I'll know that if she comes back, she'll see we never gave up on her."

Through my unspilled tears, the flames turned into a dancing blur of red and orange.

Eric was still staring into the fire. He reached over and took my hand and held it between his. I rested my head on his shoulder and we sat motionless and without speaking for a long time, while the dogs snuffled and twitched.

He stayed the night because I asked him to. No promises, no expectations, just an opportunity to feel the warmth of another person and hear the calming sound of their sleeping breath.

I slept incredibly soundly and couldn't remember a single dream when I woke to a chilly room. The crumpled sheets on the other side of the bed were cold and empty except for a note on the pillow: "Have to milk the cows. Would love to see you again very soon. Call me later. Eric".

35

Did he really want me to call or was he being polite? Would we have any conversation left after the previous day? Did 'later' mean today, or an unspecified point in the future? The sensation in my stomach was one I recognised from the day in Wales when Tom and I had walked along the promenade after our first night together, which only compounded my nerves.

That afternoon I was washing paint from my hands, trying to muster some courage, when Eric called me. On the phone his voice sounded a little different but I could picture the creases around his eyes when he laughed, which made me smile. We arranged to meet the next day, first for a walk, then he would drive us to lunch in a pub in the next town where dogs were allowed inside.

The next town; no need to explain why we shouldn't meet locally. I began to practice the conversation I would have with Dad if this became a habit, not that his reaction concerned me. Tom's displeasure at hearing about Jenni for the first time would pale into insignificance once my mother heard I had been spending time with Eric. Her mouth would be pursed shut, a deep furrow between her eyebrows as she digested the news about the man she believed had taken her daughter from her and got away with it.

The next day, with panting dogs steaming up the inside of Eric's car, we turned into the pub car park. Before we got out, another vehicle pulled up nearby. It was an old car, light blue, and with a local number plate. Eric stared at it intently until the driver got out, glanced suspiciously our way, and walked off down the street.

"Do you know him?" I asked.

Eric shook his head. "You remember the blue car – well, the one I saw and you didn't?"

"Of course. I still dream about it."

"I've never been able to stop looking for it. I don't even know what make or model it was, only that it's light blue and would probably have been a saloon car if they wanted to hide someone in the boot. Sorry, sorry," he looked appalled at himself. "I'm just thinking aloud, I shouldn't have said that."

"It's fine, honestly. It's nothing I haven't thought a thousand times."

His eyes were fixed out of the side window as he spoke: "If only I had taken a proper look instead of assuming it was a neighbour. I've always thought it's possible the driver saw me and if I stare hard enough at everyone in a blue car, and it turns out to be him, I'll see recognition in his face."

So many ways in which things could have been different.

Inside the warm pub with low wooden beams we talked for hours, stopping only when our food arrived and to move the dogs back when they snuck closer and closer to the hearth. The more we talked about Jenni, the more relaxed we became. It was liberating to bring up details no-one else had been witness to and have Eric nod vigorously in agreement instead of asking a dozen unanswerable questions.

Jenni wasn't our only topic; Eric had been mulling over a change at the farm and he wanted to share with me what he'd been thinking.

"Back when I was in Kent I studied farm management, which I've been doing all my life anyway. My uncle suggested it, said my generation shouldn't be tied to the land like his and Dad's was, and I should do something to give me options.

"Initially I was reluctant to go to college – I wasn't exactly the best pupil at school – but I was amazed how different I felt once I was interested in what I was learning. I don't want to waste that, and I have all of Dad's practical knowledge to pass on. So I've been thinking about training to become a teacher."

He wasn't suggesting anything as dramatic as selling Tremayne Farm – not immediately, anyway. "That seems a bit 'final' when I haven't even tried teaching yet. But I've been doing the sums and I can afford to employ someone to manage everything while I do a one-year course. What do you think?"

He was asking my opinion! I told him the idea made sense. "Last year you said the inheritance meant you could take time to work out what you wanted to do. So, as you say, you don't have to sell the farm in a rush then regret it."

"I forgot I'd said that. You have a great memory!" He was pleased.

"Better than I want it to be, sometimes."

In response, he rubbed my hand gently and again I was reminded how different he was from Tom.

~ ~ ~

That evening, submerged up to my ears in a hot bubble bath, I began to fantasise about what might happen if Eric were to sell the farm.

I imagined us buying our own little white cottage with a big open fireplace and cosy low-beamed ceilings. It would have an artist's studio on the side, and enough land for the dogs to roam and for us to grow all the vegetables we needed. Maybe even space for Steph and the girls to come for that retreat. I'd sell heaps of paintings in Newlyn and elsewhere, which would lead to an invitation for my own exhibition; even that felt achievable now.

By day I would paint and continue writing while Eric was teaching. In the evenings, he and I would walk the dogs in the woods together, or along the beach or coastal path, and take it in turns to cook dinner. We would travel. First to Barcelona, then Italy, and then anywhere else we wanted.

I slid lower and inhaled the steam scented with Lily of the Valley – my Christmas present from Red.

Bruno's gorgeous nose appeared over the side of the bath and I teased him, dabbing bubbles onto places out of reach of his pink tongue.

Of course, I'd have to give Bruno up when Mary came home, which would be a terrible wrench. But Eric would still have Bonnie, and we could look for a puppy together...

A half-bark from Bruno broke my reverie.

Two dates with Eric – one of which was more for the dogs anyway – and suddenly I'm picturing a life together.

"Don't be such a naïve idiot," I scolded myself out loud. It would be far too complicated, and who's to say he's even thinking that way?

"What do you think, Bruno, am I an idiot?"

Bruno was silent.

Even so, dreaming about it gave me a glow and I lay there as the water began to cool, wondering why.

Not until I was sitting on the rug by the fire, drying my hair, did the realisation hit me: I had let myself imagine the future and it hadn't filled me with dread. For the first time, my life felt like my own instead of me being a helpless passenger. With or without Eric, I knew what would make me happy.

A lump of coal collapsed in the grate, sending bright embers sailing up into the blackness of the chimney. I wiggled my bare toes in the warmth and thought maybe this winter wasn't going to be so bad.

Epilogue

In front of me is the meandering country road, its high hedgerows shining vivid green after the late winter rain. Ahead, the long white lines disappear around a corner. It is 18 months since I was last here but every blade of grass, every tree hanging over from the adjoining fields is familiar, even though the new leaves are yet to appear.

Eric and I have just picked up the piece of engraved granite from the stonemason. Despite its weight, I make him park the car a hundred feet before the spot so I have a few extra seconds to prepare myself.

My heart is pounding against my rib cage. Eric's hand wrapped around mine as we turn the bend is the only thing keeping me from bolting.

We come to a halt. It's much colder than any time I've been here before and I can't help shivering despite my thick coat. I don't want to close my eyes because I'm terrified I'll see fluttering tassels and white flowers on a lilac saddle.

Eric has two long pieces of metal, which he drives into the stone wall with a hammer, every bang making me wince. He fastens the plaque so it won't easily be removed and is half-sheltered from passing traffic. Only those who know it's here will notice it as they pass. He rips away a few wisps of long grass, snaps two large bracken leaves, and it's done.

I stand stiffly, still braced with fear against something unknown. On one side of me, Fern is gripping Dad's hand tightly between both of hers and the look they share nearly breaks my heart. On the other, Daniel's long arms are wrapped protectively around Red, who has a crumpled tissue to her nose.

When Eric reaches for my hand again, he sees the red indentations my nails have created in the flesh of my palm and pulls me close in an intense and now-familiar hug. His lips are warm against my chilled forehead.

This is where I lost my sister. Eleven and a half years ago I was here and she wasn't and everything changed. Eric understands. He holds me like he never wants to let go, kisses my hair, and lets me cry.

TO JENNI, WHO DISAPPEARED

FROM THIS SPOT ON 12 AUGUST 1982.

WE LOVE YOU, WE MISS YOU

AND WE HOPE ONE DAY

YOU FIND YOUR WAY BACK HOME.

Acknowledgments

When I started writing, I thought being an author was an isolated process. I was wrong. The Purple Bike would not be what it is without the involvement of more people than I could have imagined.

Natalie Sheridan-Smith has top billing for being an amazing cattle prod (mostly figuratively) and chief encourager from before day one. You are brilliant.

To Dad and Susan: some of this was written in your kitchen in Cornwall, where I have always felt your love and support in everything I do.

Julie Hunter, you gave me time, fabulous insights and lots of chardonnay, all of which make me grateful for you. I wish Joy had had someone like you in her life.

For the 'two thumbs up' on an early draft that barely deserved one, and for introducing me to someone as an author for the first time, Geoff Lynch you will always have my thanks.

Tim Oudenryn, you showed me I could evoke emotion (even in a grumpy old Dutchman!), which is all a writer wants to do.

Giselle Jesse, thank you for always telling it like it is and for inspiring me with your creativity. You're next.

Jacqueline Donaldson, you gave me precious time and

editorial expertise and delivered feedback with your usual grace.

Thanks Kester Sheridan for answering questions from a random stranger on studying Fine Art in Wales in the 1990s.

To the many friends who encouraged, enquired and enthused along the way: your anticipation kept me going. To the Brunchers and Lunchers, The Solids, The Legends, my fellow Tigers tragics and those who work on Inglesby Road – I hope I do not disappoint.

Above all, though, I am grateful to my wonderful partner for life and personal Patron of the Arts, Joe Sullivan: thank you for taking this incredible leap with me and keeping me in slippers and instant coffee.

About the author

Tamsin Stanford was born and raised in Cornwall, UK, in a small town not on the tourist trail.

During her languages degree at the University of Bradford, she spent time working and studying in France and Belarus. After a second spell in France in 1996, she found herself in London for a few years.

Since 2000 she has lived in Melbourne, Australia, with her partner.

After almost 20 years working in online content and communications, she took a break from the corporate world to write full-time in 2018. She now writes fiction in between projects as a content and usability consultant.

Her first bike was red.

www.tamstanford.com